THE DOOR TO THE BERLIN BUNKER OPENED

A red light in the doorway outlined a figure wearing a stiff-brimmed officer's cap, leading a dog on a leash. From the wall where he was hiding, Jonathan could see his round face and the mustache under the nose.

Hitler.

Except that the ground had been blown to hell by bombs and Russian artillery, he might have been any dog owner walking his dog in the moonlight. He strolled toward Jonathan's wall, letting the dog sniff. Sweat rolled down Jonathan's back. He could feel it soaking through his shirt.

Now Hitler was no more than five meters away, standing in the moonlight, his hands on his hips, and the dog was suddenly barking and straining at the leash. Hitler bent forward and looked Jonathan over carefully. Then he straightened up and said:

"I've been expecting you."

James N. Frey

ZEBRA BOOKS
KENSINGTON PUBLISHING CORP.

ZEBRA BOOKS

are published by

Kensington Publishing Corp.
475 Park Avenue South
New York, NY 10016

First printing: April, 1988

Printed in the United States of America

to
Bartley J. Prescop, with thanks

I was assigned to find Adolf Hitler or his body immediately upon entry of American troops into Berlin. I can state positively that I did not find Hitler nor did I find his physical remains. Despite a thorough search of the area, I have not been able to find any evidence that his body was burned . . . I feel that the melodramatic fabrication advanced by Dr. Goebbels—the theory of suicide by Hitler . . . followed by "cremation" in the Chancellory garden—is impossible.

—W. F. Heimlich
Chief Intelligence Officer,
U.S. Army, Berlin, 1945

Book I

Chapter One

"I haven't been to this part of the country in a long time," the young SS captain said. "It's beautiful. If I didn't have to take a prisoner back to Berlin with all speed, I would take a few days' leave here."

The moon was bright; reflecting off the snow, it was almost like daylight. The road twisted up a canyon through pine forests, past rocky cliffs, through tunnels.

The Gestapo man drove the Mercedes slowly and cautiously because he did not have his headlights on. The Allied fighters rarely flew in the mountains at night, but he wasn't taking any chances.

The SS captain leaned back and sipped some brandy from a flask. It warmed him. The heater was on low. The Gestapo man did not like his car too warm because it made him sleepy, he'd said.

"My wife and I enjoy the mountains very much," the Gestapo man said, lighting a cigarette. "We ski with the children every chance we get. What prisoner is it you've come for?"

"A Jew. Some professor."

"Ah," the Gestapo man said. "A Jew who needs special handling?"

"Very special."

"He wasn't involved in the underground, was he?" the Gestapo man asked. He dumped the ash of his cigarette out the window. Cold air rushed in.

"Not as far as I know," the SS captain said. "He was hiding in a chicken coop. They want him for something else, they didn't tell me what. You know how it is with Himmler, everything is a secret."

"Stuckurt, our man in Rothbaden, caught him?"

"Yes."

The Gestapo man laughed.

"What is so amusing?" the SS captain asked.

"Stuckurt is sort of a joke around here. He does his job, but he doesn't have the heart for it."

"I'll keep that in mind."

"He thinks more of his belly than anything else. And his bad back. The man is a complete hypochondriac. And thick-headed. I don't think he appreciates the necessity of our historical mission to free Europe and the world from the Jews."

"How is it such a fool can be section chief in the Gestapo?"

"You know how it is, Herr Captain," the Gestapo man said glumly. "He probably knows somebody. Watch out for him, though, he's suspicious of everyone. He'll give you the third degree if you ask for a glass of water. The man has no instincts for security work, so he makes up for it by working his fool head off. You'll see. Well, here we are, just around the curve up ahead is Rothbaden. I'll drop you off at Gestapo headquarters and be on my way. Not a bad town, you should drink the water, it's so good for your health."

"I haven't come here for my health," the SS captain said.

The worst part is the waiting, Julius Shapiro thought.

It is worse even than the pain of the welts where they beat him with the riding crop and where they had hit him with their fists and kicked him. The physical pain is bad, but not intolerable. Julius Shapiro, former professor of chemistry at Heidelberg University, could stand up to it, he told himself. Even when they kicked him in the groin, with his testicles already swollen painfully, he could grit his teeth and stand it.

The real torture is the waiting.

Like now, in between the interrogations, alone in the darkness of the small, damp, cold cell. The mind begins to play tricks. Flashes come. Hope. Maybe there's some way out. Maybe the war will end before they get around to killing me.

But then just as quickly as a flash of hope comes, it is gone. Escape? What chance is there of that? A sensible man would not think such idiotic thoughts.

How much time, he wondered, will it take until they figure out that he doesn't know where other Jews are hiding? Not long. A few more days. And then what? A quick bullet or a trip to a camp. He wondered what happened at the camps. Do they starve you? Shoot you? Let you die of dysentery or typhoid?

Don't think of such things, he scolded himself. He was letting his imagination torture him and that was just what they wanted. The camps were not death camps. The Nazis were monsters, but they weren't *total* monsters. The rumors of the mass killings going on in the camps were just that, rumors.

No, there were no death camps. When the Gestapo was through with him they would take him to some kind of camp, Auschwitz, maybe—he had heard that name—where he would be forced to do war work. That is all, that is not such a bad thing. Germany, before the war, before the Nazis, was the most civilized country in Europe, in the world. Civilized people just don't go around murdering people because they don't like them. A few fanatics might. But there were not enough fanatics in Germany, in the world even, to exterminate all the Jews in Europe. Besides it would be stupid, and though Hitler might be a madman he was not a fool, and he was not stupid. Even he would not waste lives that could be used to help win the war.

Of course they might shoot you if you refused to work. Julius Shapiro had already decided he would not refuse. He had hidden out because he didn't want to work for them, but now that he was caught he would do what they wanted. He was no hero.

His legs cramped under him. He shifted his position and his leg touched some cold water in a puddle. The sudden cold provoked a numbing sensation that wasn't at all unpleasant. That was the strange thing about pain. Once a certain threshold was reached, pleasure awaited on the other side. He had read about that somewhere. Maybe he would be lucky. Maybe if they kept it up he would experience the pleasure of pain.

Don't think like an idiot, he told himself. There was no pleasure awaiting him.

He lay down on his left shoulder and brought his knees up, relieving the ache in his groin. In this position he could smell the fresh air coming in from under the door and for a moment he felt almost comfortable. Except for the hunger pangs that came and went like little volcanic eruptions, he was at the moment feeling not all that bad.

What is it the Buddhists say? Think only of the moment.

But he couldn't think only of the moment. The waiting lay heavily upon him. He didn't want to think of what was going to happen, but he couldn't not think of it. If only he could shut the future out of his mind. He had had it better than most for a long time. He had stayed out of it, and for that he must congratulate himself, and he must thank God. For three years he had hidden from them in a small room under the planking of the floor in the chicken coop of his former professor, Dr. Heinz Muller, who had retired to the state of Wurttemberg, which the Nazis now called the province of Reinfranken. Muller had been an old man living on a meager pension, thin and pale, crippled with arthritis, vaguely sympathetic to the Nazis, who he thought had breathed new life into Germany and would erase the terrible shame of losing the Great War. Yet when Shapiro had showed up on his doorstep saying he needed a place to hide and there was nowhere else he could go, old Muller had hidden him and fed him and taken care of him for over three years.

But then old Muller decided to shovel a little snow one morning. His hired man had been conscripted into the Volkssturm. It was foolish for Muller, in his frail condition, to shovel snow, but he was expecting guests and wanted to have a clean walk for them. After a few shovelfuls he had had a stroke and died face down in the snow, the flat-bladed shovel clasped tightly in his hand.

It took his widow only one day to turn in the Jew who was hiding under the chicken coop. Shapiro should have run when he had the chance, but where was there to go? He would have been caught in an hour.

Now, in the cold stinking darkness of his cell, Shapiro tried to understand Frau Muller. And he tried with all his might to forgive her. She was a widow now and alone, he told himself, and for the whole three years she had lived in terror that one day the Gestapo would come and take them all away. He could still picture her cold blue eyes staring at him every time she would bring him food. Like he was what? Some kind of loathsome animal. A venomous snake her doting husband kept under the chickens. He knew all along that if the old man died, she would turn him in. He should have killed her immediately when the old man died. Now wasn't that a strange thought? Kill someone who had hidden you for three years? What an impossible idea. He could not kill a frightened old lady, no matter how much he feared her. Even to consider such as thing was monstrous.

The Nazis make monsters out of everyone, even

their victims, he thought.

He sat up painfully and leaned back against the sharp stones of the wall and stared off into the darkness. How quiet it was above. No one screaming. What a relief. Was it dawn yet? Each new day brought more terror, but each new day also brought the Allies closer and closer to ending the madness.

What would one make of the human race? Dr. Muller had a picture of Adolf Hitler on his wall and attended rallies and speeches given by the Nazi Party, often traveling as far as Nuremberg just to get a glimpse of Hitler. But he hid a Jew he hardly knew and kept him hidden. His wife was a good Catholic with a strong sense of right and wrong, who thought the Nazis were nothing more than thugs and criminals, yet she turned the Jew in at the first opportunity, saying "the law is the law."

Yes, *the law is the law.* But what happens when the law is made by criminals? He asked her that, but she was incapable of formulating a logical or humane answer. "The law is the law," she had kept saying, as the two Gestapo men in their leather overcoats took him to their car.

Suddenly, somewhere above him, a prisoner screamed, a scream choked off in the middle as if a garrote had been put around his neck. Shapiro felt himself gag. Well, they were back to work. A new day. The waiting was almost over. It was both terrible and a relief. Soon the Gestapo guards would be coming for him. They would go about their business in a dull, routine way. They hit whom they were paid to hit, they kicked whom they were paid to kick. With them, it was a livelihood. Only Stuckurt, the man in charge, ever spoke. He kept saying, "Where are the others, Shapiro, tell me or I shall take you upstairs and really give you the business." Even Stuckurt's threats were given in a mechanical way, as if he were bored with the whole operation. Like torture had somehow become everyday drudgery.

But Shapiro did not know where any others were. He told them over and over that he only stayed in Germany because his wife had been arrested passing out leaflets on the Heidelberg campus. He was a scientist and had never been involved in politics. All he wanted to do was teach organic chemistry and write books. He explained over and over again that when they said she had hung herself all he wanted to do was get out of the country. But he couldn't find a way. He couldn't get a visa. Then he'd heard they were looking for him, so he went into hiding the only place he could think of.

Stuckurt didn't believe any of that. "Just tell us, Jew, and we will leave you in peace. You don't and we take you upstairs."

What they were doing, Shapiro knew, was breaking him down. He had read about the procedure when he was a student. The grand inquisitors of the Catholic Church had figured it out. First you beat your victim a little to humiliate him, all the time making threats. And then when he's ready, when his will is broken, when he can no longer order his thoughts, you take him to the torture room. Most of the time you don't have to do anything. The sight of the instruments of torture—the rack, the iron maiden, the hot coals—is enough; the prisoner will confess to anything, and maybe even believe it himself.

How fortunate, Shapiro thought to himself, that he had been careful not to allow himself to be put into a position of learning anything that would be of use to the Gestapo. He could not jeopardize anyone because he knew nothing. He had worked it out with Muller the first week in hiding. They would talk only about chemistry and the war, and about nothing he wouldn't want the Gestapo to know. In a way, now, his shrewdness made him feel superior to the men who were trying to terrify him.

In the last year Muller hadn't come to the chicken coop often. He would send his wife once a day with some soup or a few small potatoes and a piece of bread. Most of the time Shapiro was alone with his thoughts and a few books. By the time the Gestapo came for him, he was talking to himself. He remembered thinking, as he saw the car with the two men in it driving around the back of the house toward the coop, *at last it is over.*

But at the time he had thought they would simply send him to a work camp. He had no idea they would first bring him here to Rothbaden and put him through "obedience school" as the guards called it.

The problem, as he saw it, was to get the Gestapo to realize that he in fact knew nothing. He pondered it as if it were a scientific question. A hypothesis is needed, he thought. What would Stuckurt say if you said to him, *Please take me to the camps where I can be with my people, where I can suffer with them, try to give them hope, where I can feel their pain and share their anguish.*

They would think him mad. Or a liar. And they would no doubt beat him all the more.

A new hypothesis: what if he gave Stuckurt some phony names and locations? Made up an elaborate network. Gave him and his goons some work to do. They might stop beating him for a day or two while they checked out his story. And by then the Allies, who were already fighting on German soil in the northwest, might be here. It could work. It was worth a try. At least it was something.

Suddenly the door burst open:

"On your feet, Jew!"

It took Shapiro a moment for his eyes to adjust to the light. It was one of the guards; he was big, brutish. His gray SS uniform was rumpled and open at the collar. Shapiro got up as quickly as his swollen scrotum would allow. He stepped into the corridor.

"Move faster!" The guard kicked Shapiro in the rump. Shapiro straightened up, squaring his shoulders.

At the moment of his arrest Julius Shapiro, professor of chemical science, swore he would not beg or plead for mercy. He would take whatever they were going to give him and keep his dignity. So far he had kept that pledge.

The guard shoved him down the hall. "I said faster, dirty Jew bastard!"

Shapiro quickened his pace slightly. He kept his eyes on the doors to the other cells. He heard someone moaning and praying.

"Keep faith!" he called out to the unseen prisoner. "Your deliverance is near!"

For that he received a fist in the back of the neck that sent him stumbling forward. He regained his balance and continued walking with his head high. And then he remembered the note he had received from his wife, Sarah, two days before she was reported to have committed suicide. The prostitute who had smuggled it out of jail said Sarah had had a strange glow on her cheeks when she had given it to her. The note said, *They have foolishly pushed me to the point where they have lost their power over me.*

He had no idea what that meant at the time, and it had haunted him ever since. He was just now beginning to understand. At some point when you are terrorized, death, pain, fear, all blur and become, in a way, impersonal. You suffer, but some part of you, perhaps the soul, is freed. Your mind leaves the suffering behind and soars into the cosmos.

What a hypothesis! If true, escape could be imminent! Escape was possible even though the evil had custody of the body.

Shapiro felt the sharp sting of the guard's stick on his back. The hypothesis, tested, fails the test. He felt his shoulders sag.

The idea of the soul soaring into the cosmos—what stupid, romantic nonsense. They pushed him into the interrogation room and suddenly he felt his knees buckle with fear and a plea for mercy involuntarily escape his lips.

Chapter Two

Bernhard Stuckurt, Gestapo Chief for Rothbaden, was, as usual, early for work. He was early despite the fact that he was feeling none too pleased about the prospect of another day of interrogating the Jew, Shapiro, who obviously knew nothing, but procedures required that he be given the full interrogation routine anyway. And Bernhard Stuckurt, Gestapo Chief of Rothbaden, always did what was required of him.

It was just becoming daylight when he parked his noisy and battered Volkswagen staff car in front of the weatherbeaten wooden Gestapo headquarters on Goschen Street. The headquarters building was rather plain, but had a certain rustic appeal. An ugly, concrete block of cells was appended to the rear, which made it look, someone once said, like an old tugboat towing a garbage barge. To make matters worse, for security reasons, the security division had cut down the tall pine trees that once surrounded the building, exposing all of its architectural faults. Stuckurt opened the car door and squeezed his heavy frame out from behind the wheel. He found the tiny seat in the car torturous, but he never complained about it. Not when Germany's youth was suffering so much on the Russian front.

It was perhaps five degrees below zero centigrade outside, and a light snow was falling. It was overcast from horizon to horizon. It meant that for the third day in a row the Allied bombers would have to stay on the ground. Good. Very good. Over the radio he had just heard the news that the Wehrmacht was counterattacking the U.S. Seventh Army near Rimling and Gambsheim and inflicting heavy losses. The front in the Ardennes was holding after the brilliant offenses the Fuehrer launched a few weeks before on 16 December. So all is going well, Stuckurt thought, at least for the moment. Soon the super weapons the Fuehrer had promised will push the enemy back into the sea.

He turned up the collar of his heavy, black leather coat and dragged his briefcase, stuffed with reports written by his six-man staff of agents, from the back seat. He always went over his men's reports before forwarding them to Berlin because sometimes his men were careless in matters of grammar and spelling and he didn't want them to look bad to his superiors. There wasn't enough time to do such work during the day, so he took it home.

He started up the icy stairs that led to the front door. His back was bothering him, making each step painful. And he would have to spend half the morning haranguing the Jew Shapiro. He cursed his fate, and he cursed the Jews for being Jews. This, despite the fact that Stuckurt never thought of himself as anti-Semitic. Not by nature, at least.

Before the war he had been a streetcar conductor. He had hurt his back in a streetcar accident. He loved being a conductor. After work he would go to the biergarten and drink beer and sing songs. He lived in Dortmund then, and he used to chant anti-Jewish slogans and paint "Death to the Jews!" on Jewish businesses, but it was only because the party rewarded such activities, and the party had gotten him the job as a streetcar conductor in 1929 when no one could find a job. He was duty-bound to be as anti-Semitic as they wanted him to be. But in his heart, he didn't really hate them. He hadn't known many Jews personally, but those he did know didn't seem so bad. He even had a Jewish teacher once, Herr Horowitz, whom he rather liked.

But Stuckurt never thought about Herr Horowitz. For him, the Jewish question had a simple answer: Duty. He rounded the Jews up and followed a carefully detailed procedure. That was all there was to it. Duty. Nothing to think about. He filed his report with his superiors in Berlin, giving each prisoner's name and employment and, if included on the lists, his assigned fugitive number. Then he interrogated them to see what they knew of other Jews and where they might be hiding. After the third day of interrogation, whether he'd found out anything or not, he turned them over to the SS. His duty done.

As Stuckurt went in through the front door, the guard, an SS corporal, gave him a salute. He was from the Waffen SS, a wounded vet from Italy, missing his left arm. A surly fellow without much brain power, Stuckurt knew, but he regularly put in a twelve-hour shift without complaint.

"An SS captain is waiting up in your office, Herr Stuckurt," the corporal said.

"I did not see a staff car," Stuckurt said.

"He said he came by train, sir."

Stuckurt was puzzled for a moment. "Was there a train during the night? I thought the bridge near Mengin was still out."

"I don't know, sir, I'm just reporting what he told me."

Stuckurt nodded and went into the lobby to the counter where permits and travel passes were issued; it was manned during the day by a couple of female clerks and an old man. The night clerk was still on duty. During the day he was a postal clerk. The clerk looked up with red eyes and a forced smile and said good morning. Stuckurt nodded to him and went upstairs. Stairs were the worst thing for his back. He had already taken four aspirins, but he had gotten very little relief.

He pushed the door to his office open and found the SS captain sitting behind the desk with his feet up, his collar open, and his cap at a jaunty angle. An Iron Cross, second class, dangled from a hook on his shirt collar. He was reading reports and correspondence Stuckurt had left on his desk. Ah, Stuckurt thought to himself, here was one of these cocky young officers who thought they owned Germany. Who enjoyed their rank and privileges just a little too much.

"Heil Hitler!" the SS captain said.

"Heil Hitler. I am Herr Stuckurt," Stuckurt said, taking off his coat and hanging it on the hook by the door. The fire was going in the old iron stove.

The SS captain put down the reports and smiled. He had a square handsome face and blue eyes. A scar ran down one cheek, jagged, like a lightning bolt. A dueling scar, no doubt. Stuckurt thought, a status symbol among the young SS officers.

"And who might you be?" Stuckurt said.

"SS Captain Hans Shroeder," he said, standing up suddenly and giving an off-hand salute. "I hope you don't mind my sitting in your seat, your man downstairs said I was to wait here. Your chair was the most comfortable in the room, so I took the privilege. I have warmed it up for you." He gestured with a flourish for Stuckurt to sit down.

Stuckurt threw a few more coals on the fire. The room was already warm, but it was a habit of his. He sat down gingerly, being carefully not to jar his back. He straightened his blotter, centering it in the middle of his desk, and put the pen holder precisely in the right-hand corner. "Now then," he said, folding his hands on the blotter, "what, Herr SS Captain, have you come for? Certainly not to read my reports on the lack of mush to feed the prisoners, the lack of fuel for the staff cars, the lack of . . . everything."

"I'm here to pick up one of your prisoners. His name is, let me see . . ." He produced an envelope of papers from inside his shirt. "Ah yes, Julius Shapiro. Number 10987124."

"Show me." Stuckurt said. The SS captain dropped the papers on the desk. A standard transfer of custody order, a circular description of the prisoner, a transit pass, all pretty much routine. Then Stuckurt noticed the order of transfer was signed by Horst Rasten, Deputy SS Reichfuehrer, himself.

"Must be an *important* prisoner," Stuckurt said with raised eyebrows. He handed the SS captain back his papers.

"Perhaps," the SS captain said with a shrug. "My orders are to take him to Berlin, so that's where I'm taking him."

"What was he doing in my sector, one might wonder?" He drummed his fingers on his desk.

"His field of study before the war was shellfish toxins, that's all I know about him;" the SS captain said. He produced a large silver flask from his pocket and took a few swallows. "French brandy," he said. "Nineteen thirty-three, a very good year." He passed Stuckurt the flask, who stared at it blankly for a moment before accepting it. Stuckurt then reached behind him and took a water glass out of a small cabinet. He wiped the mouth of the flask with a clean napkin he kept in his desk and poured himself a modest amount. Normally he didn't drink so early in the morning, but he thought it might relieve the pain in his back. The brandy had a delightful, sweet aroma. He let it trickle down his throat. His opinion of the young SS captain was improving.

"Now then," the SS captain said. "Might I have my prisoner and be on my way?"

"Yes, yes of course." Stuckurt reached for the house phone and began dialing.

"I will also need a car and driver," the SS captain

said.

"I'm sorry, but there is a shortage of transport, I don't think we could spare a car until sometime this afternoon."

"Not when the transfer order is signed by a deputy Reichfuehrer, surely." He took another swig of brandy from the flask. "My orders are to take this man to Berlin with all due speed. All I want you to do is to give me a car and a driver to take us to the station at Westheim. Your driver and the car will be back in two hours."

"But the bridge south of town is out, you can't get a train at Westheim."

"I know. I came as far as Thule last night, and was given a ride here by a Gestapo man. A bus is going to pick me up at Westheim."

"Oh, and who was the Gestapo man?"

"Wiebe, his name was. An inspector of some sort."

Stuckurt nodded. "I know Wiebe well. Terrible about his family being killed in an air raid, wasn't it?"

"Strange, he said he liked to go skiing with them. I had the distinct impression they were still alive."

"Oh yes, of course." Why was he so suspicious of this man? he asked himself. He was supposed to be suspicious of everyone, was the answer. "How will you get from Westheim to Mengin, Captain?"

"They are running a special bus from Westheim to Mengin for prisoners."

"Are you quite certain?"

"Check with the ministry if you wish," the SS captain said. "Why all the questions?" He passed him the flask. "I am not going to steal your car and driver, I assure you. On my honor!"

"Of course you're not," Stuckurt said with a chuckle. "It is just the unusual nature of your mission. A signed order from a deputy Reichfuehrer, no transportation of your own. But you have answered all my questions to my complete satisfaction." He poured himself some more brandy, mutely toasted a large photograph of the Fuehrer on the wall, and drank it down. It was truly amazing, but his back was no longer hurting.

He pushed a button on his desk and a moment later his sleepy-eyed young assistant, Gunther Epp, entered the room. "Heil Hitler, Herr Stuckurt." Epp, an emaciated and nervous young man, stooped forward in a servile manner, rubbing the cold out of his hands.

"The prisoner Shapiro, have him made ready for transport," Stuckurt said. "Get a car and driver for a trip to Westheim."

The assistant eyed the young SS captain and his flask, nodded, bowed, backed to the door, bowed again, and left.

"The SS get all the good men, see what I'm left with?" Stuckurt grumbled.

"By the time it is over," the SS captain said with a grin, "we may not have any men at all." He wiped his mouth on his sleeve. Stuckurt's opinion of the man was once more deteriorating. The man had the manners of a French whore, he thought.

"Let's go downstairs," Stuckurt said, wanting this man out of his office. "They'll bring the prisoner to the reception room."

Stuckurt found himself quite unsteady on his feet. Once in his youth he had drunk a full litre of brandy without so much as a slur in his speech. It was creeping old age, he thought. He was headed for liver trouble, perhaps.

Holding onto the railing, he took the stairs one at a time on the way down. He felt lightheaded and giddy, and even found himself humming. What a remarkable beverage, brandy. The French know how to live, he thought, even though they fight a war like old women.

At the bottom of the stairs, they passed through a doorway and down a long hall, then descended another set of stairs. Stuckurt unlocked a door and they went through to a vestibule near a side entrance. The room was half in the new concrete cell-block building and half in the old wooden building, which had once been the town constabulary. The part in the old building had once been a holding room for town drunks and juvenile offenders who would wait for their parents to come for them. Now the drunks and the juvenile offenders were all in the army or the cemetery. He burped, cupping a hand over his mouth.

The two men paced around for a few minutes before Gunther Epp appeared with a guard and Shapiro in tow. "Ah, here he is," Stuckurt said. "Ready to go."

The guard shoved Shapiro into the room. Shapiro had a large bruise over his right eye. Caked blood covered his lower lip and chin. He struggled to hold himself erect. He still had pride, Stuckurt thought, but in few more hours he would break like a twig.

He would weep like a woman giving birth.

The SS captain looked Julius Shapiro over carefully. "Well," he said after a couple of minutes, "he doesn't look like such a big shot now, but apparently he is a very powerful enemy of the State, Herr Stuckurt. And the Fuehrer himself will be told you are the man who captured him."

Stuckurt beamed. As far as he was concerned, Shapiro had been just another worthless Jew who gave up without even a whimper. In fact, he had the distinct impression the man was glad to be caught, that he was tired of hiding. It was not an uncommon thing.

The SS captain said, "I wish for the man to be shackled."

"See to it," Stuckurt said to the guard. The guard hurried away.

"It is difficult to keep a high efficiency rating these past few months, believe me," Stuckurt said. "Especially since we've had to go through so much with the plot against the Fuehrer last July. Do you know we made seventy arrests right here in our district? Unbelievable, is it not?"

The SS captain nodded his head. "So much treachery." He grinned. "It makes one almost ashamed to be German."

"It does indeed," Stuckurt said, then quickly realized it was not a good thing to admit in front of one's subordinates.

Stuckurt's assistant Epp appeared. "I'm sorry, sir, but there are no drivers available at the moment until Schiller returns from his meeting this morning."

"Nonsense!" Stuckurt snapped. "Drive the captain and his prisoner yourself. Go on, get your overcoat!"

Julius Shapiro said weakly, "Where are we going?" The guard told him to shut up and jerked his arms behind his back and put the shackles on.

"Talking not permitted, Jew!" Stuckurt said, hitting him in the mouth with the back of his hand.

The SS captain said, "Herr Shapiro, I assure you, you are going where you least expect." He grinned at Shapiro. It was a strange grin, Shapiro thought, half-amused, half devilish.

The guard handed the key to the shackles to the SS captain, who put it in his shirt pocket.

"Here we are," Stuckurt said, looking out a window. Epp drove up with a car. It was an old gray Mercedes with a red and white Nazi flag on the fender. Epp got out and opened the rear door.

"Would you like it if I sent along a guard?" Stuckurt said. "I'm sure we can spare someone."

"I can handle him," the SS captain said, taking Shapiro by the arm and yanking him out the door into the biting wind. Shapiro shrank from the cold. The SS captain turned and gestured a salute to Stuckurt, who waved and said, "Heil Hitler!" Stuckurt closed the door, walked over to the window, and watched them drive off, turning right out of the driveway and heading down the hill through town.

The SS corporal with the missing arm came in. "Herr Stuckurt, where are they taking the prisoner?"

"Westheim, where they will get a bus to Mengin where they will catch a train."

The guard shook his large head. "But that is not

possible. With my own eyes I have seen them taking up track between Mengin and Stuttgart so they can use the steel in the tracks."

"Surely you must be mistaken," Stuckurt said.

"I know what I know," the guard said.

Stuckurt gave him a hard glance as if he had made an insolent remark and went back upstairs to his office. He drank some hot coffee and tried to clear his head. Perhaps he had misunderstood the SS captain. There was much misinformation given out by the ministry of transportation. The damnable enemy bombings were making a mess of everything.

But then again, there had been something odd about that officer.

Stuckurt got up and dropped a couple lumps of coal into his stove, then sat in his chair sipping coffee and staring at the portrait of Hitler on the opposite wall. Hitler was giving a salute from the balcony of his suite outside the Reichchancellory in Berlin. Hitler looked like a true man of destiny in the photo, his face rigid, his arm extended stiffly, his stare piercing.

What was there about that SS captain? He was young, dashing devil-may-care. Much like the new breed. Nothing odd about that. A little bold, slightly ill-mannered. Common today. Something else. Something not typical.

He shared his brandy.

Stuckurt got up from his chair.

Yes, yes, that was it! The man was generous with a very superior and scarce brandy!

The SS men he knew were all arrogant and selfish, and looted whatever they could whenever they could.

But would they ever share any of it? Certainly not. Not a single one Bernhard Stuckurt knew. Not with a Gestapo man!

And then there was the signature on the document. How did he know it was Deputy SS Reichfuehrer Horst Rasten's signature? Had he ever seen a document signed by him? Yes, once maybe. When did Horst Rasten bother to sign documents in person? Especially over the capture of some Jew?

Bernhard Stuckurt, Gestapo Chief, Rothbaden District, shuddered.

He picked up the phone and told one of his assistants he had to speak to SS Headquarters in Berlin immediately, to Deputy SS Reichfuehrer Rasten, even if they had to wake him up.

"Urgent, most urgent!"

Chapter Three

Gunther Epp drove hunched over, holding onto the wheel with thick leather gloves, a felt Army hat pulled down over his ears. The heater in the car didn't work, and the wind whistled through a broken wing window on the right side. The prisoner sat shivering in the back seat, pressed up against the door. The young SS captain, sitting in back with the prisoner, kept sipping brandy and singing the SS anthem to himself:

When all are disloyal
Then we remain loyal
So that always upon this earth
There may be a banner in front of you.

The snow was falling as they wound their way through the streets of the town, which was just coming awake. Peddlers with carts and wagons and shopkeepers and children on their way to school hurried about. The town still retained its medieval character; many of the houses were of gothic architecture, built of stone with gray slate roofs. A group of boys were throwing snowballs at each other. The war had so far not touched here; there were no burned-out buildings, no bomb craters, no antiaircraft guns. Only an occasional Nazi banner or poster showing men in battle, urging the citizens to greater sacrifices, to donate food, clothing and blankets to men fighting on the front. These posters and banners were the only obvious manifestations that this was a country at war. Except, of course, that there were no young men anywhere to be seen.

Julius Shapiro, looking out the window, felt a pang. The town somehow reminded him of how things used to be in the Kaiser's day, and what a quite pleasant and civilized country Germany used to be.

Once through the town, they turned west. They drove through the snow-covered countryside, past dairy farms and thick pine forests dusted with snow.

Julius Shapiro found it too painful to look out the window. He turned his interest instead to the young SS captain, who in Shapiro's estimation was everything the Germans thought of as the perfect Aryan type. He was handsome, blond, filled to the top of his skull with his own self-importance. But there was something strange about him, about the way he looked at Shapiro. There wasn't any hate in his eyes. It was something else. Not pity, certainly not pity. It was as if he had a joke to tell him, but he wasn't ready yet to let him in on it. The look was not unfriendly. It had humanity in it.

Ah, you're fooling yourself, Julius Shapiro told

himself. This man is the very essence of the enemy and there is not one drop of humanity in him.

Suddenly the SS captain said, "Driver, I have to relieve myself, pull over."

Gunther Epp did what he was told.

"Not here," the SS captain said. "Up there near the trees would be good."

Gunther Epp continued on for half a kilometer, stopped the car, got out and opened the door for the SS captain. The wind was blowing the snow across the nearby field. The SS captain got out. It was then that Shapiro saw the gun in the SS captain's hand, which he brought up and shoved in the driver's face.

"March to those trees," the SS captain said, jerking Gunther Epp's sidearm out of its holster.

Shapiro watched the gawky Gunther Epp tremble and his breath puff out of his mouth like a steam train going uphill. He tilted his head forward and pushed his lower lip out. *"Nein, nein,"* he sputtered.

The SS captain pulled a length of cord from his pocket. "I'm only going to tie you up. March over there."

Gunther Epp looked toward the trees, then at the SS captain. He had his hands in front of him, waving them, then suddenly he pushed the SS captain and made a dash for the field across the road.

The SS captain cried out: "Halt! Halt!" But he didn't halt. He was flying across the field, his arms waving crazily, his feet kicking up snow behind him. The SS captain took aim with his pistol, held it, didn't fire. Instead he walked behind the car and stood under a telephone pole and fired a few shots at the insulators, cutting the lines. Then he climbed into the back seat and unlocked Shapiro's chains and gave him a biscuit and a piece of veal sausage.

"It's all I have to offer for breakfast," the SS captain said. "I hope it holds you until lunch—in Zurich."

Julius Shapiro just stared at him. He didn't know what to say. Or do.

The SS captain patted him on the shoulder, gave him a wink, then got into the driver's seat, put the car in gear, and pulled out onto the road. Accelerating quickly, he piloted the car down the road like a racecar driver, cutting the turns, glancing off the snow banks, leaving a great cloud of snow in their wake. As he drove he kept taking swigs of brandy.

He glanced back at Shapiro and said, "I suppose you're wondering what the hell's going on?"

Shapiro had eaten the biscuit and was now devouring the sausage slowly, letting each piece dissolve in his mouth. "When you've landed in the madhouse," he said, "everything is madness. You stop wondering."

"I suppose you think I should have shot that man back there."

"I'm glad you didn't. I don't like to see killing. Even a Gestapo man."

"There wasn't much purpose in dropping the poor *schnook*. By the time he puts out the alarm, we'll be gone like the magician's rabbit." He turned off at a fork in the road and headed up in the mountains toward Brendt. As he dropped down into third gear, the engine whined. He glanced back at Shapiro and said, "If it looks like we're going to be stopped at a routine checkpoint, chain yourself to the door post.

I'll complain about having no driver because of the manpower shortage. Just play your part, look stupefied. Can you handle that, Professor?"

"I am just a Jew, no one will ask me anything." After a moment he said, "You shouldn't be risking your life to save me. I didn't ask you to. I'm thankful, but I don't want to be the cause of another man's death."

"Relax, I've done this all before. They see my SS epaulettes, they just salute and say 'sieg heil.' Nazis are so brainwashed they haven't got a brain left." He guided the car through a couple of sharp S turns and headed down a straightaway.

After a moment, Shapiro said, "Might I ask who you are?"

"I'm a German and a Jew, the same as you. Only my mother had the good sense to take me to America when I was twelve."

"Not the same as me. I am terrified. Please tell me your name."

"Jonathan Becker."

"Thank you, Jonathan Becker."

"My cover name is Hans Shroeder. We'll just go on as we were. You're a Jew and you just got caught by the nasty SS. Finish that sausage, in case we're stopped. Wash it down with this." He passed him the silver flask of brandy.

Julius Shapiro tipped it up and let it trickle over his tongue. He had not tasted liquor of any kind in three years. He'd never been a drinking man, but he would take a drink on a special occasion. The brandy tasted sweet and a moment later a softening sensation went through his limbs. He felt momentarily light-headed, then he just relaxed, leaning back into the seat.

He remembered reading a story by the American Ambrose Bierce. In it, a man is about to be hung from a bridge. As he is pushed off the bridge with the rope around his neck, he imagines all kinds of things. How the rope breaks and he hits the water, how he runs away, how he eludes capture, how he makes it home to his beautiful wife—and it turns out to be a dream. At the end of the story he is hanging from the bridge.

He took his last bite of sausage. The meat was soft and moist and spicy. Real veal sausage. He leaned back and savored it, watching the snowbanks and the fields and the pine groves flash by the window. It had to be a dream. Being rescued by this handsome young man who gives you food and brandy. Surely this could not be happening.

The pain and the cold seeped out of his body. He felt warm now, and comfortable. Happy. It was not a dream. He had been rescued by this very brave, very bold young man, and he was going to have lunch in Zurich.

Bernhard Stuckurt kept telling himself to keep a cool head. The phone call to Berlin Headquarters produced little. With the Russian army closing in they no doubt had more important things to think about than what was going on in his sleepy little sector. They refused to wake up Deputy Reichfuehrer Rasten, but at Stuckurt's insistence they did check their files on Julius Shapiro. The Jew Julius Shapiro had been listed as having fled the country. He was just a professor, they said, of no particular importance. But they would check further and let him know.

Relieved, Stuckurt drank some coffee and looked out the window. Army trucks full of wood chips were rolling through town on their way to synthetic fuel plants. He knew they would be pulling off the road just south of town where they would be kept hidden from the Allied fighters, which were more numerous by day. He paced around. Ten minutes went by, then twenty. Finally the phone rang again. An angry Deputy Assistant of Weapons Development was on the line. Julius Shapiro had valuable knowledge useful in the manufacture of superweapons and he should be recaptured with all deliberate speed. He was not to be killed. And the man posing as the SS captain should be taken alive if possible and held for interrogation.

Posing as an SS captain. Incredible! The man was an agent for the Allies. Right here in the office, Stuckurt thought, drinking brandy!

Stuckurt wiped the perspiration from his face. The tongue in his mouth felt like a lump of leather. A sudden terror took hold of him. He had turned a valuable prisoner over to an Allied agent! If he did not act quickly, he would be facing a discipline hearing by the end of the week and then—

And then what? A trial? There was no time for trials these days. Perhaps not even a hearing. He would be simply and summarily shot. Despite the fact that he had handled the matter in a routine way, the way that anyone would have handled it.

Bile rose in his throat. The Jew and the counterfeit SS captain must somehow be captured. Yes, yes! They couldn't have gotten far. He reached for the phone. The mountainer SS training station was five miles away. He called the commandant of the trailing station and said he needed a dozen combat-ready men and transport immediately.

"Might I ask what is the problem, Herr Stuckurt?" the commandant asked.

"This is a priority request," Stuckurt stammered, "There's been an escape of an important prisoner by an Allied commando unit!" There, that would make them act fast.

"Responding immediately, Herr Stuckurt, we are on our way! Heil Hitler!"

Stuckurt then ordered his car fueled. His hands trembled. He decided not to take any of his men with him. He'd rely on the SS men, who were combat trained. Besides, if they failed he didn't want his men there to witness it. He loosened his collar. The room seemed impossibly stuffy.

He studied the map on the wall. He had seen with his own eyes that they had driven through town. That meant they would either be going to Westheim as the impostor SS captain had said, or they would turn off and head toward Brendt. Brendt was eighty kilometers from the Swiss border. At Brendt there was a detachment of the *Abwehrpolizei*, the border police. Stuckurt figured he could call and have them send some men to intercept. He picked up the phone and asked his clerk to make the call. He kept his voice well controlled. A moment later his clerk called back.

"Sorry, Herr Stuckurt, the line to Brendt is out."

"Get them on the radio, then."

"Their radio tower has been down since yesterday. It may have been sabotaged."

Stuckurt felt a cloud of gloom forming in his soul. He went back to his map. Precious minutes were ticking away. The Volkssturm—the Home Guard—checkpoint, manned by old men and boys, was his only hope. They at least had a shortwave radio.

He hurried off to the radio room. He wanted to give them their instructions personally.

The car came suddenly to a stop. Shapiro sat up and looked out the front window. The road led into a vast forest, and above the forest was a mantle of dark, brooding clouds.

"Snow, coming from the north," Jonathan said. "We'll have to hurry." He started driving again, fast. "Don't worry, I'll get you there."

Julius Shapiro suddenly and inexplicably burst into tears. "But why me?" he said. "Of all the millions?" A moment before he had been serene and calm, quietly looking out the window. And now tears. He must be having a breakdown, he thought.

"Why you? Because of what you know about shellfish toxins. They're afraid the Japanese might in their last desperate struggle turn to chemical agents and you know something about likely toxins. They want your brain."

Julius Shapiro sank back into his seat and wiped his eyes with a sleeve. "I'm sorry, I'm not usually given to emotionalism. Nor do I often cry like a baby."

"It's okay, Professor, cry all you want. My last customer, who I snatched from a transit camp in Belgium, had a laughing fit. I had to put him to sleep to get him to calm down."

Shapiro leaned back and looked out the window again, feeling the soft motion of the car as it glided along the snowy road. He was thinking that if his life didn't last another hour he had had at least one moment of hope. If there were men like this in the world, evil could not triumph.

A few kilometers further on, they went around a sharp bend in the road and came to a halt again.

"What is it?" Julius Shapiro asked.

"Transit checkpoint."

A kilometer ahead was the standard little hut, a crossbeam across the road, and a few guards.

"I'm afraid I may not have given Herr Stuckurt enough to drink. That, or our friend was a faster runner than I gave him credit for. Take a look. There are eight men—they look like Volkssturm—waiting for us, rifles pointed this way."

"What will we do?"

"I for one will have a little more brandy," Jonathan said. He put his hand back over the seat and Shapiro handed him the flask. He took a couple of swallows and put the cap back on and slipped the flask into his inside pocket. He handed Gunther Epp's pistol, a standard Walther P-38, to Shapiro. "The safety is on the side. Push it forward and it'll be ready to shoot."

"I was in the Great War," Shapiro said. "I assure

you I know how to shoot."

"These men are Volkssturm," Jonathan said. "They will not fire on Stuckurt's orders. The fools will stand there until we open fire. They have rifles, probably, but no automatic weapons. I will approach slowly. When we're within twenty meters I'll accelerate and head for the ones on the right. Shoot the ones on the left. Then keep down. Once we're through the gate, keep shooting out the back window."

There were high snowdrifts on either side of the road and the gusting wind was blowing swirls of snow into the air. Jonathan gunned the engine, shifted into low gear, and started forward. The red and white Nazi flag was blowing straight to the right in the strong wind.

Julius Shapiro prayed in Hebrew, *"Oh Lord, my God, in Thee do we put our trust: save us from all them that persecute us, and deliver us."*

"I don't think the Lord is listening to us Jews much these days, Professor. Better check to see how many bullets you have."

They were fifty meters from the checkpoint, approaching slowly. The car swerved gently on the slippery pavement.

Forty meters.

Shapiro said, "Fully loaded."

Thirty meters.

The guards kept their rifles pointed at them. Jonathan rolled down his window and stuck his hand out, waving to them.

Twenty meters.

"When mine enemies are turned back, they shall

fall and perish at Thy presence . . . Thou hast rebuked the heathen, Thou hast destroyed the wicked, Thou hast put out their name for ever and ever."

Jonathan suddenly accelerated and turned to the right, heading straight for the three men who suddenly stiffened as they recognized the danger. The crossbeam snapped. One man fired; the windshield shattered, spraying glass over Jonathan and Shapiro. The men screamed as they disappeared in front of the car.

Julius Shapiro, in the back seat, fired to the left, shattering the glass in the door, hitting the first man in the shoulder, then the second, then the back of the third as the car careened to the left into a parked truck, then bounced on down the road. Bullets thudded against the car.

They went around a curve and headed down a long straightaway.

"Nice going, Professor!" Jonathan yelled over the cold air rushing in through the hole where the windshield used to be. "Perhaps the Lord has woken from his long slumber and is listening once again."

Julius Shapiro said nothing.

Jonathan looked back over his shoulder. Julius Shapiro was slumped down on the floor, blood streaming out of his neck.

Chapter Four

Julius Shapiro opened his eyes. He was lying on his side in the snow with Jonathan bent over him. Jonathan was tying a bandage to his neck, securing it under his arm. Above, the clouds were dark and the wind was blowing wisps of snow across Jonathan's face. Julius Shapiro turned his head and saw the snow on the ground red with his blood.

"I can't stop the bleeding completely," Jonathan said. Julius Shapiro could see the fear dancing in Jonathan's eyes.

"Then leave me," Julius Shapiro said.

"How do you feel?" Jonathan asked.

"Weak," Julius Shapiro said. He strained to raise his head, but couldn't. The wound itself throbbed, but the pain was not excruciating. "You tried very hard, Jonathan Becker," he said. "I can die a happy man. Now go, save yourself."

"I promised you lunch in Zurich, remember?" Jonathan said, wiping his mouth with the back of his hand.

Julius Shapiro grabbed Jonathan's sleeve and held it. "Don't give your life to save mine, I won't have it!"

"I'm not giving my life for anything, Professor. We're in this together, now just hang on." He gave him an encouraging pat, but there wasn't much hope in the tone of his voice. "Listen, we've got just a short distance to go, right across that field. Can you walk? The car's gas tank was shot out." He helped Julius Shapiro to his feet; Shapiro took a step, but his legs collapsed from under him. "It's no use."

"Then I will have to come back for you," Jonathan said. "Here, take this." He handed him his Luger. "Here are eight bullets. Ammunition for the Germans is in short supply and an officer transporting a Jew would not be allowed any more than a few extra bullets, so I didn't want to risk carrying more. If they come before I return, hold them at bay." He lifted Shapiro into the back seat of the car. It was hardly warmer in the car than it was outside, but it was slightly more comfortable.

"Try to get an officer if you can," Jonathan said.

"I will shoot him right between the eyes."

"Good."

Jonathan took off running. Julius Shapiro watched him cross the field next to the road and head up the hill, disappearing into the trees. He had no idea where Jonathan Becker was going. Perhaps there was a town in that direction. He knew it would have been stupid for Jonathan Becker to say where he was going. If Shapiro knew and he got caught, the Gestapo would get it out of him. He was glad he didn't know.

Strange, but at the moment he felt so at peace.

The snow was falling more heavily now. It looked beautiful, Shapiro thought, swirling down on the field. Shapiro remembered his youth, in the town of Bemen, outside Leipzig, where he and his friends would ride a toboggan from the top of the hill down through the church yard, narrowly missing the gravestones. How daring! How thrilling!

He had taken his wife Sarah tobogganing once or twice in the first years when they were married. He had been working hard on his researches then, trying to earn his degree. Right after the Great War.

Yes, the Great War. Even now, thinking about it brought tears to his eyes. The defeat had been a terrible thing for Germany. He remembered weeping at the armistice, weeping for Germany. He was a sergeant in an artillery unit at the time. He had liked the army. The camaraderie. Perhaps there were some in his unit who despised him for being a Jew, but most of the soldiers forgot he was a Jew because he was a good sergeant, and they generally liked him.

But that was the Kaiser's Germany, where a Jew belonged to the "national brotherhood," as they said. Not Hitler's Germany, where Jews were considered "racial tuberculosis."

He closed his eyes. So peaceful. He could feel the warm blood trickling down his chest. Jonathan would have to come back soon, he thought, or all his blood would be gone. He wondered how much one could lose and still stay alive. An interesting problem in biology.

Fatigue overcame him and he drifted off to sleep.

* * *

Jonathan was on the other side of the hill now, out of breath, his face hot from running, weaving his way through a thicket of scrub pines. Already he could see the meadow and the steep cliffs beyond. It was snowing even more heavily here, and the snow was swirling in the stiff winds that were coming down from the upper valley to the north.

He came to the edge of the meadow and halted. Ski tracks. They were nearly covered over, but they were definitely ski tracks. Two sets of them. They appeared to have come down from the upper valley, followed along the edge of the woods, then, a few meters from where he was standing, headed to the east across the center of the meadow. Border patrols? Unlikely. It was almost a hundred kilometers through rugged terrain to the Swiss border. Border patrols would not be this far north. It could be that his tracks had been spotted the night before and they were looking for him. Then again, maybe they were just a couple of skiers. He examined the tracks closely. An hour or two old, he figured. He looked across the meadow. There was a trail beyond, he knew, that led down through the woods to Brendt.

He would circle the meadow, staying hidden in the trees. That would be the safest way to go. But Julius Shapiro was wounded and there was no telling how close the pursuit was. He didn't think that Stuckurt and his men would be there yet, but they might in forty-five minutes; if he took the time to circle the meadow, he might not return in time. He would have to chance it and make a mad dash for the woods on the other side.

He took a couple of deep breaths, scanned the other side of the meadow for the spot he wanted, and started running.

The snow in the meadow was drifted in places, almost waist high. His legs began to ache as he pushed himself forward. Now, exposed, he called himself a fool for not having stayed in the woods. If anyone was around he was sure to be spotted, and would be an easy target set off against the white snow.

He was making mistakes now. The mission was falling apart. He'd left the man he was supposed to be saving bleeding at the side of the road. Now he'd put himself in a vulnerable position.

He kept pushing, pumping his legs through the deep drifts, scanning the edge of the woods on the far side of the meadow. He was almost halfway across. So far, so good. He glanced back over his shoulder. No one following. The only sign of life was his own tracks. Faster, he told himself. He was gasping for air. Didn't his trainers have the goddamn sense to train him for high-altitude work? He was going to raise holy hell with Willis when he got back. If he got back.

That was no way to think, he told himself. You think *if,* you don't make it. You think positive, that's what they told you. Think positive. Positive. Anything a man can conceive and believe, he can achieve. Goddamn Americans! Everything a matter of believing in yourself!

Faster, he told himself, running now with his arms held high. He was less than a hundred meters from the other side of the meadow now. What was that?

To his right, back in the woods. Movement?

He hit the ground, burying his face in the snow. He lay still, trying to keep his breathing regular and slow. He listened. Quiet. The wind whistled through the trees. He reached for his Luger, then remembered he had left it with Julius Shapiro.

He raised his head slowly and looked toward the spot where he thought he had seen something. Whatever—or whoever—was gone. Maybe it was snow falling off a tree. Maybe it was his imagination. Agents must not let their imaginations run away with them, he'd been told a thousand times. There is danger enough without making it up in your stupid head, they'd said over and over.

He stood up and dusted the snow off. His muscles burned with exertion. He checked to make sure he was heading in the right direction, then started off walking with long strides. He was almost to the trees when he saw two Volkssturm soldiers with rifles aimed at him. He stopped and put up his hands, and let a slow smile come to his lips. They were just boys in ill-fitting uniforms, their helmets down over their ears. One looked about nine or ten, the other a year or two older.

"Heil Hitler!" Jonathan said, trying to sound slightly angered, but amused. "I am SS Captain Schroeder." He kept his hands up, but he looked at them in a kindly, fatherly way.

"Come over here, sir," the older one said.

Jonathan locked his fingers behind his head and kept smiling. He put his eyes on them, as he knew they were probably trained to tell a deserter by his lack of eye contact. He figured they would think of him as a deserter; it was not likely that they would have been alerted about the shooting at the checkpoint yet. The Volkssturm did not carry radios on their patrols.

"I'm going to put my hands down now, this is very uncomfortable."

"Nein!" said the older one. "Is it you who has the airplane over there?"

"Airplane? No, of course not. But I've been marching all over these hills all morning looking for it."

The two boys glanced at each other.

Jonathan smiled and said, "I brought a detachment of men with me this morning to search for an airplane which belongs to an Englisher. A spy. My men are searching on the other side of the hill there."

"I am sorry, Captain, but we must take you to Brendt," the older boy said. "Our orders are to take whoever we find in these mountains in for interrogation. Heinrich, please take the officer's sidearm."

The smaller one clicked on the safety of his weapon, leaned it next to a tree, and ran over and put his hand in Jonathan's holster. "He doesn't have one, Rudolf."

"I must have dropped it," Jonathan said.

"Check his pockets," the older one said. The younger one patted Jonathan down for a gun, but didn't find one. He ran back to his rifle.

"May I show you my papers?" Jonathan said.

The older one said, "We were told not to believe papers, they can be made by the enemy. Please start walking in that direction." He indicated the direction with a wave of his gun barrel.

"May I at least put my hands down?"

He hesitated, then said: "Yes, but keep them in your pockets."

Jonathan put his hands in his overcoat pockets and smiled an easy, confident smile. "Boys, you are making a terrible mistake. I can see you mean to do your duty well. Then you must listen to me. I am on a secret mission for the Fuehrer. I must get to that plane. I have to go to Berlin this moment, the future of the Reich may be at stake."

The smaller one said, "What if he tells us the truth, Rudolf?"

"We have our orders," the older one said. "We must obey them. Please, sir, begin walking in that direction or I will have to shoot you." And from the illogical, childish, but resolute look in his eye, Jonathan believed him.

Jonathan sighed and started walking.

Julius Shapiro awoke with a start. In the distance, he could hear engines. He pulled himself up and looked out the shattered back window. The snow was still falling. There, down the road and around the bend, he could see vehicles moving in the trees. Two, no, three of them. One, a truck.

He clutched the pistol. It felt as if it was made of lead. For a fleeting moment he thought of turning the gun on himself. But Jonathan had said to shoot one. An officer.

A good idea. If he did, it was just possible that he might save the life of some other Jew. Remotely possible, but possible. All right, he would do that. Kill one officer.

Strange, how having a purpose seemed to give him strength. He was hoping it would be Stuckurt. God, if only it would be Stuckurt.

He had to do it right, he told himself. Had to make it appear that he was going to give himself up. Then they'd come close. If they sensed any danger they would open fire. He would have to show them he was a groveling Jew. They wanted Jews to grovel. They expected it. They, the supermen, would never grovel. Yes, that was it. He'd pretend he was begging for his life. They would find that amusing. They'd come close to watch, to make him beg all the more. And then he would give them the surprise. He would aim and fire quickly and without warning.

Stuckurt first, then the next highest ranking.

Jonathan's Luger had a full magazine. Epp's Walther had one round.

The vehicles were closer now. A kilometer, perhaps a little less. He could see the flag on the fender of the first one. They were coming slowly. He could make out men with rifles getting out of the truck. Black uniforms, filing out in perfect order. They were SS. Crack troops. Maybe a dozen of them. He felt a shiver go up and down his spine.

They spread out now on either side of the road, approaching cautiously, bent forward, with their weapons held across their chests. A feeling of cold dread came over him. Now, looking death in the face, it was not nearly the same as when he had said he would shoot one of them between the eyes. How would that save another Jew anyway? Why was he telling himself those stupid lies?

He looked around for Jonathan. Where was he? He hoped he'd stay away. He closed his eyes for a moment. If only they would get it over quickly. That's the best he could hope for.

Julius Shapiro felt calmer now. He raised Jonathan's Luger, took the safety off, and pulled the receiver back. Everything was quiet. He looked around. A breeze swirled some snow. Lightly. Like a ghost dancing across the field. And for a moment his mind went back to his childhood in Bemen and to the steep hill behind the church where he and his friends used to toboggan. Funny, but at a distance the SS men, crouched low, dark against the snow, looked like his playmates pulling their toboggans up the hill from the cemetery.

Chapter Five

Jonathan walked as slowly as he could. The older boy kept ordering him to walk faster, but Jonathan kept the same slow pace, trying to think it out. Soon the heavy snow would come; if he didn't act quickly, he wouldn't be able to take off from here or land in the field near Shapiro, even if he got there before Stuckurt.

He had always been able to rely on his ability to bluff and act. He was an actor by profession. His mother had been an actress, the toast of the Berlin stage in the wild twenties, and she had trained him in the trade since he was four years old. He knew there were few actors of his skill in the world. But at the moment his skill wasn't doing him a bit of good.

Until now, his performances had always worked. But these boys had their orders fixed in their heads like nails driven into hard wood. He glanced over his shoulder. They were twenty paces behind, both pointing their rifles at him.

What had they taught him in training? In a tight spot, remember your cover.

Don't think like an agent, think like who you're supposed to be. All right, he said to himself, what would you do if you were a real SS captain? You would not tolerate the insolence of these two boys. Of course you wouldn't. You're a member of the SS, the elite. You're an Aryan superman on a secret mission for your Fuehrer. You wouldn't obey two small boys. You'd bark orders at them. You'd bully them into submission. Demand they follow your commands.

The German nation runs on orders. Everyone obeys. The German character lends itself to obedience. He could rely on that. These children were trained like circus seals. That was his chance.

He stopped walking.

The older boy said, "Keep moving."

Jonathan turned and faced them. "I am an SS officer!" he shrieked. The boys jumped back, startled. Jonathan took a few steps closer to them, putting his hands on his hips: "I am countermanding any and all previous orders you may have received! I order you to put down your weapons immediately!"

He marched toward them, resolutely. The younger one backed up, but the older one stood his ground, bringing his rifle up to his eye and aiming it at Jonathan. "I will shoot! I will shoot!"

"In the name of the Fuehrer, Adolf Hitler," Jonathan said in a commanding voice, "I order you to put down that rifle. You will shoot no one. I am an SS captain, and if you do not put that rifle down I will have you executed by firing squad!" He moved a few steps closer.

The younger one looked terrified, backing away. The older one didn't move. "H-H-Halt!" he ordered.

But Jonathan didn't halt. He could see the indecision in the boy's eyes as the boy sighted down the gun barrel.

Jonathan screamed: "Put down that rifle, I'm giving you an order!"

Jonathan was almost close enough now. One more step. He lowered his head and lunged for the boy's weapon.

The rifle crack split the air and echoed up the valley. Jonathan felt the bullet nick his left ear as he grabbed hold of the rifle, jerking it from the boy, raising it up and crashing it down on the boy's head. The smaller boy turned to run, but then, as if remembering his duty, turned back toward Jonathan, raising his rifle to fire. He was a few meters away, the heavy gun wobbling in his grasp.

"Nein!" Jonathan yelled, working the bolt action of the older boy's gun, slamming a shell into the chamber. *"Nein! Nein!"*

But the boy was going to shoot.

Jonathan ducked. The boy fired, the bullet going wild. The boy struggled with the bolt. *"Nein!"* Jonathan yelled. The boy brought the weapon into position to fire, but Jonathan fired first, hitting the boy in the chest, slamming him backward; a puff of breath escaped the boy's lips as he hit the snow.

Jonathan checked the older boy. His head was caved in, blood ran out his ears. The second boy was hit in the center of his chest and he wasn't breathing.

Jonathan flung the rifle away and stared, trembling, at the boys. Vomit rose in his throat. He gagged and spit, then caught his breath and slowly turned away and stumbled off in the direction of his plane.

To Julius Shapiro, the approaching SS no longer looked like school boys pulling toboggans. Those who were closest looked like the Four Horsemen of the Apocalypse, four dark figures in the whiteness. They crouched low, their machine guns held tight to their chests. The rest of the SS fanned out behind the four in a half circle perhaps a few meters across. Then Shapiro saw that Stuckurt was one of the first four. Stuckurt hollered something.

Julius Shapiro listened. The wind whistled softly through the smashed windows. There it was again: "Throw down your guns and surrender. This is a lawful order. You will not be killed."

Shapiro chuckled to himself. He was amazed at how clear-thinking he was. How unafraid he felt at the moment. He found that fact singularly strange. Death was a half kilometer away, approaching steadily, yet he felt no fear whatever. He felt instead a kind of elation. Why was this, he asked himself? He was not a particularly brave man. He had never considered himself a hero. He tried to form a hypothesis, but couldn't.

The answer came to him like a jolt. They could kill him, yes, but they had not defeated him!

And men like Jonathan Becker, brave men, cunning men, determined men, would carry on the fight. Adolf Hitler was doomed, and his evil empire was doomed. And nothing could stop it. He, Julius Shapiro, might die, but every man must die. He was forty-seven years old. He had lived well most of those forty-seven years. He had had a lovely wife, had done some important work, he had stayed out of the war for five years.

So what did his death matter in the grand scheme of things? Very damn little. Men were dying everywhere. Only one little task left to do. Kill as many of them as he could. At least he had his chance to die like a fighting man instead of a stewing hen. For that he must be thankful to God.

All he needed now was a little help from the God of Israel with his aim. *"Into Thine hand I commit my spirit for Thou hast redeemed me, O Lord, God of truth."*

Straining with the effort, he raised himself up and pointed the gun out the back window. His vision was blurry for a moment. He rubbed some snow on his face. That helped. The four dark figures trudged forward. He aimed high. *Wait until you see the whites of their eyes.* He had read that once, but couldn't remember in which famous battle it had been said.

Suddenly they stopped moving, just out of range. The ones further back started running in a wide circle to completely surround the car. When they were in position, Stuckurt came closer and yelled, "You cannot escape, give yourselves up!"

Ah, so they didn't know Jonathan Becker had gone off, Shapiro thought. That was good.

Shapiro didn't answer him. He didn't want to spend his strength shouting. A gust of wind blew a cloud of snow between them and they disappeared for a moment. Then they appeared again, trudging forward relentlessly.

The fear started in Shapiro's belly now. It was like this when he was a soldier, seeing the thousands of enemy troops charging madly at them. He held fast and kept his gun firing even when it seemed that they would be overrun. Back in the days when a Jew could serve his country and be a part of the National Brotherhood.

Fifty meters.

He could not see the whites of their eyes, but he could see their faces. The fear in his belly had formed a solid ball. He had planned to put on a show of weakness for them, but now that the moment had come, he couldn't do it. He couldn't let them come any closer. He sighted down the barrel of the gun. Stuckurt had slipped back a little. One of the others was circling in from the left, fast as an attacking leopard. Shapiro put his finger on the trigger and squeezed slowly.

The sharp crack of the pistol sounded and the man went down.

Julius Shapiro felt a burst of glee. He fired quickly at a second one, then a third, but he missed both. He fired both guns now with two hands as quickly as he could pull off shots. Then suddenly machine gun bullets peppered the snow all around the car. He drew back and slid down on the floor. Two more bursts danced around, kicking up the light snow. Then the firing stopped. They had missed. How could they miss?

He took a look. They were lying down in the snow

now; he could barely make out the tops of their helmets.

Why hadn't they fired on the car? A sudden terror gripped him. They wanted him alive!

For what cruel purpose?

He checked the magazine in his gun: four shots left. And in Jonathan's Luger: one shot.

He would have to save that one, he thought.

Jonathan's plane was an American-built Graumann two-seater originally intended for photographic reconnaissance, modified to carry a recoilless thirty-caliber machine gun in each wing. The construction of the plane was cloth over metal, light, relatively slow, but with a low stall speed. It was painted white, with no markings. When he got to it, the white tarpaulin had been pulled away. He climbed into the cabin and sat in the cold cockpit. He touched his ear and felt the warm blood. He was definitely missing the lobe.

He advanced the throttle, pulled out the choke, and hit the starter. The engine coughed and sputtered, then roared. He held the choke out until the engine smoothed out, then pushed the throttle forward. He put the flaps down and slowly advanced the throttle further. The plane began to move forward on its skis. The drifting snow and uncertain winds would make it difficult to get airborne.

He headed down the slope, along the edge of the woods. The bodies of the two boys were shadows on the snow as the plane swooped past. He looked away. He turned the plane to face up the valley, increasing the throttle. The plane began to gather speed. Forty, fifty, sixty, seventy, eighty, eighty-five miles an hour. He was bouncing over the drifts. He pulled back on the stick; the nose of the plane came up, then went gently down again, tipping slightly to the right; the plane bounced along the ground, then the nose gently rose again. He pushed the throttle all the way forward, pulled back the stick, and the plane rose into the air.

He felt a sudden sense of relief, of strength.

He leveled off at five hundred feet and looked back below him. A cloud of snow blown by his propeller was blowing down the valley. He couldn't see the boys any longer. He pulled back on the throttle. Air speed, one-eighty.

As he crossed the ridge at, he guessed, fifteen hundred feet, he could see the car where he had left Julius Shapiro, and he could see the truck and the SS men surrounding the car.

He gunned the engine and pushed the stick forward, banked to the right, and went in for a low pass. He closed in on them quickly, pushing the button on the top of his stick; the rattle of the machine guns on the wings let loose, kicking up the snow all around the SS men. Four or five fell, the rest scattered.

He banked to the right again, ignoring the truck and the car up the road. The men in the open field were running for the car and the truck, their black figures easy targets against the white snow. This was different than bashing in the heads of boys. These were full-grown, committed Nazis.

He came in again low, raking them. He cut down

three more. A bullet whistled through the canopy as he made his turn, missing his head by a few inches. He felt a wave of fear and nausea wash over him. In the cold cockpit, sweat rolled down his forehead.

As he came in for his third pass he caught a glimpse of a car heading down the road. He went after it. The car went around a curve and headed into a wooded area for cover. Jonathan stayed at a couple of thousand feet, then dropped straight down, firing as he went. The snow all around the car burst forth like a flower, and suddenly the car itself burst into flames and rolled onto its side.

Jonathan turned back again toward Julius Shapiro. The SS men had made it back to the truck, which was heading over the field toward a stand of pines. He let it go. He could maybe chance it and kill them, but there had been enough killing and the truck might be equipped with a machine gun that could bring him down.

Jonathan landed on the road and came to a stop near the car, leaving his engine idling. He got out of the plane, taking a sten gun with him. He raked the fallen SS just to make sure they were dead. Then he opened the car door. Julius Shapiro was huddled in the corner, his hand on his pistol and a bullet hole surrounded by powder burns in his right temple, blood and brains splattered on the seat cushions.

"Damn it, Professor, if you had waited just a few damn more minutes!"

Bernhard Stuckurt, at the wheel of the truck, had a pair of good 80-power binoculars. He had seen

Jonathan get out of the plane and knew he was vulnerable. Stuckurt felt hope rise. He looked around at his men. Only a few were still capable of fighting. He had been grazed in the leg but it was nothing serious. What was serious was that the Jew had not been taken alive.

He figured if he came back with the impostor SS captain at least he would have had some success. He would be disciplined, but not given the firing squad. He ordered the two men who were not wounded to climb onto the running boards of the truck. He shoved a clip into an MP 40 submachine gun and started the truck moving. It had taken a hit in the radiator and steam was pouring out of it. He started back down the road toward Jonathan.

He could see Jonathan turning the plane around by hand so that it was facing his truck. Yes! Yes! The wind was behind the truck, Stuckurt noticed by the way it was blowing the snow. The plane would have to come at him if it was going to take off. How perfect! He pressed the accelerator down. The truck gathered speed. He shifted into second. He could see Jonathan climbing into the plane. "Prepare to fire!" he yelled to the SS troopers on the running boards. He hit third gear and came around the little bend in the road. It was straightaway to the plane. There were snowdrifts on each side, which the plane couldn't possibly get across. We got him!

"Fire when I fire!" he yelled, sticking his machine gun out the window.

The plane was coming right at him. Stuckurt shifted into fourth gear. Steam poured from under the hood, obscuring his vision. The truck engine whined; it was overheating. The bearings are going, he thought. He yelled to the men on the running boards: "Hold your fire, hold it . . ."

The plane was dead ahead now, coming toward him at perhaps sixty miles an hour. "Fire! Fire!" Stuckurt fired through the truck's windshield.

Light flashed from the plane's wings and suddenly bullets ricocheted everywhere in the truck. The men on both running boards fell off. The truck began weaving out of control, first to the left, then the right. Stuckurt dropped his submachine gun and grabbed the wheel to hold on, aiming straight at the plane. Gun flashes again erupted from the wings, this time hitting the snowbank to Stuckurt's right.

Stuckurt kept the accelerator to the floor. The truck shuddered violently, then a loud clunk came from under the hood and Stuckurt knew it was a piston rod going through the engine block. Suddenly there was no power. The plane was dead ahead and coming at them. Stuckurt fumbled for his gun. Bullets slammed into the truck. Stuckurt ducked and fired wildly until the gun emptied.

The plane lifted off the ground, its skis scraping the top of the truck.

Stuckurt opened the door, jerking his Luger from its holster. He stood on the running board and fired eight shots at the plane as it disappeared into the clouds.

That night, from a hotel near Bern, Switzerland, Jonathan Becker sent the following telegram, in code, to his control in London. Decoded, it read:

Mission failed. Shapiro dead. Am resigning as of this date, request transportation to New York.

Book II

Chapter Six

The bare stage, lit by a few spotlights in the center, seemed cavernous.

Jonathan Becker felt strange to be standing on it. He was a man who had gone into hell and had escaped, and now just being with ordinary men seemed odd.

It had been two months since he'd turned in his resignation and so far he had heard nothing from the S.O.C., Special Operations Corps, the spy agency he'd been working for. He figured they must have known he was losing his nerve and they didn't want him. He'd had the surgically implanted fake scar removed from his cheek, and his ear lobe replaced with a piece of plastic that looked almost real. He felt himself once again. Jonathan Zalman Becker, actor.

He tried not to think about his old bosses. They were leaving him alone, he would leave them alone.

It just felt good to be where people felt passionately about things like giving a good performance. Things like pleasing an audience so they would have a good evening of theater. Nothing life or death here. Simply the pleasure of art.

But Jonathan could not forget completely the hell he had so recently visited. The image of Julius Shapiro, his brains spread over the back seat of the car on the road from Rothbaden to Brendt, would not leave his mind. Neither would the image of two boys in baggy uniforms, dead on the snow.

"Are we quite ready, Mr. Becker?" This is from Miss Melrose, the assistant director. She was sitting at the front of the stage on a stool with a clipboard and pencil and a copy of the script; she was giving him what she called *individual psychic direction.* Miss Melrose was, Jonathan thought, a befuddled young woman who, because so many really talented people were off fighting the war, had managed to rise far beyond her talents. He smiled at her and nodded. "Ready."

"I consider this soliloquy a moment of epiphany," Miss Melrose said, "and therefore one of the axes on which the play turns."

Jonathan knew better than to argue Shakespeare's authorial intent with a director, even an assistant director puffed up with her own self-importance. But he knew her theories were nonsense. *Hamlet* had a flow like a symphony, and the idea of epiphanies—one of her favorite words—was so much pseudo-intellectual bunk. But then Miss Melrose was a Vassar woman, which she didn't mind reminding people of whenever possible, and was therefore filled to the brim with irrelevancies.

She said, "Pick it up after the ghost says:

The glow worm shows the manten to be near,
And 'gins to pale his uneffectual fire:
Adieu, adieu! Hamlet, remember me!"

She said the lines with a faraway look in her upward-turned eyes, voice solemn, as if she were reciting a prayer. Not, he thought, like the ghost of a man pleading with his son for revenge.

"All right, Mr. Becker," Miss Melrose said. "Begin." She pointed her finger at him as if pushing the start button on an electrical appliance.

Jonathan stook in the center of the circle of light on the stage and brought his arms around himself tightly. That was the way he saw Hamlet in his mind's eye. As a man fighting to hold himself together. He thought of acting as taking on the personality of another, of bringing that character to mind, seeing him, feeling him, and letting that character descend upon him, like a spirit taking possession.

He began:

"O all you host of heaven! O earth! What else?
And shall I couple hell? O, fie! Hold, hold, hold my heart;
And you, my sinews, grow not instant old,
But bear me stiffly up. Remember thee!"

He let his arms unfold, stretching them outward. Then he lifted up his eyes:

"Ay, thou poor ghost, while memory holds a seat
In this distracted globe. Remember thee!
Yea from the table of my memory
I'll wipe away all trivial fond records,
All saws of books, all forms, all pressures past . . ."

As he turned to gesture toward the front of the stage, he thought he saw someone in the shadows at the edge of the stage, watching. He stopped and peered into the darkness. There *was* someone. A man wearing a wide-brimmed hat.

Miss Melrose said, "Don't be so easily distracted, Mr. Becker. Go on."

"Who's there?" Jonathan asked. He felt a sudden pang of fear.

The man stepped from the shadows into the circle of light on the stage. He was about forty, broad-shouldered. Jonathan knew the man. He didn't know his name, but he knew he was an errand boy for Willis, his so-called "mission coordinator," the man who had sent him into German-occupied territory.

"The Coordinator wants to see you, Jonathan,"

the man said. He had an expressionless face and a mechanical voice.

"Who are you?" Miss Melrose asked sharply. "How did you get in here?"

"Don't be alarmed," he said. "I'm just delivering a message."

"You've delivered it," Jonathan said. "Now go."

"I'm supposed to bring you with me."

"I'm finished with all that," Jonathan said. "I told Willis last time that it was the last time. Period."

"I wouldn't know anything about what you said to Willis or what he said to you, all I know is he told me to collect you. And I mean to do just that."

"Just what is going on?" Miss Melrose asked, climbing down off her stool. "Sir, you'll have to leave, we open in two weeks and Mr. Becker is far from ready."

"Mr. Becker has another job, lady, that he has to do. Stay out of it."

"Get out of here," Jonathan said. "Tell Willis I said 'no'."

The man looked down and shuffled his feet as if he was cleaning something off the soles of his shoes. "Mr. Willis said I was to bring you whether you wanted to come or not. You know what that means? I either bring you to Willis or send you to the hospital."

Willis had an unhappy face. His eyes were large and sad, and his mouth seemed forever in a petulant curl, like a spoiled child who couldn't get his way.

He was sitting behind a desk in a nearly empty office in a warehouse in the Bronx. The warehouse was full of canned goods, army uniforms, and unpainted pine coffins. Jonathan was given a folding chair to sit on by the man who had brought him there. The office was cold. Gray light that filtered in from the frosted window put a strange pattern of shadows on the wall. Another man stood by the window. Not at all the kind of man Jonathan was used to seeing in the company of Willis. This man was sixty or so, with a round, rather pleasant face. Willis didn't say who he was and Jonathan didn't ask.

Willis lit a cigarette with a kitchen match. "Nice to see you again, Becker."

"Just say what you brought me here to listen to, Willis," Jonathan said.

Willis took a long drag on his cigarette, not taking his eyes off Jonathan.

"You comfortable? Like a cigarette? A drink?"

"No. I'm not doing it, whatever you've got in mind. You been reading the papers? The Ludendorf Bridge over the Rhine at Remagen is intact and the Allies are pouring across it. Cologne has been taken. The Soviet Army is in East Prussia and speeding toward Berlin like a pack of ravenous wolves. The war in Europe is over."

Willis said, "Tell that to the people doing the dying."

Jonathan looked at the man by the window. He hadn't moved. He was looking Jonathan over in a curious way. As a man might admire a prize fighter.

Willis said, "We want you to go to Berlin."

"Not a chance," Jonathan said.

"The Germans are shoring up what little strength they have for two last-ditch defenses. One in Berlin, the other in Bavaria, near a small Alpine village called Obersalzberg."

"They won't hold up the Allies very long."

"Long enough for you to do what you have to do."

"There isn't anything I *have* to do."

"Listen for a moment, will you? Please." A look of pain appeared on Willis' sad face. He took a long drag on his cigarette. "The Germans can and will hold out for another month, maybe two or even three. What we propose for you to do will shorten the war by a couple of weeks, maybe as long as a month or six weeks."

"I'm not going to Berlin."

"Right now they're killing Jews at an astronomical rate, more than seven thousand per day. Per *day,* Jonathan. Fifty thousand a week. Think of it. If the war were to end three weeks earlier you would save a hundred and fifty thousand lives."

Jonathan said, "Get someone else."

"But you're the best. There's nobody as good as you."

"Perhaps I was once the best, when I thought I was invincible. When I thought my damn glib tongue would get me out of anything. But it won't. I lost the magic, Willis. My hands shake just thinking about it. Last time out I killed two boys. I close my eyes to sleep and I see them. And I never got

Shapiro out. I bungled it top to bottom."

"Nobody gets a home run every time at the plate."

Jonathan leaned over Willis' desk. "But I can't do it any more. When I started, I told you. One time only. And I did it. That was the Gypsy spy, Tobeck his name was. Then you said just one more time. To save a Jew. And I went again and saved a Jew. Then again, because some Jew was important for the war effort. I was lucky. I was good, too, maybe. Bold as hell, which is what you have to be. Twenty-one times I've gone in. It's enough. I don't have it in me any more. I can't do it, and that's that." Jonathan turned away from him.

There was silence in the cold room for a moment. The sun was going down and the light against the window was orange now. The man standing by the window looked half orange, half gray.

"Besides," Jonathan said, "There's no one I could get out who would possibly make that much difference to the war." He looked at Willis whose sad expression didn't change.

Willis said, "I guarantee you there is."

The man by the window shifted his weight on his feet and said, "Perhaps we ought to tell him, Mr. Willis."

"There's nothing you could tell me that would change my mind," Jonathan said, wiping his forehead with his sleeve.

Willis nodded toward the man by the window. "All right," he said. "This is Mr. X, Jonathan."

The man approached and shook Jonathan's hand and said, "I'm sorry for the theatrical alias, but they tell me it's necessary." He smiled softly. "I'm not a spy. I'm a scholar. A political psychologist, really."

Willis said, "Hear him out, Jonathan."

The man folded his hands in front of him and leaned back against Willis' desk. He said, "Here is what we know now. Hitler wants to make a deal with the Soviets. He is in deadly fear of Germany being partitioned. If the Soviets will agree to an immediate truce, he believes he can push the Allies out of the country and will allow the Soviets to occupy the whole of Germany. He hates and fears Bolshevism, but he hates and fears the democracies even more, we believe, and would fight to push us out and let the Soviets in. It is even more possible, given the nature of the man's psychology, that he thinks he might maneuver the Soviets into allowing him to operate a semi-autonomous Nazi state within their sphere. Included in the deal is all of Germany's rocket and jet technology, certain bacteriological weapons, and so on, which we believe the Soviets would dearly like to get hold of. You can't imagine how attractive this deal would be to the Soviets. The Ruhr and the Rhineland are the industrial heart of Europe. It would guarantee the Soviet postwar domination of Europe, militarily and economically."

Jonathan got to his feet, staring first at the mysterious Mr. X, then at Willis. Finally, he said, "You want me to kill Hitler, don't you? You must be crazy, both of you. You can't ask me to do that. It's a suicide mission. They put people on meat hooks in Germany for even whispering such a thing."

Mr. X shook his head. "No, Mr. Becker, you don't

understand. We don't want you to kill him."

Willis said, "We want you to bring him out alive. We can't try him for crimes against humanity in a world court if he's dead."

Jonathan Becker stared at him again for a long moment, then burst out laughing. "I am a Jew, and you want me to save Hitler's life! Even if it could be done, which it can't, what makes you think I would do it? You're out of your goddamn minds."

Mr. X put his hand on Jonathan's shoulder. "Listen to me. Here is our reasoning. The men who operate the death camps will continue the killing until Hitler orders them stopped or the Allies overrun them. If Hitler dies, Himmler will step into his shoes and the killing goes on. Before he gives up he will make sure that every camp inmate is dead. But if Hitler can be brought out alive, his orders will be obeyed."

Jonathan said, "If he's ready to deal with the Russians, why should he come over to us?"

"Because," Willis said, "you are going to show him how he can still win the war."

"How am I going to do that, Willis?"

"Your cover will be that of a loyal SS officer who has a consignment of poison gas—Tabun. Made in a secret lab outside of Germany. Very lethal stuff."

Jonathan shook his head. "I actually believe you think this fool scheme would work."

Willis said, "Mr. X has been studying the mind of Adolf Hitler since '37. Tell Jonathan what we know."

Mr. X stuck his hands in his pockets and leaned on the desk. "Hitler has a fixation on death. It fascinates him. He's in love with it. And even though he's threatened suicide on at least twenty-three occasions that we have documented since the suicide of his niece and lover, Geli Raubal, in 1931, it is our considered opinion that he would not go through with it. He will tell himself that he will die with his troops, but when the moment comes he will not be able to pull the trigger. You see, at his core he's two men. One ruthless, obsessed with power. The other, tender, a failed artist, a mama's boy. When the moment of suicide comes, it will be proposed by the man of power, but it will be left to the man of tenderness to do it. And he won't be able to."

Jonathan turned to Willis. "Berlin is about to be encircled by the Soviets. There will be terrible chaos. Even if they don't shoot me for a spy, I could get killed walking down the street. I might just as well shoot myself now."

Willis said, "I won't tell you the odds are good, but if we could stop all the killing, why not stop it?" His sad eyes closed, then opened again.

Jonathan said, "It's no good anyway. You can't perform if you haven't the conviction. If you don't totally believe in yourself, and I don't. You will have to send someone else."

Willis leaned back in his chair. "You've made twenty-one missions, and you're still alive. Forty-one percent of our people who are sent in never come back even the first time. No one else has even made a dozen missions. You've made twenty-one. What are the odds on making twenty-one missions? A thousand to one? Yet here you are, breathing in and breathing out."

Mr. X said, "I agree the person who attempts this mission has very little chance of succeeding, Mr. Becker. I won't lie to you. It is an exceedingly dangerous mission, with perhaps only a chance in a hundred of succeeding. But those in the camps have no chance at all."

Jonathan said, "Excuse me gentlemen, but I have a play to rehearse." He got up and started for the door.

Willis said, "If you don't come with us, we'll arrange for the army to conscript you."

"Go ahead. I like peeling potatoes."

Chapter Seven

"Gypsy Love," the folk song on the record, lamented lost love and lost youth. It was an overly sentimental song with soft violins in the background. Jonathan had always loved it, he didn't know why. He was sitting on the window sill, sipping brandy out of a coffee mug, wondering why, after almost a pint of the stuff, he was still feeling so damn sober.

Jonathan's room was tiny, but neat. There was barely enough room for the brass double bed, bedside table with an old lamp with a red shade, an old-fashioned ornate dresser, and a stuffed chair with a horrible green floral pattern which clashed with the red-striped wallpaper. His small record player was on the floor. He shared a bathroom with the roomer next door, and he had a view of the alley, but the accommodations were adequate. The hotel catered to theater people and was expensive, but it was just two blocks away from the 45th Street theater where he was rehearsing *Hamlet.*

One thing kept going through Jonathan's mind. Something Mr. X had said. *But those in the camps have no chance at all.*

He had been to the camps, and he knew. He'd seen the hollow empty eyes, the frail bodies, the smokestacks of the crematoriums.

But to go into Berlin. Now, with it under bombardment every day. What insanity! The very thought of it made him shudder. He just couldn't do it.

He leaned his head back against the wall and shut his eyes. He had never thought of himself as a coward, but he perhaps had to face the fact. But is it cowardly to want to live? He wasn't a spy. He was an actor. All he ever wanted to be was an actor. His father had been an actor, and his grandfather. His father had died of cancer when he was three, but he could still remember his father's great booming voice playing Othello in blackface.

Jonathan had acted in Germany as a child and the first thing his mother did when they came to America was to enroll him in a children's theater ensemble. His mother could speak English, and they took voice lessons together to learn to speak American English. She wasn't rich, but she'd managed to get her jewels out of Germany and sell them for a few thousand dollars. That gave them a start. And soon his mother was working.

He remembered how much she wanted him to be an American. When he wasn't acting or taking speech lessons, he went to public schools, played baseball, ate hotdogs, shot marbles, went to the movies. She had him to to Hebrew school for one year to make his Bar Mitzvah in a Reformed Temple. He forgot Germany and its horrors. And then the war came. When he joined the army to fight Nazis they found out he could speak German like a native. He was quickly transferred to the S.O.C.—the Special Operation Corps.

Willis told him, "You will be able to strike a blow directly into Hitler's heart."

He took a drink. It had all seemed so romantic, so exciting. Get into a role, jump out of a plane with a parachute. Fly his own plane. Errol Flynn. John Wayne. What an adventure!

Now, even the thought of it made him tremble. Ever since the day in '43 he'd been caught by an ordinary policeman in France for ignoring some traffic sign. The policeman didn't believe his papers and was going to call his superiors. Jonathan shoved a knife into his belly. The man threw up blood. After that Jonathan no longer felt invincible.

After that, he began to sweat whenever they seemed to be closing in on him.

Vicky Norris, another member of the theater company, popped her head in the door and said, "Heard you had a little problem at the rehearsal." She stepped in, but left the door open. She had to leave the door open. House rules, at least until eleven o'clock. But the manager went to bed at eleven, and after eleven the rules changed.

Jonathan said, "Miss Melrose is a bitch." Funny, but even though it had only been that afternoon, the session with Miss Melrose seemed like the dim past.

He reached down and switched off "Gypsy Love."

Vicky said, "We all know she's a bitch, but what about the man who came and dragged you out?" She seemed genuinely concerned. She lived down the hall. They'd had dinner a few times. Talked after rehearsals in a bar called *Indigo Blue.* Jonathan had only known her a month, but he was already extremely fond of her. She wasn't beautiful, she was a girl-next-door kind of cute; bouncy and alive, full of that American optimism he found so abominable in military men. In her it was delightful. She had a heart-shaped face, short auburn hair, and nice even teeth. She was at the moment understudy for Sheila Meers, who was playing Ophelia. Jonathan thought Vicky played a pretty bad Ophelia. Too damn perky, no tragic power. He would never tell he that, of course.

"You seem to have a case of the mopes," Vicky said. She sat down in the chair with the flowered pattern. He got up from the window to pace, but there really wasn't any room, so he sat on the bed. They couldn't both sit on the bed. Another house rule.

"Brandy?" he asked.

"Not supposed to drink in our rooms," she shook her finger at him. "Rule number four."

"Coffee then?" He passed her a coffee cup and poured some brandy in it.

"That's much better," she said.

She reached over and closed the door.

"It's only five after nine," Jonathan said.

"I know," she said, with a devilish grin. "Well, you going to tell me what that man wanted or aren't you? The whole company is bubbling with theories, most of them supposing that you're really a German agent provocateur."

He didn't answer her, he just smiled. He sat and admired her for a moment. She was wearing a white ruffled blouse and a pearl choker, a plaid skirt, white buck shoes and bobby socks. She looked back at him with blue blue eyes, with a look of complete innocence on her face. Vicky Norris from Coldwell Corners, Vermont, U.S.A. Sweet as maple sugar. But she was more than just sweet; she had Yankee practicality and a basic honesty that he rarely found in actresses.

"Is that what you think of me?" he asked. "That I'm a Nazi agent."

"I think . . . you're a very talented actor, Jonathan."

"And a Nazi?"

"No. Of course not. But they do ask why it is you've never been in the army." She curled her feet up under her.

"I have trouble with my inner ear, I lose my balance."

"I knew it was something like that. Rodney Webber—the one who played Joe Crowell Jr. in 'Our Town' last year—said you were probably a homosexual and that's why you weren't in the army. I told him he was an idiot."

Jonathan laughed.

"So who was that man who came to rehearsal today?"

"Somebody I owe money to. Rather, he works for the man I owe money to."

"Oh."

She took a gulp of brandy, then said, "I have a few dollars saved, maybe I could let you have some."

"Thanks for the offer, but the problem's been taken care of." He poured them both some more brandy.

"So how come you aren't in war production?" she asked suddenly. "A man who has trouble with his ear can work on an assembly line punching rivets."

"You certainly are suspicious."

"I'm sorry, I don't mean to be."

"I don't mind telling you. My mother knew someone on the War Productions Board and got me an exemption so I could act. She and I have done some USO work to make up for it. They count that as being for the war effort. That's why I've been away from New York so much."

She shook her head. "I don't believe you," she said. "You know what I think?"

"What do you think?"

"I think you've been a spy of some kind.

He laughed.

"And you know what else I think? I think they want you to do something terribly dangerous, and you've told them no. That's why you've been sitting here in your room all alone drinking brandy. You know what else? I'll bet you've done your bit. Whatever it is they want you to do, you've a perfect right to say no."

Americans, he thought, were wonderful. Almost childlike in their simplicity. Moral dilemmas could always be reduced to a simple equation. *You did your bit*. Simple enough. Damn if he didn't like the way her eyes sparkled.

"I'm not a spy," he said.

She said, "You must be very proud."

"I'm not a spy," he said again.

She took a sip of brandy and stared wide-eyed at him. "They want you to go on a suicide mission, don't they? Deep behind enemy lines."

"Come on now, do I look like a spy?"

"They want you to assassinate some baron or somebody. Someone terribly evil."

"All right, have it your way. You're right. I'm an assassin. They want me to shoot Baron von Klauswitzmeinklunk, the Tiger of the Rhineland, Hitler's bootmaker."

"There, I knew it!" she exclaimed, laughing. She got out of her chair and sat next to him. He kissed her on the cheek. "Thanks," he said.

"Thanks for what?"

"Just thanks."

She turned his chin toward her, the pressed her lips against his. Her lips were warm, and he felt the warmth float down his body. The kiss left a sweet aftertaste. Maple-sugar sweet. She pulled back with a smile on her face. Then she locked the door. She turned the record player on low and started unbuttoning her blouse.

He went to his bureau and took out another pint of brandy. She took it away from him.

"You won't need any more of that tonight," she said.

The dream was the same: Men and women with

faces twisted in agony, packed into cattle cars. The doors of the cattle cars open. The men and women walk down a ramp. Suddenly he is at the head of the line. At the end of the ramp a door opens. Inside is a fire. An SS officer in a black uniform smiles and gestures that he may go on in. He approaches. The coals of the fire are human skulls.

Jonathan awoke, sweating, to the sharp ringing of the phone. A thought struck him: *But those in the camps have no chance at all.*

He clicked on the light. The clock said four-fifteen. Vicky was gone. The phone rang again. He answered. The desk clerk said, "A lady to see you, Mr. Becker."

"I'll be right down."

He didn't ask who it was. He knew. His mother. Goddamn Willis must have talked to her, he thought. He dreaded seeing her, but there was no way to avoid it.

He got up and dressed. He had a slight headache, but he was alert and rested. Vicky had succeeded in lifting his spirits. He splashed some cold water on his face.

His mother was waiting for him in the lobby.

She was wearing a cloth coat with a fur collar buttoned tight to her neck, a small, stylish fur hat, gloves, and black boots. She was standing very erect, her chin high. Regal. She had finely chiseled features and very dark, piercing eyes. Her hair was iron gray.

He kissed her on the cheek. "Where can we talk?" she said in English. She had insisted they speak to each other in English since the day they left Germany. She had wanted nothing more to do with those "damnable Prussians," she'd said, "and their sick little corporal king."

The odd thing was, she was more German than the Germans in many ways. She clung to the traditional German virtues of punctuality, neatness, "correctness," the worship of order and orderliness. Before the Nazis came to power she had been, like most Jews, completely assimilated into German society. She'd been a star of the German stage and radio drama, she moved among the German aristocracy with the brilliance and ease of a meteorite through the heavens.

They went into the small sitting room and closed the double doors. He helped her off with her coat. Through the translucent drapes he could see the snow falling outside, large flat flakes swirling down into the street.

He said, "Willis talked to you, didn't he?"

She nodded. Her dark eyes seemed frozen deep in their sockets. "Mr. Willis came to see me in Hartford. He left at nine o'clock last evening. Since then I've been pacing the floor."

She sat down in a chair. He sat opposite on a settee and rubbed his face.

"You've come to convince me I ought to go."

"No," she said. She was stiffly erect, her hands folded in her lap. Her eyes searched his. "I would never try to convince you of anything you knew in your heart to be wrong."

"Did Willis tell you what my mission would be?"

"No, but I assumed it was a particularly dangerous one."

"Dangerous in the extreme." He couldn't look at

her eyes. "It's a simple as that. The courage has all been used up. And to go into Berlin itself would be suicide. Bombed by the British and the Americans day and night. Just to find a contact would be nearly impossible."

"I see," she said.

"Haven't I haven enough, Mother? Twenty-one times I have gone in there. Twenty-one! I have brought out twenty-six people. Twenty-six important people, people who have helped to win the war."

"Yes," she said. "And I am proud, supremely proud."

"I want to live," he said.

"And I want you to live, Jonathan. More than anything. You are all the family I have. You are my only child. You mean more to me than I can ever tell you."

Jonathan stood up and began pacing. "I am an actor, not a soldier, not a spy. I don't want any part of their filthy war. You wanted me to become an American. I am an American. Europe and its sickness is none of my affair."

She said nothing to that.

He turned to her now and saw tears streaking down her face. He had seen her cry only once before, on the day they left Germany, the time she told him from then on English was their language and America was their homeland.

"Listen to me," she said. "They took us captive in Egypt, and we survived. The Romans destroyed the Temple and dispersed our people, and we survived. Their brutal empire is in the ashes of history and here we are. Others, the Russians, the Ottoman

Turks, the Spaniards, have had pogroms and inquisitions against us and we are still here, while all their empires have turned to dust. We have met this Adolf Hitler before, when he had a different face and a different name. Always we survived. We sometimes moved on. We sometimes fought. We have endured prisons and famines and beatings for millennia and we are still here."

"I know, Mother."

She suddenly stood up and hugged him, then walked to the door. "I have a matinee tomorrow," she said. "I should get some sleep."

Jonathan felt a sudden sensation of fear, a powerful sensation that made him shudder. He closed his eyes and told himself, *no matter what, I can't go.*

"Is it true," she said, turning back, "that this mission would save many Jews?"

"Possibly," he answered after a moment.

She nodded, then she kissed him on the cheek and went out without saying anything more. He followed her outside, where a cab was waiting. He opened the door for her.

He said, "If I go, I will be killed."

"No one knows what the Lord has in store for him.

He watched the cab drive down the street and turn the corner, then he watched the large flakes of snow float to the pavement in the cone of light from a nearby street light. He felt peculiar. Like a man taking a last look at his home town before leaving it forever.

He headed for the stairs to his hotel and there was Willis with his overcoat on and his collar turned up.

"Do you believe in God, Willis?" Jonathan asked.

"No," Willis said. "I believe in fate."

Jonathan said, "There's a girl I'd like to say good-bye to."

"Not permitted," Willis said.

Chapter Eight

Emma Rolf was a stern, sixtyish German, an intellectual, a communist, anti-fascist to her core. She had broad peasant shoulders and a flat, square face with large yellow teeth.

She had a passion for martyrdom and couldn't tolerate anyone who didn't. Hitler and his gang of thugs, as she called them, were the worst evil in history, and it was her mission in life to blot them out. Once in Munich before the 1923 Beer Hall Putsch she had attempted to stab Hitler with a bread knife and had been beaten unconscious by his bodyguards. She loved to tell the story. It always ended with her pounding her fist on a table or wall while she said: "If only I had had a gun, there would have been no Third Reich!"

Despite her bullying ways, Jonathan liked her.

"I am to get you ready for your mission," she said to Jonathan on his first day, a cigarette wet with spit stuck between her lips. She spoke in guttural German that came out of her mouth like a growl. "From now on, Mr. Becker, no liquor, no idleness, no wandering thoughts. Work, work, and more work!"

He clicked his heels and saluted with a smile. He wasn't feeling all that good-natured about it; he was showing a little bravado.

"A comedian," she scoffed. "Well, we shall see. You have ten days to get ready. We shall see how much you will want joking when we finish."

They were at what once had been some kind of resort in either upstate New York or Vermont, Jonathan wasn't quite sure which.

Near the resort was a lake, some mountains, a lot of pine trees. The days were warmer and the snow was melting. A few birds had arrived to announce that spring was here.

The resort itself was made up of a huge brown-shingled, rough-hewn, deliberately rustic house and a few outbuildings: a boat house, a stable, some small cabins. The training teams were kept separate from one another. Altogether there were possibly a hundred people staying there, Jonathan guessed. He saw some of them going jogging or to the showers. Mostly young men and women with eager, serious faces, aglow with the spirit of adventure.

His orders were to speak to no one except to members of his own team, which consisted of Emma Rolf, Mr. X, and a martial arts expert he had had dealings with before by the name of Ott. Ott, as far as Jonathan could tell, was a psychotic killer who was so profoundly artful at killing they put him in charge of teaching others. Jonathan detested him.

Emma Rolf's job was to get him prepared to

assume his new cover identity; Mr. X's, to teach him about Hitler; Ott's, to give him a quick brush-up course in killing. Jonathan was already feeling afraid. He was being prepared for a trip into hell. *Abandon all hope, ye who enter here.*

Emma Rolf took Jonathan to his first morning session with Mr. X. They met in an attic room; it was airless and overly warm and smelled of dust. It had plank floors and a blackboard and a window that looked out on the lake.

Mr. X sat across the table with a bundle of notes in front of him. He was wearing a pair of bifocals and a bow tie and blue suit with wide lapels. He smiled pleasantly when Jonathan entered the room and he offered him a seat. Jonathan took him to be an American with the typical American naivete, and thought all he would hear from this man would be pleasing falsehoods that would not serve him well when the time came.

"You are an expert on Adolf Hitler?" Jonathan asked.

"Yes."

"Did you ever meet him?"

"Personally? No."

"Did you ever see him?"

"No, not in person."

Jonathan leaned back in his chair and said, "Then how is it you are an expert?"

Mr. X raised his eyebrows. "A fair question, Mr. Becker. All right, I will tell you how I know what I know. I have interviewed personally four hundred people who knew him, some intimately. From fellow students to close relatives. We have had a panel of fifteen top psychologists working on this project since 1938, inspecting every aspect of the man's character."

"If I do get into Hitler's presence, Mr. X, my performance will have to be perfect. I have to know the audience I will be playing to, and he is the audience."

"We are making educated guesses, the best guesses the best minds in the field can make."

"All right, tell me what you know."

"Adolf Hitler was born 20 April 1889 in Braunau am Inn, Austria. His father, Alois Schickelgruber Hitler, a retired customs inspector, was then fifty-two, stern, a drunkard, and a brute. Adolf's mother, the former Klara Poelz, was 20. She doted on Adolf and often fought pitched battles with her husband because of it. Young Adolf was a poor student, a dreamer, moody, lazy, and discontented. He had a deep and abiding hatred for his father and his younger brother. Adolf's mother died of cancer in December 1908, which was a terrible blow to young Adolf, who by then was thoroughly a mama's boy."

"I already don't like him," Jonathan said. "And we haven't yet met."

Mr. X smiled, then went on, hardly needing to refer to the bundle of notes in front of him:

"Young Adolf had dreams of becoming an artist, and while it's true that many of his critics have since said he was not very good, he was in fact *quite* good. I have some samples here of his work." He produced a picture of a house, another of a boy fishing, another of some soldiers. Jonathan glanced at them, then nodded.

"I'm not a critic," he said.

"I'm not either," Mr. X said, "but I've had them analyzed by good critics, who tell me he might have had a future. Let's see, where was I? Oh, yes, where he left school to go to Vienna with grand illusions of becoming a famous artist. He failed to gain acceptance into the art academy, and went on to live as a sort of bum, painting a few postcards, living in what we would call flophouses. Here he fell in with fellows who were rabidly anti-Semitic, and it was during this time his hatred of the Jews began. He attended anti-Semitic rallies where he first heard of such concepts as 'blood purity,' the 'Eternal Jew,' and other racial nonsense, mostly from a defrocked monk and lunatic named Lanz von Liebenfels." Mr. X took his handkerchief out of his pocket and blew his nose with a loud honk. Then he continued:

"In 1913 Hitler left Vienna and went to Munich, where he lived the same sort of life as a down-and-outer leading a hand-to-mouth existence, going to political rallies and anti-Semitic club meetings, and dreaming about becoming a great artist or architect without really doing anything about it. When war broke out in 1914 he joined the Sixteenth Bavarian Infantry Regiment. He was a clerk and dispatch runner through most of the war, rose to Lance Corporal—equivalent to a Pfc in the American army—was wounded twice, and gassed once, right before the end of the war. He recovered and remained in the army after the war, spying on fellow soldiers about their revolutionary activities and getting a few of them sent to the firing squad."

"Such a nice fellow," Jonathan said, "even then."

Mr. X honked into his handkerchief again. Then he continued without commenting on Jonathan's sarcasm: "One of the groups he was sent to spy on turned out to be the German Workers' Party. It had only a few dozen members. He joined, and shortly it became the National Socialist German Workers' Party, and he became its *Fuehrer.* His first contributions to the party were its new symbol, the swastika; its greeting, 'Heil!;' and the first formations of storm troopers."

"What wonderful gifts to the world," Jonathan said. "So far what you've told me is in the encyclopedia."

Mr. X frowned. "Hitler was instrumental in formulating the party's twenty-five point program of February 24, 1920, which proposed the exclusion of the Jews from the *Volk* community."

"Couldn't we just pass by the history lesson and get to something I might be able to use? Like what does he eat for lunch?"

"You must know his whole life story."

"I'd rather know the man. The details. The minutiae that make up his life. What does he eat?"

Mr. X closed his notes. "He's a vegetarian."

"Does he like women?"

"Yes, and men, too, apparently."

"You mean he's queer? Never heard that one before."

"Bisexual, probably. Many of the flophouses he

stayed in were known to cater to homosexuals and he's been known to address a few close male friends by the name 'Bubie,' which homosexuals often use to refer to their lovers. He was registered in the Vienna police files as a pervert, at least there's some evidence he was. In the beginning of his political rise many of his closest associates were homosexuals—including Ernest Rohm, the head of the S.A., whom, as I'm sure you know, Hitler had murdered."

"What about Evae Braun? What's his relationship with her?"

"Heterosexual."

"He's heterosexual *and* homosexual. He's a dreamer, a mama's boy, and a man of action. An artist and a militarist. So far, Mr. X, you've painted a very confusing picture."

"Hitler is two men. One is the mama's boy. Sensitive, moody, a dreamer, an artist. When he went into politics he realized that this personality would never do, so he created another. A quite remarkable achievement, I think. He can adapt this personality at will to hide his real self, the mama's boy who cried, I've been told, when his canary died. I wish we could open a window in here." He fanned himself, then went on: "He made himself into the superman he dreamed about. The triumph of the will. Iron discipline. He developed this personality first as a device for public speaking. He was making speeches to people who had lost everything in war, to inflation and unemployment, people who had no hope and no goal. Germans have always loved the strong man, who they want to lead them. Hitler set out to make himself that man in every way."

Mr. X got up and tried the window, then sat down again. "The manufactured personality, the strong man, you cannot deal with. He is an imaginary man and quite irrational."

"So we deal with the mama's boy. How do I do that?"

"You have to wait for the personality to shift on its own, I suppose."

Jonathan said, "And if it doesn't shift?"

Mr. X shrugged. "I have a few more points I want to make before getting into his bizarre sexual proclivities and other elements of his rather warped personality." He flipped through some pages and said, "Ah, yes, he was arrested for the Beer Hall Putsch in 1923, when he attempted to overthrow the government. He was imprisoned in Landsberg Fortress for nine months, during which he wrote his famous book *Mein Kampf,* which he had originally planned to title *Four and a Half Years of Struggle Against Lies, Stupidity, and Cowardice.*

Mr. X found that amusing; he chuckled over it for a moment. "I see our time is up for today. I'll give you some things to read, which will help you get to know the man better."

"Hold on, Mr. X, you still didn't answer me," Jonathan said. "What happens if his personality does not shift to the mama's boy mode?"

"We think that it will."

"What you think is not good enough. My damn life is on the line."

"Everytime in the past he has faced a disaster, he

has retreated into his mama's boy personality."

"The Russians banging on the door of Berlin is not exactly going to improve his disposition."

"In a way it will. Each disaster in his past drove him closer to what we believe is his present psychological state. First, his mother's death drove him into despair and rage. A rage that fixed itself upon the Jews. Next, his failure to get into art school. Here he again fell into despair and rage and withdrew into the underworld, so to speak. Next, after the war, he fell in love with his niece and they had a rather open and torrid love affair. Of course he dominated and brutalized her, but he loved her as he loved no one else before or since, including Eva Braun. But he so dominated Geli, not letting her see her friends, forbidding her to come and go as she pleased, that she committed suicide. Again, the same pattern followed. Withdrawal, more rages. Only this time he threatened suicide, and supposedly tried to kill himself, but to the great detriment of the world he didn't. Following the defeat of General Paulus' Sixth Army at Stalingrad in January '43, we get the same pattern. Withdrawal, followed by rage. Again, the same pattern following the assassination attempt on July 20th last year. This time the rage resulted in the assassination of ten thousand Germans in the most grisly way. We have just received good intelligence that he has within the past few days ordered the virtual destruction of Germany: all bridges, schools, factories, power plants, everything. You see, Mr. Becker, he is heading into the state of psychological withdrawal. In that state you will be able to manipulate him. What we believe is that during these periods of withdrawal, he takes off the personality of the superman and becomes the mama's boy, where he dreams up a new version of the superman. If he has gone into one of his withdrawal periods he will be ripe for your picking. You will show him he can rebuild the superman and he will listen, and you will be able to lead him into our trap."

"And if he is not in the withdrawal period?"

"He will probably have you shot."

Chapter Nine

Jonathan was sitting alone at a small table in the kitchen eating a tuna fish sandwich while three women who belonged to another team chatted amongst themselves about how wonderful it will be when the war's over and nylons will again be available. They also talked of penetrating the enemy's embassy in New York, which gave Jonathan a jolt. What enemy had an embassy in New York? And then he suddenly realized they were talking about the Soviet Union. Germany was not even crushed and there was a new enemy. Americans, what a wonder, he thought.

Emma Rolf suddenly burst into the kitchen and marched over to Jonathan and said, "What, Herr Becker, is the motto of the SS?"

"Believe! Obey! Fight!"

"Very good," she said, giving him a satisfied smile, displaying her large, yellow teeth. "Now then, if you are to be the mad little corporal's messiah, you first must be someone whom he will trust. We must make your story credible."

"Credibility is always the key, I've been told," Jonathan said.

She was wearing a padded army jacket and she had one for him tucked under her arm. "Come with me," she said, throwing him his coat. "I've got someone you must meet."

He followed her out the back door of the kitchen and down a flight of unpainted wooden stairs to a waiting car. It was a pleasant afternoon, sunny and warm. Spring in the air. She drove. The road was full of ruts and curves, but it didn't slow her down much.

"You think you're going on your last mission to die, Mr. Becker," she said, "and that is why you are so cynical and sarcastic. Believe me, you are not going to die. You will carry out this mission and you will be successful. We will have Herr Hitler and we will try him and hang him. And you will have saved the lives of a hundred thousand people. You should feel honored and privileged."

"And if I don't make it?"

"You will have the honor to have died in a great cause."

"Which is something I never aspired to do. Where are we going?" he asked, hanging on to the door handle as the car bounced along.

"Not far."

The road turned into two parallel paths, twisting up the mountain. They came to a halt below a small shack built into the side of a hill. Emma Rolf got out and gestured for Jonathan to follow. They walked up the hill into the shack. Inside were two

U.S. Marines with Thompson submachine guns. They saluted and opened a large wooden door that led into a cave in the mountain.

The cave was cool and the air was moist, but fresh, blowing up from what seemed like a deep cavern in the earth. Jonathan followed Emma Rolf through a narrow passage lit with a string of low-wattage naked bulbs. Water dripped from the walls. The tunnel floor was covered with crude planks in places. At last they came to a stairway that led down to a well lit, huge room cut out of rock with other passageways leading off it.

Here, a Marine sergeant sat at a large desk with a few telephones and a stack of papers in front of him. He stood up when Emma Rolf and Jonathan entered the room.

"Number four," Emma Rolf said.

The Marine sergeant produced a large key ring from his desk and indicated that Jonathan and Emma Rolf should follow him. He went down a narrow, dark passage, where it was warmer but the air was no longer fresh and smelled vaguely of cooking odors. After fifty yards, the passage widened. Here were a series of heavy metal doors built into the rock. The sergeant opened the one marked #4 and Jonathan and Emma Rolf went in.

It was like a monk's cell, only larger—the size of half a tennis court—with a cot, a table, and a small bookcase. A young man approximately Jonathan's age lay on the cot. He got up when they entered, and rubbed his eyes. He was wearing tan pants and a rumpled white shirt. The Marine sergeant said, "Company, Herr Lieutenant." Then he turned on some lights and left them alone.

"I speak English, I prefer it," the lieutenant said.

"Hello, Fritz," Emma Rolf said. "Meet Jonathan."

"My name is Lieutenant Mohne," he said stiffly, "and I expect to be so addressed."

"It is a pleasure to meet you, Lieutenant Mohne." Jonathan gestured a willingness to shake hands, which Mohne declined.

"Being a member of the super race," Emma Rolf said, "Fritz does not want to touch the flesh of inferiors. Afraid he might catch something."

"You are jealous and make jokes," Mohne said, "because you know it is true, we are the super race."

Jonathan said, "You supermen don't seem to be doing so well at the moment."

"We have not quit, don't say anything until we do."

Emma Rolf said, "Lieutenant Mohne has been in South America."

"Where I was illegally and forcibly kidnapped by Jewish scum and brought here. Wherever *here* is."

"Tell Jonathan what you've been doing down in South America."

Mohne said nothing, he merely sneered.

"You might as well tell it," Emma Rolf said, "you've already told the whole story once."

He looked pleadingly at Jonathan. "I have been tortured."

"He cracked," Emma Rolf said, "in fifteen minutes. I never touched him, that is the honest truth."

"What sense was there in holding out?" Mohne said. "They would do what they would and I would be broken eventually anyway. We Germans perfected the methods used by interrogators all over the world."

"The lieutenant has been setting things up for Herr Hitler," Emma Rolf said, "so he will have a home after the war is over. Should the Germans lose."

"It is a long way from over," the lieutenant said.

Emma Rolf sighed. "You see, Herr Becker, this is the man you will become when you go to Berlin. You will be Lieutenant Friedrich Franz Mohne."

Jonathan raised an eyebrow. "I have never played an actual person before."

"We know. But it's just possible Hitler will have you checked out. We want to make sure that if he does your cover story will hold up. You see, even though you have no faith in this plan, we do. Tell him, Herr Lieutenant, what you were planning to do when you were apprehended in Argentina."

"I was going back to Germany."

"For what purpose?"

"To take the Fuehrer to safety."

Emma Rolf turned to Jonathan. "You see. A simple thing, we merely send you rather than Herr Mohne."

Jonathan looked at him closely. He did in fact resemble Mohne. Mohne was perhaps an inch taller and his hair was darker, which would not be a problem. His cheekbones were higher, but perhaps that could be taken care of.

Emma Rolf said, "In faded old photographs you will be close enough to pass."

"What if I run into someone who knew him?"

"Then you'd better learn to walk and talk and

think like him, and maybe you'll get by."

Mohne said, "No one could impersonate me, it is not possible. But it will be amusing to see how long you live in Berlin. I give you five minutes."

Jonathan, with identical inflection in his voice, said: "No one could impersonate me, it is not possible. But it will be amusing to see how long you live in Berlin. I give you five minutes."

Mohne stared at Jonathan in astonishment.

And at that moment, for the first time, Jonathan thought he just might make it. They had gone to a lot of trouble on this one. Perhaps, if his nerve held up, he just might be able to pull it off.

Newspapers were not allowed at the training center, but Jonathan found one stuffed between the door and the seat of Emma Rolf's car. He read it sitting on the john.

It was full of war news. The Philippines were again invaded by the American Army's 185th Regiment. Danzig on the Baltic coast was overrun by the Russians, who were advancing on Germany in three massive fronts. The American First Army had crossed the River Eder. Forces of the French First Army crossed the Rhine near Speyer.

Damn, he thought, if only the end would come now. Can't the idiotic Nazis see it's over for them? Why the hell don't they just shoot Hitler and call it quits?

After supper he had a few minutes before he had to see Mr. X. He took a short walk up one of the nearby trails and watched the sunset, which caused the mountain that towered above the lodge to glow pink. Was it possible, he wondered? Could this crazy plan work? After dark it quickly turned colder. He came back down and warmed himself by the fire for a few moments before climbing the stairs to the attic for another session with Mr. X.

Mr. X was wearing the same suit he had on that morning, but with a sweater underneath. Jonathan was late. Mr. X seemed perturbed by that. There was so much he had to know, and so little time, he scolded.

Mr. X began by pointing out that Hitler had a phenomenal photographic memory and that Jonathan should make sure that whatever he told Hitler, he should not change it even in the most minute way. The next thing he should know was that Hitler was a great mimic and that one of his favorite tricks was to perfectly portray one of his underlings and embarrass him. He was a genius at that sort of thing.

And that Hitler had an irresistible hypnotic glare, and that his glare alone had brought many hundreds of people into the party and many millions of marks into the party's coffers.

That he fervently believed in astrology and that he at no time would have no less than three astrologers close at hand. That he believed in providence. Once when he was sitting in a trench during the Great War he heard a voice say, "Get up and go over there." He did, and the men who were sitting with him were all killed a moment later by an artillery shell. That from that moment on he believed providence was guiding him.

Mr. X seemed to take on a glow as he talked about

his subject.

"Hold on here a minute, Mr. X," Jonathan said. "You know how I work. I go in posing as a German, usually a high ranking SS officer."

"I know."

"I've fooled a good many people. High ranking people. What are the chances of fooling Hitler?"

"I can't answer that one. I have no crystal ball." He turned a few pages of his notes. "Hitler has three major themes upon which he harangues endlessly: the treason of the November criminals; the rule of the Marxists must be broken; the world domination of the Jews. And he identifies himself with the Teutonic knights, and once had himself painted as a knight of the Holy Grail. Below the painting was the inscription: *in the beginning was the word.* He has incredible powers of concentration, can endure several days with little sleep, can break down a complex problem into a few simple factors, more by intuition than by logic. He often boasts that he has no conscience. 'My conscience is Adolf Hitler' is one of his favorite phrases."

"Will he go for what I'm selling him? Will he want to leave Berlin if I show him a way out?"

"Please pay attention. I was about to give you his primary rules of leadership: Never allow the public to cool off. Never admit a fault or a wrong. Never concede that there may be good in your enemy. Never leave room for alternatives. Never accept blame. Blame one enemy at a time for everything."

Jonathan said, "You've still given me nothing I can use. The plan is that I am going in to persuade Hitler to come out with me. Will he believe me? Will he go for it?"

He averted his gaze. "I cannot answer that."

"You think Hitler will see through me in five minutes."

Mr. X looked around as if he were making sure he was not about to be overheard. "Let us say it would be foolish to underestimate him."

It was late when he finished with Mr. X and Jonathan was tired. But first he had to spend an hour down in the boat house which was being used as a gymnasium. Ott was waiting for him when he arrived. He was an evil-looking little man with oriental eyes, even though he was a German, and had a narrow chin, which gave him a satanic look.

"Hello, Becker," he said. He said, "Becker" with a hard "B" as if there were something wrong with the name. Jonathan had always suspected Ott didn't have much liking for Jews. Or anyone else for that matter.

"All right, Becker, let's see what you remember from the last time I tried to teach you something."

"I've had a long day and I'm tired," Jonathan said.

"You have several hours to spend with me over the next few days, you might as well get used to the idea."

Jonathan kicked off his shoes and got onto the mat. Ott invited him to attack, then threw him a few times using standard judo throws. Jonathan got up slowly each time.

"I see you have not been practicing much," he

said. "Let's see how you do with kicks."

Jonathan was working up a sweat. He tried first a punch, then a kick to Ott's head. The next thing he knew he was on the mat looking up. He got to his feet.

"You never were any good," Ott said. "You have none of the killer in you."

"Maybe if I had had a better teacher."

Ott pointed at him and said, "You'd better watch your smart mouth. I can make it rough for you."

Jonathan retrieved his shoes. "I've had enough for tonight."

"You've had enough when I say you've had enough!"

Jonathan just ignored him.

Ott called after him, "I got you down for two tomorrow, you aren't here, I tell Willis."

"Yeah, yeah," Jonathan said over his shoulder.

When he got to his room, Jonathan had a surprise waiting. A woman was standing at the window in the darkness.

"Did I get the wrong room?" he asked, clicking on the light.

She turned to him. "I don't think so," she said.

It was Vicky.

Chapter Ten

"Aren't you happy to see me?" Vicky asked.

"More than you could ever imagine." Jonathan wrapped his arms around her and they kissed. She exuded a clean aroma, like fresh soap and talcum powder. "My God, how did you get here?" Jonathan asked. "I never in a thousand years—" He drew back from her suddenly. "Willis brought you here, didn't he?"

She nodded. "Yes."

"How?"

She shrugged. "I was at rehearsal. He came on stage with Miss Melrose and she introduced him simply as a man from the government and said that if I was willing to do what he wanted me to do the company would spare me for a few weeks. Then I spoke to Willis and he said you needed me, and would I come with him to visit you at a very nice lodge. He said it was most important to both you and the government. So I wanted to do my bit. What's the matter, Jonathan? You're sweating."

"I'm not sweating." He walked to the window, wiping his forehead on his shirt sleeve and looked out on the darkness.

"Come and sit by me," she said. "Would you please tell me what's going on around here? What is this place?"

He ignored her question. He kept looking out the window. "Those bastards," he said finally.

"I wish you'd explain, Jonathan."

He swung around. "Tell me something. How is it you happened to be playing stand-in for Ophelia?"

She shrugged. "I tried out for the part and I got it. The usual way . . . Would you please come and sit by me?"

He stayed by the window. "How did you hear about it?"

"I was in Herb Cohen's acting workshop and I got a phone call from someone who said they saw me in Mr. Cohen's class and thought I should try out for the part."

"Who was this person?"

She shrugged. "Howells—Fowells—something like that, he said his name was. I thought he was a scout for the company."

"Scout for the company, bullshit! Where's Willis now?"

"In the room at the end of the hall. He said if I wanted to go back with him tonight I should tell him before midnight. I don't want to go back."

Jonathan started out the door, but held up. He turned to her. "Wait a minute, wait just one damn minute. I'm not buying it, Vicky. All that talk the other night about me being a spy. You knew then I was with S.O.C., didn't you?"

"I, ah—"

"No lies now, if we're going to mean anything to each other, we've got the tell the truth."

"I've known Mr. Willis for some time, yes."

"He has you date spies?"

"Well, in a way. It isn't what you think, Jonathan, I like you, really I do. I wouldn't have come here if I didn't."

"Wait here." Jonathan stormed out of the room, marched down the hall, and kicked open the door.

Willis was sitting behind a desk, facing him, signing his name to some papers. He looked up and said, "Close the door."

Jonathan slammed the door behind him, grabbed the edge of Willis' desk, and threw it to one side.

Willis blinked at him. "If you touch me, I'll have you killed." His voice quivered, but his face was as placid as if he were ordering a cheese danish.

Jonathan said, "If I touch you, there won't be enough pieces left to know you were ever on this planet."

"My, my, what has managed to upset you so?"

"You and your damn little organization. Planning my love life. Arranging things."

Willis leaned back in his chair and crossed his legs. "You like her, don't you? You'd be amazed at the selection process we used to find one just the right type. You like them young, innocent, and naive."

"You maggot!"

Willis shrugged. "I have a job to do and I do it any way I can. I have to arrange a little romance, I do it. You were a fucked-up mess. Resigned to dying. A man resigned to dying will not fight hard enough, will not use all his tools. A man resigned to dying is already dead. A dead agent is no good to me. Now I suggest you go back down to your room and enjoy yourself."

"Take her away, I don't want her."

Willis shrugged.

"I mean it, Willis, get her out of here, now!"

Willis got up and put on his overcoat. "You're a fool."

A few minutes later Jonathan watched Vicky and Willis walk down the stairs. She gave Jonathan a cold look as she passed by, but she didn't say anything. He went to his room and looked out the window. She got into a black Packard sedan with Willis and they drove off down the road.

Jonathan went down to the kitchen where he found two young men from another team drinking cocoa and talking about going on a hike the next morning. He asked them whether they knew where Ott's room was. One of them told him to check the south wing, room two.

Jonathan went up to Ott's room and pounded on the door. Ott opened it. "Hey, what's up? The war over?"

Jonathan hit him square in the face, staggering him.

"I'll be down at the boat house," Jonathan said. "You want to do anything about that?"

In the boathouse Ott said, "What the hell got into you, man?"

"You always wanted to teach me something, now's

the time."

Ott moved in low with amazing speed, taking Jonathan down. Jonathan kicked him on the roll, and Ott returned the favor.

"Teach me to be a killer," Jonathan said, rolling onto his feet. "Teach me everything you know."

Jonathan awoke bruised and sore at seven-thirty in the morning. Ott had thrown him around for over two hours. Punched him, kicked him, and put him in arm locks and head locks. Jonathan had thrown him as well, and got in some good kicks and punches. It felt good. His head was clear. And even though he took a beating, he had felt no fear.

Ott had then shown him what he wanted him to learn. How to take a man with a piece of wire concealed in the sleeve, how to go for the eyes first. How to freeze your mind when you kill, so that plucking a man's soul out of him means nothing more than plucking a ripe peach.

The gray morning light filtered through the curtains and made a strange pattern on the wall, almost like a swastika. Jonathan got up stiffly, showered and dressed. It was while dressing that he had the overpowering feeling that somehow there was an unseen force controlling his destiny.

Over the next two weeks he worked fourteen to sixteen-hour days. First there were films to watch of Friedrich Franz Mohne, the officer they had locked away in the cave. He had some characteristic gestures Jonathan wanted to get down pat, the way he arched his eyebrows when he was being sardonic, which was often. The superior way he paced, his hands behind his back, chin held high. When he was being particularly arrogant he curled his lower lip out and spit out his words.

Jonathan found the man thoroughly disgusting.

Mohne had a scar on his back in the shape of a scythe. A doctor came and marked Jonathan with an identical scar. Next, they shoved some kind of dental cement high into his cheeks to give him Mohne's high cheek bones, then they dyed his hair. The transformation was good, but not perfect. But then Mohne had been in South America for nearly two years, and they were counting on that. A man changes in two years.

Emma Rolf kept telling Jonathan it was extremely unlikely that he'd meet anyone who knew Mohne, but they weren't taking any chances.

Meanwhile, every morning in the attic, Mr. X kept up his discussions with Jonathan about Hilter:

"He's two people, never forget that. One soft, who can cry at the death of his pet canary, the one who likes dogs. He's the one who wants nothing more out of life than to sit around and have women take care of him. Now that the Reich he built out of his twisted fantasies is crumbling, you can expect him to vacillate much more frequently between his two personalities. Perhaps even several times in the space of a few moments. Work on the weak one. Do not confront or try to influence the strong one. Work on the one that has nightmares, the one that must sleep with a light on. The one that must have someone in the room with him to read him to sleep because he cannot face the terrors of the night. The weak character will be ready to grab at any straw. Be sure the straw he grabs is *our* straw."

The afternoons were spent with Ott in the boat house learning new ways to kill. How to shatter a man's neck vertebrae with a twist of the head. How to shove a knife into a man's neck and push outward, cutting the carotid arteries. How to choke a man to death with one hand.

Meanwhile, Emma Rolf made him practice being Mohne until he could take on the cloak of his character at will. He could strut like him, throwing his hip out to one side; he held a cigarette between the tips of his fingers; he snarled when he said the word "Jew;" his eyes glowed when he mentioned the sacred name of Adolf Hitler.

She had him do skits, ordering a subordinate to shine his boots, expounding Nazi crack-pot philosophy in the officers' barracks, having a drink of schnapps with a superior. She'd sit on the couch and yell, "You've got it! Perfect!" At times. At others, "No, No! Shoulders more square, the glint in the eye, proud, not angry. Proud, damn it!"

Jonathan Becker was becoming Friedrich Mohne, right down to the click of his heels on a hard floor.

He read the file they'd put together on Friedrich Mohne's life. He was a member of the East Prussian aristocracy. His father, Franz, was a general, killed on the Russian front. Friedrich played polo while in school, learned swordsmanship. Excelled in mathematics and physics. Joined the Waffen SS in 1939 at eighteen, befriended by Himmler, sent to explore possible overseas escape routes for high-ranking Nazis in 1943. Jonathan memorized the names of

Mohne's friends, relatives, and classmates, the names of his polo ponies. The name of the Lutheran church where he was christened, the women he had affairs with.

Then Jonathan started on profiles of the people he would be likely to encounter if he ever got close to Hitler. Men like Himmler, the SS chief, a scared rabbit, a scatterbrained intellectual, ruthless, nervous; Goebbels, the slick propaganda minister who loved Hitler; Goering, the overindulgent, corpulent head of the Luftwaffe; Albert Speer, the genius armaments czar; the mysterious Martin Bormann, Hitler's point man; Eva Braun, the party girl. And there was Hitler's crackpot physician, Dr. Morrell, who had addicted Hitler to amphetamines and was injecting him with a pharmacy of unknown palliatives every day. Jonathan studied them all, the generals, the ministers, the party lackeys.

It started raining on April tenth and didn't let up. The grounds around the lodge turned to mud. On the evening of April fourteenth, Willis arrived with wire service photos of the Belsen and Buchenwald death camps, which had been liberated the day before. He called Jonathan into his small office and spread the pictures out on the desk. Hundreds of them, showing walking skeletons in striped uniforms, stacks of bodies, the gas chambers, the crematoriums.

"Look at them all, Mr. Becker," he said, "That is what you can stop if you do your job."

Jonathan said, "I've been there, remember?"

"I want you to refresh your memory as to what it's like. I don't want you to forget. Here's a good one of a child they impaled on a fence post. They shoved it right up in her, split her wide."

Willis stuck the picture in front of him. It was a little girl, four or five, with a doll clutched in her hands.

Jonathan went down the hall to the bathroom and threw up.

Willis was waiting for him in the hall when he came out. "You're ready," he said.

The following morning Emma Rolf brought Jonathan an SS uniform, identity papers, travel orders, a Nazi party card, an SS song book, Argentine underwear, and a pair of boots. She waited for him downstairs. It was still raining heavily as they ran to the car that took them back up the road to the cave.

Lieutenant Mohne was still eating breakfast when the Marine let them into his cell. Mohne shoved his plate away and lit a cigarette.

"Well, well, the monkey in his costume." He smiled sarcastically and got up, with his arm cocked, the cigarette at the tips of his fingers, resting his elbow in his other hand. He circled Jonathan, looking him up and down.

"A poor imitation," he said. "It will fool no one."

Jonathan cocked his arm in a similar way, holding it with the other hand as Mohne did, then he circled around Mohne inspecting him the way Mohne had inspected him. Then he said. "A poor imitation. You can't hide a Jew in a nice uniform. The inferiority seeps out."

"Bravo!" Emma Rolf said, clapping. "Perfect,

Jonathan, perfect!"

Mohne put his face to Jonathan's and said, "You may look like me, but you can never *be* me. You stink of fear."

Emma Rolf said, "Enough insults, Lieutenant. We must be on our way. Did they give you a good breakfast?"

"Better than usual."

"Good," she said. "We wouldn't want you to go without having a last meal."

Jonathan didn't see where she had the gun hidden. He saw it in her hand suddenly, and she was aiming it at Mohne. Mohne took a step back, his face showing first disbelief, then terror. His jaw dropped open to say something at the moment she fired, the shot echoing off the cavern walls. Mohne clutched his upper chest, blood squirting between his fingers, he stumbled backward, a look of surprise and pain on his face, and fell over the desk, his legs flopping comically like a stunt in a Keystone cops film.

Jonathan froze, watching Emma Rolf, who circled the desk and stood over the man she had just shot, a strange, cold twisted expression on her face. She aimed the gun downward at Mohne and fired five more times.

Jonathan hadn't moved. He was too astonished to move. He still kept his eyes on Emma Rolf; her features had softened and then she began to smile like a child who had just been opened the gate to Santa's toyland. Jonathan came around the desk and looked down at Mohne. His chest was awash with blood and his face looked like it had been smeared with red vomit, his eyes fixed and staring. Jonathan backed away, feeling strangely chilled and nauseated.

The Marine came running, a .45 in his hand. "What the hell?"

Emma Rolf turned to him, still smiling, and said: "Superman just found out he's not."

It was a rough eighteen-hour ride in a B-17C to London with a stopover in Greenland, which was scheduled, and one in Ireland, which was not. The second stopover was necessary because black smoke was coming from behind the instrument panel. It turned out to be smoldering electrician's tape left behind by a workman that was shorting out the windshield wipers.

The plane was loaded with blood products and airplane engine parts. There were six other passengers, diplomats on their way to some conference. Five men and a woman. The main topic of conversation was the news of President Roosevelt's death the day before and what it would mean to the country now that Truman had taken over. It was supposed that Truman was a hayseed and a buffoon, and everybody had better get ready for a Republican in '48.

Spring rains were lashing the runway when they were lowered from the belly hatch of the plane onto the tarmac. The lady diplomat got out first, standing on unsteady legs, and was led off to a waiting car. A young man in a gray raincoat met Jonathan and gave him the recognition code:

"Mr. Reynolds?"

"Yes, are you Phil Morrison?"

"Is it raining?"

"From here to Tennessee."

"I'm Morrison, would you follow me please?"

The young man was no doubt a new recruit to the S.O.C. He might be Belgian or Flemish. By the proud way he walked and kept looking around, Jonathan figured he liked using recognition codes and coming out to airports on rainy nights. The young man took him to a wooden shack used in the daytime by a maintenance supervisor. The light was on inside. He opened the door for Jonathan and let him in, but he stayed outside in the rain.

Willis was waiting inside. He was smoking a curved pipe, sitting on an old straight-back chair. The office was packed with boxes of cleaning fluids and rags; there was a stack of brooms in the corner. A huge calendar with a semi-nude woman hung on the wall opposite. The calendar was for 1939.

"Nice flight, was it?" Willis asked.

"A real joy. When do I leave for Germany?"

"When I say so."

Jonathan took this to mean he was leaving immediately. "How's the weather to the east?" Jonathan asked.

"Never mind the weather." Willis took out an envelope and handed it to him. "Your instructions, a few hundred Reichmarks. Recognition codes in case you're taken by the Allies."

Jonathan reached for the envelope, but Willis pulled it back. "First we've got to make sure, Becker, that you are perfectly clear on your orders. You are to make every effort to get the subject out of Germany. In this envelope are your routes in and out. If he decides to go over to the Russians you are to kill him. But you are not to kill him for any other reason. Do you understand that, Becker?" His usually petulant mouth took on a cruel cast. "If you do kill him for any other reason," he said, glaring at Jonathan, "there will be grave personal consequences."

Jonathan felt a jolt. Now he knew why Emma Rolf had killed Mohne. To impress Jonathan. To let him know how damn brutal they could be.

"And don't imagine that the hero who kills Hitler will be immune to disciplinary action."

"You're a contemptible bastard, Willis."

"It's good you feel that way, because hate will keep you alive." He handed Jonathan the envelope. "We've got a lot riding on this, Becker. We've spent a great amount of our resources on this project. We picked you because you're the best. Perhaps no man alive could pull this off, but we think you can. You do this, and you'll be in history books five hundred years from now. They'll build statues of you in Central Park."

"I can't wait."

"We've concocted a scenario you're to tell Hitler. It's all there in your written orders, which you are to destroy as soon as you read them."

"And if he doesn't go for this scenario?"

Willis sneered. "It's up to you to see that he does. If he doesn't, I suggest you tell him to contact me—it's all written down how you're to have him contact me. Got it?"

"Yeah."

"I can't impress on you too much, you're not to

kill him. We want him."

"Just tell me where I go from here, Willis."

Willis stood up. He attempted a smile, but his sad face still looked sad. He shrugged nervously. "I guess I am a contemptible bastard, but I'm a contemptible bastard with a good cause."

"That excuses everything, does it?" Jonathan asked, then added, "It's doubtful I'll ever see you again, Willis. If there's a next life, don't look me up."

Book III

Chapter Eleven

Brigadier General Reinhard Hanover, 42, Group One Tactical Commander, sat in his office at Brensof Luftwaffe base near Prague, confronted with a problem. What to do with this SS Lieutenant Friedrich Mohne, who had appeared suddenly the evening before at the front gate, in an SS uniform, demanding air transportation to Berlin. All he had on him were old orders and old identity papers, signed by an SS colonel back in September, 1943.

The brigadier's office, deep in an underground bunker, had a strange odor, something like cow dung, and the ventilator rattled incessantly. The walls were concrete; the roof dripped water and the dim lights continually flickered. The only sound that penetrated was a bomb blast. He'd had no sleep for forty-eight hours because his group had received twenty brand-new "People's fighters" equipped with jet engines and capable of speeds of five hundred miles an hour. He trained all his men personally and got them into the air as quickly as he could.

Brigadier Hanover was a pilot by profession, with fast reflexes and killer instincts in the air. He'd been an ace in the Great War, having shot down 22 enemy planes and four observation balloons. Later he helped design the Messerschmitt-109 and the Heinkel 219 Owl nightfighter. He was a flyer and a fighting man, not a desk man. On the ground, he was out of his element.

In the air, he could make a decision in a split second and invariably be correct, as so many of his opponents had discovered. But on the ground, when so many unknown factors had to be inserted into the decision-making process, he was at a loss. Particularly when it came to political questions. Hanover did not like politics; he was a man of direct action. He was not a party member. He could not reconcile his Catholic religion to the Nazi creed. Otherwise he would have been a major general, at least.

At first he thought the problem of what to do with Mohne to be an easy one. Get through to Berlin and ask his superiors. So he did just that. The angry deputy Reichfuehrer he spoke to said at the moment they were too busy preparing for the Russians who, rude shitheads that they were, had invited themselves to dinner. Hanover would have to make a decision on his own initiative, the deputy Reichfuehrer said.

Hanover went down the hall for coffee. Every muscle in his body ached. In the cramped dining room a group of four flight officers were drinking synthetic coffee and smoking rank-smelling cigarettes. He joined them for a few moments. An argument was in progress. One officer said now that Roosevelt, the chief warmonger, was dead, maybe America would come to its senses. The others disagreed. They asked Hanover what he thought. He never got involved in these kinds of arguments because he was always unsure of his facts. International relations were a mystery to him. But this time he agreed it might be possible, even though he thought it not likely. War, like a plague of locusts, had its own momentum, he said. Once it's rolling, nothing can stop it.

All four of them seemed to agree with that.

Lieutenant Colonel Lammers asked Hanover what he intended to do with the SS officer. Lammers was short and swarthy. Hanover knew him to be a braggart and overbearing as a man, but he'd shot down sixteen four-engine bombers and was one of the best pilots in Hanover's group, so Hanover was always patient and indulgent with him. He'd given Lammers the job of interrogating the mysterious SS lieutenant. It was Lammers' recommendation that he should be shot without delay, or turned over to the Gestapo. He argued that Mohne had no doubt seen the People's fighters and, if he were a spy, had already seen too much. If he wasn't a spy, he must be a deserter whose conscience bothered him and that was why he wanted to come back. Either way, he should be shot.

"What did Headquarters say about Mohne?" Lammers asked now.

"They say they are busy with their own problems."

Lammers shrugged. "Just shoot him. I will take care of the matter if you wish."

Lammers' lack of respect for human life irritated Hanover. Killing was part of war, but one didn't kill someone simply because he didn't quite believe their story. Especially a fellow German. He decided no matter how tired he was he would have to talk to this man Mohne himself and make up his own mind.

They had no facilities on the base for holding prisoners, so they had put Mohne in an officer's sleeping room, which was little bigger than the space occupied by one cot. These rooms were insufferably stuffy without the door open. A sleepy private with a rifle stood guard; he saluted sloppily as Hanover approached.

Hanover knocked on the door out of military courtesy. The lieutenant opened the door sleepy-eyed, his tunic unbuttoned. He saluted the brigadier, sticking his chest out and rising high on his toes, clicking his heels together. Hanover returned the salute casually and invited the lieutenant to come with him. The private followed behind with the rifle.

Already, Hanover had sized up the lieutenant. He was obviously a Prussian, born and bred into the German military tradition, arrogant and class conscious. Hanover, who came from peasant stock and had to work for every break he ever got, felt a certain distaste for the man.

They walked down the long concrete hall, which dripped with moisture. Rust streaks marred every wall. Mohne lit up a cigarette with a pearl lighter. It was a sweet-smelling American cigarette. He didn't offer one to Hanover.

"I take it," the lieutenant said, "you are the commander here. That buffoon I spoke with upon my arrival is one of your men, is that correct?"

"Yes."

"I think I would have that man shot for being an

idiot. I have wasted many hours of valuable time. I told him it is absolutely imperative for the war effort that I get to Berlin immediately. Instead of speedily getting me to Berlin, he asks me many stupid questions about the nature of my mission, which I told him was of a top-secret nature."

Hanover said, "How old are you, Lieutenant?"

"Twenty-six."

"How long have you been in the SS?"

"Are you going to ask a lot of stupid questions yourself, Brigadier?"

"I was simply wondering why it is that you are only a lieutenant."

"I've been out of the country on a mission of utmost importance. I have had little contact whatever with my superiors for twenty-seven months."

The end of the hall opened onto a large repair facility where a dozen mechanics were at work on engines. The lieutenant took a long look.

"These are jets?"

"Yes," Hanover replied.

The lieutenant nodded, but that seemed the extent of his curiosity. Hanover thought: If he were a spy, he would pretend not to be curious. He would not ask questions.

"Do you think they will win the war?" the lieutenant asked.

"I cannot answer that," Hanover said. "If I say yes, you might think me a foolish dreamer. If I say no, I could be accused of defeatist talk. Let us say they are making a contribution. My group has shot down two dozen heavy bombers and nearly seventy fighters in the last eleven days."

The lieutenant nodded approvingly. "Impressive. And your losses?"

The brigadier held up one finger.

"Very impressive. It seems that you know what you are doing. Can you get me to Berlin today?"

"We shall see."

They walked through swinging doors, down another hallway, and up a flight of stairs into the sunlight. They were at the end of a runway, surrounded by tree-covered hills. The weather was clear, but it was cool. A strong cold wind was blowing from the west. Crews were hard at work patching bomb craters in the runway.

Hanover turned to the private and told him he could go get a cup of coffee. The lieutenant arched his eyebrows, but said nothing. The private headed back into the bunker. The lieutenant looked off in the distance with his hands behind his back, his shoulders square.

"Now then," Hanover said, "we can talk in private."

The lieutenant said, "The Fuehrer has been betrayed by so many. If it were not for the traitors, the war would not be going so badly. But I for one have faith in the Fuehrer. He says more super weapons are coming and I believe him. Look, here they are, and flying."

"What is the nature of your mission to Berlin?" Hanover asked.

"I am not permitted to say. You have seen my papers. You have no doubt contacted Berlin so that you know I was ordered to go to Argentina clandestinely. I request that you now, with all due speed, get me to Berlin." He rocked back and forth on his heels, looking at Hanover with cold eyes.

"Berlin has not confirmed anything," Hanover said. "They are too busy fighting the Russians, who are, as I'm sure you know, pounding on the door."

"That is why I must get to Berlin *immediately.*" He took a deep drag on his cigarette, holding it in his mouth with the tip pointed upward.

"You won't tell me anything about your mission?"

"Nein. I have sworn an oath on my honor to speak to no one about it. I will only say that it is of immense importance to the future of the Reich and the sacred principles of National Socialism."

Hanover leaned against the concrete bunker and looked over his captive for a few moments. There was absolutely no sign of fear in the man, only anger. And he was every inch a Prussian militarist and a Nazi fanatic. Still, Hanover had his doubts. These questions of security often troubled him. He could call in the Gestapo, but he had an abiding hatred for the Gestapo and would not call them except in an extreme emergency. The local Gestapo chief was, Hanover thought, a moron and a coward, and was spending all his time planning for a quick getaway at the moment the surrender came.

Finally Hanover said, "If you won't tell me anything about your mission, perhaps you might tell me something about yourself."

The lieutenant shrugged. "What's there to tell?"

"Are you related to Baron von Mohne?"

"Yes." He flicked away his cigarette. "My father."

"Ah." Hanover smiled. "There is an SS Colonel Poulin who I believe served with your father in the

Great War and is now serving in an SS security detachment not far from here. I think I will have him speak with you. If he believes you are who you say you are, then we shall see about getting you to Berlin."

"Don't have me wait in that stinking little room, Brigadier, I beg you."

"All of our rooms are stinking and little, Lieutenant, but I will see what I can do."

They put Jonathan in the briefing room, where he could read some magazines that featured the early days of the Ardennes offensive, when the German Panzers were rolling west. Jonathan wasn't much interested in the magazines. He was worried about Colonel Poulin and how much he might know about the elder Mohne. If he knew much at all the game was up, and Jonathan would have to swallow the suicide capsule he carried in a hollowed-out wisdom tooth. That, or let them shoot him.

A clammy feeling came over his back.

They served him dinner at six. A potato, a little sausage, fresh bread, some greens. Coffee that tasted like burnt tree bark. He was surprised at how well he could eat, knowing that his judge and possible executioner were going to show up any minute.

He was getting somewhat comfortable wearing the cloak of Mohne's personality. At first he'd decided to play him one-dimensionally. Arrogant. But then he decided that it was possible to give the portrayal more facets of character than simple arrogance. True, the real Mohne was full of Nazi platitudes, hatred for Jews and Slavs, awe for Hitler, and the rest of it. But Mohne was also brilliant in mathematics, ascetic in his personal habits out of a sense of historic mission, and had a subtle, sardonic sense of humor. In addition, he was intensely loyal to his country, his friends, his fellow officers, and above all, his family. In an attempt to humanize him, Jonathan decided to make him an amateur poet. Not a very good one, but a poet nevertheless.

Now, while he was waiting, he scribbled some verse on a pad:

The eagle soars on outstretched wings
against the outstretched sky
With savage, bloody, talon claws
Living free, in obedience to his own laws . . .

Jonathan knew it was drivel, but the Mohne characterization needed something.

Jonathan next worked on Mohne's walk and gestures to be sure he had a full range of them. He practiced summoning a waiter with a snapping of his fingers. Arguing a point with a contemptuous expression. Ordering men to their deaths with his jaw set firm and his eyes ablaze with a sense of mission.

Then he asked himself how Mohne would react to his mother's death. To a pickpocket? To a case of the pox? How would he seduce a woman? A performance could only be perfect if the actor knew the answer to any such question without hesitation. He was not yet to that point of perfection.

Suddenly the door swung open and Hanover and an SS colonel came in. Jonathan stood up and saluted with a click of his heels.

"I am Colonel Poulin, I knew your father," the colonel said, returning the salute.

"So I've been told, Herr Colonel. I'm so glad you've come, I have been having great difficulty convincing these men of the importance and urgency of my mission."

"To take you to Berlin, that is a difficult assignment. You must understand the sort of dilemma this puts on Herr Brigadier Hanover." He glanced at the poem, and a slight smile came to his lips.

"Forgive me if I can't at the moment feel compassion for his plight," Jonathan said, giving a hard, angry look in Hanover's direction.

The colonel smiled faintly. He seemed to be a good-natured man, Jonathan thought, well fed, pink-faced, with an easy smile. But, Jonathan noted, he had cunning little eyes, and he was, after all, an SS colonel. Which meant he would do his duty and show no mercy.

"Now then," the colonel said. "I last saw your father some years ago, but as I remember him, he was a man of keen intelligence and a marvelous sense of humor. He treated the men under him well and was a consummate tactician. He loved Schubert and Wagner and, for relaxation, played the cello. I am telling you this so you know that I knew him well."

Jonathan had no way to know whether the man he was describing was Mohne's father. All Jonathan knew about Mohne's father was what he'd read in the file. A Prussian general who fought in World War I, was wounded twice, had rapid promotion, backed Hitler early, and was killed on the Russian front in 1944. Jonathan felt sweat rolling down his back, but he maintained his stiff posture and a smug grin on his lips. One thing he knew for certain about the father was the kind of son he raised.

Jonathan shook his head and said:

"I do not mean to disagree with the colonel or imply that his memory may be flawed, but my father was a cold-blooded bastard with no sense of humor. His men feared and hated him more than they feared and hated the enemy and so they fought like tigers. My father was not a dolt, but neither did he have a 'keen intelligence.' He fought wars by the regulations he learned in the war college. He thoroughly memorized Clauswitz and followed it like a churchman follows his gospel."

The colonel clapped his hands together. "That's the man. And you no doubt are his son. A pleasure to meet you." He bowed, clicking his heels together. He turned to Hanover. "I suggest, Brigadier, you give this man every possible assistance." Then he gave them both a curt salute. "Well, I must run. Lots of work to do. We have a thousand Jews to take care of. What with the camps working beyond capacity and transportation so difficult, we must devise our own methods. Well, the woes of command, eh? Good luck on your mission." He saluted again and hurried out the door.

Hanover turned to Jonathan and said, "After you get to Berlin, you may wish we just shot you."

Chapter Twelve

Lammers volunteered to take Jonathan to Berlin, which Brigadier Hanover went along with, even though Lammers obviously had ill feelings toward the arrogant young lieutenant. Hanover agreed mainly because he was too exhausted to try to find someone else.

Lammers and Jonathan took off at eight o'clock in the evening, Monday, April 16, in a Messerschmitt BF 110 Destroyer, an old two-engine fighter. Jonathan was in the front gunner's seat. The BF 110 was no longer used as a fighter; the Spitfires and Hurricanes and the new American P-51's could fly faster and higher, were more maneuverable, and carried more firepower. The BF 110 was now equipped with night-vision radar equipment and was used for night attack only. This particular plane was badly in need of maintenance. It chattered, one engine sputtered frequently, and a cold wind blew through the cockpit. And the enemy aircraft detection devices were not working and, according to Lammers, never had.

The weather forecast was for clear skies, Lammers said, which was bad news. The skies would be full of American planes. They usually came at midnight, but they could come earlier. He'd gotten clearance to land at Templehof Airfield. If the Americans were coming in for a raid, Jonathan would have to jump.

Jonathan was terrified of jumping out of planes, especially in the dark. He'd only done it once before and he'd landed in a lake and damned near drowned.

Once they'd achieved altitude, Lammers tapped Jonathan on the shoulder and gestured for him to put on a headset. When he had it on, Lammers said, "I was in favor of having you shot," he said, "when you first showed up."

"Why is that, Colonel?"

"It wasn't that I didn't believe your story, I did. I thought you must be working for some party big shot. Himmler maybe. Someone who wants to get away from Germany and find a nice safe refuge in South America. I thought, why should they escape when we have to fight?"

"But now you're taking me to Berlin."

"I would have to fly out later anyway. This way I can go back early and get to bed. I am so tired of this war. Everyone is so tired. Why don't they end it? They would end it if it were not for men like you. Dedicated Nazis. What are we fighting for now, can you tell me that? Except to show how bravely we die."

Jonathan said nothing for a moment. He looked

out over the horizon, still pink with twilight. There were dark clouds ahead, gathering around the peaks of some mountains. Finally Jonathan said, "If you don't want to die, why don't you just fly east and surrender to the Allies?"

"Maybe because I am a good German, and we Germans always fight to the end, even in lost causes."

Jonathan lay back and closed his eyes. He had a tightness in his throat that seemed to spread down like fingers into his chest.

He drifted in and out of sleep for a while. His mind was a jumble of thoughts and images, memories and fantasies. He saw himself floating to earth in a parachute, while thousands of men on the ground fired guns at him. Then he saw himself burning in the wreckage of a plane, followed by another image. He was standing in front of a firing squad and a corporal was giving the order to fire, and when he looked closely he saw the corporal was Adolf Hitler.

He opened his eyes, suddenly aware he'd been sleeping. It was cold in the plane, but he was sweating. The air was bumpy. Darkness had enveloped the sky. The sputtering starboard-side engine ran smoothly now. Beneath them he beheld a vast darkness, as if they were in the middle of nothingness. As if this plane and the two men in it were the total universe. Above him, stars by the billions. The feeling that he was somehow a man of destiny once more took possession of him.

Lammers' voice came through his headset: "You have been mumbling in your sleep. Something about the Fuehrer."

"Obey the Fuehrer, probably," Jonathan said.

"I think it was something more like 'Kill the Fuehrer,' but what man controls his thinking while he's asleep?" He chortled. "I knew a man once who carried a baby picture of himself and used to take it out and show it anytime someone would show pictures of their children. Isn't that funny? What made me think of that now?"

"How much further is Berlin?" Jonathan asked.

"Look ahead of you."

Jonathan leaned forward in his seat and wiped some vapor off the glass of the canopy. There, far in the distance, he could see the faint glow of flames and tiny pinpricks of bursting light. Bombs falling. Fires. Searchlights. A circle of fire perhaps two hundred kilometers in diameter.

"The bombers came early tonight," Lammers said. "We'll have to turn back. Try again tomorrow night."

"No! I'll jump!" Saying it brought a wave of fear through him, but he knew it was the only way.

"I can't take you into all that," Lammers said. "There'll be a hundred enemy bombers and three hundred fighters there. And we could get killed by our own anti-aircraft. We wouldn't have a chance in this old garbage can. Not me. We can try it again tomorrow."

Jonathan had no way to stop him from turning back. He had no gun. The man outranked him.

The plane banked to turn back.

"Wait!" Jonathan cried. "Take me as close in as you can. I'll jump. It's imperative I get to Berlin immediately!"

The plane straightened out and returned to course. "I can't take you in much closer," Lammers said. "The American fighter escorts know we're coming in from the southeast and sometimes come to greet us. The Russians, too, hang around the outer rim, but they are not that good fighting at night."

"How far are we from the city?" Jonathan asked, even though he knew it was at least seventy kilometers to the southern edge.

"A hundred kilometers," Lammers said.

Suddenly a burst of gunfire erupted off the starboard side and bullets smashed through the plane. A fighter plane whizzed past in front of them, a second one passed overhead.

"Yaks!" Lammers said. "Russian fighters. Damn them!"

Black smoke was filling the cockpit. Something in the instrument panel was burning. Jonathan grabbed a fire extinguisher and sprayed underneath. The plane banked right and the engines roared to full power.

"Here they come again!" Lammers cried, banking to the left. The wing guns clattered, the plane dipped, then started into a steep climb. "We still burning?" he called to Jonathan.

"Yes, I can't get it out. It keeps sparking and smoldering."

"Switch off everything electrical."

Jonathan threw all the switches. He sprayed with the extinguisher again but it quickly fizzled. Smoke continued to pour out. Lammers pulled back the canopy, letting the smoke escape. The temperature in the plane dropped dramatically.

The starboard engine sputtered and clattered. In the darkness, Jonathan saw something coming at them. He cried: "Enemy at two o'clock high!"

Lammers cut the engines and went into a dive, peeling off to the left, then rolled and came up again. Dead ahead was one of the Yaks. Lammers gunned his engines; the plane shook all over. Lammers fired. Bright orange flames burst from both sides of the Yak, then the plane rolled over and headed straight down.

"Now to get the bastard's brother," Lammers said.

Jonathan felt a sudden admiration for Lammers. He knew how to fly a damn plane.

Lammers headed down into a power dive. "He's behind us!"

The starboard wing suddenly seemed to dance. "We're hit!" Lammers cried. The starboard engine sputtered, then began streaming a thin streak of yellowish flame. Lammers leveled off, then put down the flaps and cut the engine. Air speed fell. Bullets slammed into the fuselage.

Jonathan turned and saw the yellow bursts of machine guns behind, and then the dark figure of the Yak come over them. Lammers pulled the stick back and the plane pointed up. He hit the throttle and the old Messerschmitt started shaking wildly, the starboard engine coughing smoke and flames. The Yak was exposed for just a moment. Lammers yelled, "My fire control's out!" Jonathan grabbed the stick in front of him and pushed the firing mechanism button. The fuselage guns clacked for a moment. The Yak rolled over twice and exploded.

Jonathan watched the fiery pieces float downward.

"The dumb bastard let me sucker him," Lammers said, then added, "Nice shooting. You handled yourself well under fire. I'm glad they didn't let me take you to the wall."

The starboard wing suddenly blazed up again and the whole plane began to tremble. Lammers pulled the canopy back all the way and said, "Looks like the end of my career. I suggest you bail out yourself."

"Will do," Jonathan said, "soon as I can get in a little closer."

"Have a nice time in Berlin, say hello to the Fuehrer for me."

He stepped out onto the wing and disappeared into the blackness.

Jonathan took hold of his stick and put his feet on the pedals and tried to bank. Everything seemed sluggish. He cut back the throttle. The port side engine hummed along. He looked at the starboard side and the flames were still leaping from the engine, but they had died down some. The fuel in the wing tanks must be expended, he thought. If the damn thing had wing tanks.

He wiped the smoke off the front screen. He was closer to the ring of fire now. He couldn't see any planes in the air, but he knew they must be there. There were hundreds of bomb bursts on the ground.

It was too dark to read the altimeter, but he knew he was losing altitude. If he got too low he would not be able to jump because there would not be adequate distance for his chute to open. If he got any closer, the flak might get him. Or he might draw another fighter. An American, one of his comrades-in-arms. Not quite fair, but that's war for you.

He could see the flashes of the anti-aircraft batteries in the distance. Below him, fields were on fire, so he knew he was not over the city yet.

He looked to the peaceful heavens above him and a strange kind of fear came over him. Not fear of death. Fear of something worse than death. A moral fear. As if he were putting his soul in danger of damnation.

But then he did not believe in the soul, or in life after death. Still, the feeling was overpowering. Suddenly, in the glow of the fires, he caught a glimpse of a fighter coming down on him. He unbuckled his safety belt and banked to the right. He pushed the throttle forward; the plane began to shudder violently and the port engine began a high-pitched whine. He was losing altitude faster. He glanced to his right and saw that the wing was coming apart.

Only one place to go. Only one thing to do. He stood up to bail out, feeling around behind him to give his parachute one last check. Something was wrong. There was a hole burned in the canvas parachute bag, and the parachute inside felt hard, like crystalized sugar. It had melted. Sparks from the fire must have hit it.

There was no time to think out alternatives. He had to find a flat spot and bring the plane down. And he had to do it now.

The fighter coming down on him made a pass, bullets slamming into the fuselage. The end of the right wing tore away. The plane tipped violently right, then left. Jonathan fought to hold the stick straight. He looked around for a lake or a pond. He saw something ahead reflecting the glow of the flames. He pulled the throttle back. The left engine sputtered and smoke billowed out of it. The plane was now losing altitude quickly.

Suddenly it felt as if the plane was being kicked from underneath. Flak from the ground. He looked around for the fighter and couldn't see him. No doubt he'd fled from the flak.

The plane seemed to be coming apart. Flames and smoke poured out all over it. He looked ahead. Shimmering blackness. Flames reflecting off water? It damn well better be.

He lowered the flaps without any idea whether they actually went down and pulled the throttle back. The engine coughed, then stopped. All he could hear now was the crackle of the flak above him and the thumping of the guns and bombs below. He put his head back and looked up at the stars. For a moment he was paralyzed with fear. Sweat poured down his face. He gulped air, then clenched his teeth and closed his eyes. For some reason the image of Julius Shapiro in the back of the car with his brains blown out flashed through his mind.

He opened his eyes. The ground fires were so intense that he could see the inside of the cockpit now. He grabbed the stick and looked out toward the front of the plane. The plane was gliding, but losing altitude rapidly. He pulled the stick back. He remembered what they'd told him in training a thousand times: Keep the nose up. Keep the nose up.

There was a slapping sensation below him, then

the plane seemed to rise up again and twist to the side with a great roar. He saw the starboard wing tear off as a propeller blade smashed through the canopy. Then the plane nosed over. For a moment all was quiet and he saw the stars and the flames around him reaching up for them.

And then the blackness swallowed him up.

Chapter Thirteen

He opened his eyes. Gray light.

His head ached. That was the first sensation. A dull throb started at the base of his head and spread upwards, wrapping around his brain.

He could make out a door. Some shelves. A wooden chair. The place had the smell of earth and decay, and faintly of exploded bombs and smoke. His mouth was dry. It took him a moment to remember. The plane. The flak. The wing burning. Heading for the water. Then what?

Vaguely, he remembered someone dragging him along the ground. Dreams. Someone whispering in his ear. A woman. A woman's soft, soft whisper.

He lay still for a moment and listened. In the far distance, an air raid siren. He felt around him. He was on a cot of some kind. A blanket over him. He patted himself down. His right arm had a crude bandage. Another bandage on his head. A wave of dizziness came over him and then subsided. His whole body was sore, but in one piece. He moved his feet, his hands, turned his head. Everything seemed to work.

He heard footsteps. The door opened and a figure appeared in the doorway framed by the gray light. A woman.

"Hello," he said.

"Hello," she said.

The door closed. "I see you're awake," she said. "I thought you weren't dead, but I wasn't sure." She lit a candle. It took his eyes a moment to adjust. She was young, eighteen, twenty, perhaps. Thin, stringy blond hair, a tattered schoolgirl's uniform. Dirty face. She came over to him, staring down at him and he could see in her eyes she wasn't right. A far-away, unfocused look about them.

"I know your secret," she said.

"Pardon?"

"You're a Jew, don't try to lie about it."

"I am Lieutenant Friedrich Franz Mohne, SS."

"No you're not." She shook a finger at him.

"I have credentials that prove that I am."

"You are Jonathan Zalman Becker and you've come from New York. You told me all about it when you were dead. The Jews are bad people, everyone says so. They have corrupted the race. The Jews have been rounded up, and are all gone. Like the birds that go south in the winter. The Jews have all gone south where they can no longer corrupt the race."

She sat down in the straight-back chair, putting the candle down on the floor. The light flickered on the ceiling, making a wave pattern. She rocked back and forth, her hands in her lap, humming to herself, looking like a specter in the light of the candle.

"Have you reported me to the authorities?" Jonathan asked.

"Authorities?"

"The Gestapo?"

"No. Why would I do that?"

"Because the Jews are bad people and you think that I'm a Jew."

"I'm a mole person now. I have no purity. I'm like the Jews. Dirty Jews. We always said that. Dirty Jews. Threw stones at them. Our neighbor Herr Krigbaum was a Jew. The Gestapo took him away in a truck. We stood on the corner and yelled 'dirty Jew' at him until he went down Gerberstrasse. We never saw him again, the dirty Jew. He used to give me ribbons for my hair when I was little and tell me how pretty I looked. Red and blue ones. He owned a shop. Ribbons and yarn. The dirty Jew."

Jonathan sat up. "I appreciate what you've done for me. Is there anyone else? I mean, are you staying here alone?"

"Just me and the rats. The rats are my friends. Except when they bite me. Then I have to scold them. Are you here to kill the Fuehrer?"

"No, did I say I was?"

"No, but everyone wants to kill the Fuehrer. The Russians are coming to kill him with their tanks and everything. Armies and armies of Russians. The Americans are trying to kill the Fuehrer with bombs.

And the Brits. Everyone wants to kill our Fuehrer. Not me, of course. I love the Fuehrer. He brought us the Thousand Year Reich. He proved we are supreme. The triumph of the will. All Germans love the Fuehrer, and we must obey him."

"But you don't?"

"I am no longer German," she said bursting with a wide smile. What the smile meant, he had no idea. Was she joking with him?

She said, "When I was a German I made flags. Big red and white ones. I used to march in the parades. Don't you like parades? Thump, thump, thump, with all the marching feet." She thumped her feet on the hard earth floor. "It was good being German. The master race, you know. That has been scientifically proven, over and over again. The Jews and the Slavs are inferior races. Would you like something to eat? Do you think the Russians when they come will rape all the women? I cleaned you up, you had mud all over you. You crashed in a plane."

"How long have I been here?"

"Two days. I have some soup, but I can't heat it up. Would you like some soup? My father used to say before it was over the Germans would be eating each other. That proves something, don't you think?"

"What do you mean?"

"That the Germans are the super race."

He had no idea what she was getting at, but she seemed quite pleased with the insight.

"Where's your father now?" Jonathan asked.

"He refused to join the Volkssturm. He said the very idea was stupid. There was enough killing and the war was lost, and he would not be a party to any more killing. He was a gardener, what did he know about killing, he said. He said he knew how to fertilize roses and transplant lilies, but killing was not something he wished to do. He would not be able to shoot his fellow beings. So they hung him with a rope. My father was always so stubborn, even with the rope around his neck and they gave him one last chance, he still refused. They let me take him down and bury him. He dirtied his pants." A terrified expression came over her face, then faded.

"What's your name?"

"Heidi Luden."

"You wouldn't mind if it was our secret that I'm a Jew."

"I can keep a secret. I haven't told anyone you're here. You landed in the duck pond at the botanical garden. It's not a garden any more. It's now the moon. Is this war to end or will the killing just go on and on? I think it will go on and on. We Germans love killing. Except those of us that have become mole people. Did I offer you food?"

"I am very hungry."

"I'll get you something."

She brought him some crackers. "It's all I have," she said. "Except for cold soup. The crackers are not bad. My father hoarded them, even though it was forbidden."

"Is my jacket around here?" he asked.

"Yes. I wouldn't steal anything." She handed him the jacket. He took out a couple of tins of field rations and offered her one of them.

Her eyes went wide.

"What a nice present. I'll tell your fortune."

"Eat first."

He opened the tin with the key and handed it to her. Inside was some biscuits and processed meat. She ate ravenously, like a starving animal. He found it tasted good and tried to savor it, but when she was done she still looked hungry, so he gave her the rest of his.

He felt stronger, but the meal did not sit well on his stomach. He got up and tried his legs. He was weak, and he was dizzy. He felt his head where she'd bandaged it. There was a lump that felt about the size of a hand grenade.

He sat back down again.

"It's been raining," she said. "And so we've had no bombs. But the rain's stopped now, and so they will be back. They're killing us with the bombs. Do you think they don't know there are people down here? I mean the ones in the airplanes? How could they do it if they knew there were people down here? Let me tell your fortune." She went to a cupboard and pulled out a small jar full of a brown liquid. She took it over to him and had him hold it in his lap. Then she took off the top. The stench was overpowering, but he managed to sit still. She held the candle over it and blue flames appeared on the surface of the liquid, dancing around. He watched her eyes glow in the candlelight.

She intoned:

I see the Fuehrer and you
locked together in mortal fight
One would kill the other
And steal his might

She blew out the candle. It was at that precise moment the first bomb of the evening fell.

Jonathan and Heidi spent the night huddled under a sturdy bench in the corner of the room. She nestled under his arm and cried and wept and squeezed him every time a bomb shook the earth. He understood now what was meant when they said that strategic bombing terrified the enemy. He was terrified. Each time a bomb hit nearby and the room shook and dirt rained down on him he had visions of being buried alive, and the fear rose up in him like a giant anaconda squeezing his chest and he had to fight for his breath.

The bombing stopped a little after midnight. Heidi continued to whimper for an hour or so until she finally fell asleep, and a few minutes later he did too.

In the morning they had the last of his field rations. He was feeling stronger. She seemed different somehow than she had the night before. Quiet, sullen.

"What is it, Heidi?"

"You are leaving today."

"I didn't say that."

"But I know you are. I know things."

They went through the door and down a partially caved-in hallway of some sort. It had no doubt once been part of a basement storeroom. They crawled through a small space, then up a ladder. She showed him how to slide the heavy metal covering.

"Look first," she said, "make sure that no one's around. If they find this place, the rat people will take it over. Steal the crackers."

He nodded. She poked her head out, then motioned for him to follow.

It was a brilliant day, a bright blue sky. It took a moment for his eyes to adjust to the bright light. Columns of smoke rose into the sky. A squadron of fighter planes was strafing a few miles away, but there were no bombers. The smell of death was overwhelming. Death and the stink of sewage and smoke.

Then he heard the sound of artillery in the far distance, like the rumble of thunder.

He looked around. He had been in Berlin as a child and he remembered the wide boulevards and the beautiful, quiet neighborhoods. It was sickening to see the destruction. He tried to tell himself the Germans have only gotten what they deserve, but somehow it seemed hollow. Not every German was a Nazi. He remembered how his mother's friends had helped them get their exit papers, and how many of them had urged her to go.

"Follow me," Heidi said.

She showed him a large, twisted piece of pipe sticking up out of a pile of rubble.

"This is how you find your way back," she said, "if you want to come."

He followed her down a path of bricks. Rows of bombed-out buildings. Half a kilometer down the path, there was a twisted pile of wrought iron, part of what might have once been an entrance gate, and beyond it was an open area.

"The garden," she said. "The roses here, up there some lovely lilies. Hedges by the paths where people used to walk with their children. Over there, tulips."

It was now pockmarked with bomb craters. Uprooted trees, mud holes. Paths broken up.

"The pond is over here," she said.

She took him to the edge of the pond, which stank of rotting bodies and sewage. A few feet away the Messerschmitt BF 110 Destroyer, a crumpled mass of tangled iron, sat half-submerged. Across the pond was more rubble, like waves of the sea, surrounding the thousands of bombed-out buildings. Between the buildings were burned cars and trucks and artillery pieces. A few fires were burning. Fire brigades were trying to put them out.

Berlin, he thought, is no more.

A stunned feeling of the miraculous suddenly took hold of him. Somehow he had survived. Somehow, his plane had found this one safe place to land.

Then he thought, no, it wasn't merely luck. He had seen the pond, and he put down there. Training. A little luck.

Many men had survived worse, he thought. He once had seen a building in Belgium hit by a bomb. A man inside had reached down to pick up his handkerchief at just the right moment and was spared. Eleven people around the table dead, but the man who dropped his handkerchief was saved. No guiding hand of fate. He had the sniffles and wanted to blow his nose.

She took Jonathan's hand. "You were saved by God," she said, as if she knew what he was thinking.

"Saved for what, I guess, remains to be seen."

The artillery rumbled again in the distance. She squeezed his hand in terror.

"Never mind," he said. "They are still a long way away."

The firing was coming from east and north of the city. That, he figured, would be Zhukov's First Belorussian battle group and Konev's First Ukraine Battle Group. He knew they had amassed an assault force of over two million men, 6,000 tanks and 5,000 to 7,000 aircraft. The Germans had a million men to stop them, very few tanks, and very few aircraft. Rokossovsky's army from the north would be moving to the west soon, to encircle the city. Soon there might be no way out of Berlin.

That meant he would have to hurry.

"I have to go now, Heidi," he said. "Thank you for everything."

"I want to stay with you."

"It's just not possible. I shall be forever grateful. And when it is over, we'll meet again. Right here, when the gardens bloom again."

He kissed her on the forehead and hurried off to the north and east, to the citadel section, which he figured would be the innermost circle of defense, and where he would find the command posts.

He walked quickly, glancing over his shoulder from time to time. He never saw her following, but somehow he had the feeling she was there.

Chapter Fourteen

The two sentries who encountered Jonathan on Potsdammerstrasse in the Schoenberg district took him to their battalion commander.

Lieutenant Colonel Adrian Schaft of the *Grossdeutschland,* the Berlin Guard Battalion of the Wehrmacht, was a patriot of the old school, who had backed the Nazis when they were coming to power in the early thirties because he opposed international Marxism. He had been in the Imperial Army in 1914 as a young man, wounded nine times, and was promoted to the officer ranks from a common soldier, an extreme rarity in the Kaiser's army. He had stayed in the Army between the wars and in this war had fought in Greece and Italy before being assigned to Berlin. He, along with Otto-Ernst Remer, had broken the back of the July 1944 plot against Hitler by refusing direct orders to seal off the ministries in the Wilhelmstrasse. He considered mutiny to be a blot on the record of the army.

He did not think much of the SS. He regarded it with both envy and loathing. The SS had gotten most of the glory during the war because, he reasoned, they had the first pick of the recruits and suffered least from the shortages of supplies.

In addition, he had met Himmler, the Reichfuehrer, Commander-in-Chief of the SS, on several occasions, and had heard him spouting some of his beliefs in faith healing, mesmerism, homeopathic medicine, and so on, and thought the man was unbalanced. Someone once said Himmler was a man with his feet squarely seven inches above the ground. Lt. Col. Adrian Schaft concurred with that assessment wholeheartedly.

Now, here was this SS lieutenant standing in front of him with the most fantastic story. That he had flown in from a secret Luftwaffe base near Prague and had crashed his plane in the duck pond at the botanical gardens.

Schaft offered the lieutenant a piece of dried meat, which he accepted. Schaft didn't like this lieutenant much, an arrogant Prussian. They were in a small room of an underground bunker, surrounded by sandbags and boxes of hand grenades and ammunition. An artillery barrage was in progress overhead, but they were protected.

"So you wish to see the Fuehrer, is that right?"

"I *demand* to see the Fuehrer."

"He demands," Schaft said to his men. "And by what right do you make this demand?"

"I am on an important and secret mission. What I have to say must be said only to the Fuehrer himself. I demand you take me to him at once."

"He demands," Schaft said again to his men. He put a piece of dried meat into his mouth and tore it with his teeth. "The Fuehrer is in Berlin," he said. "But exactly where he has set up his command post is a closely guarded secret."

"Then," Jonathan said with an imperious sneer, "have me blindfolded and escorted. I don't give a damn *where* it is, I just want to be there. I suggest you get moving, or I will report you to the highest authorities, who just might have you shot."

Schaft was not a man to be bullied, especially not when his command, not to mention the entire social order, was collapsing around him. Schaft stood up stiffly and smiled at him. "You may not understand my position here, Lieutenant. I have the authority to have anyone shot who is not attached to a combat unit or who has no valid orders. You have neither. For all I know you are an Allied spy."

Jonathan grinned and glanced over his shoulder at Schaft's men, as if to offer sympathy for those who must serve under such a moron. Then Jonathan offered Schaft a cigarette.

"American?" Schaft asked, taking one.

"I was in Spain only a few days ago." He gave Schaft a light, then lit one up himself.

"I tell you what, Colonel," Jonathan said, "why don't you contact Reichfuehrer Himmler, he will verify my mission."

Schaft took a long drag on his cigarette. "Perhaps you have not heard, but Herr Reichfuehrer Himmler has tried to usurp power rightly belonging to the Fuehrer. He surrendered part of Army Group Vistual to the Americans, and then attempted to make a peace accord through the Swedish Red Cross. He has, as a result, been branded a traitor by the Fuehrer, stripped of all rank and privileges, and has gone into hiding."

Jonathan shook his head in disbelief.

Schaft said, "You have sought the wrong man to support your claims." He leaned back against the sandbags, stroking the stubble on his chin. Schaft was a soldier, not an assassin. He would hang a deserter or a coward without a qualm, but this man was neither, and the idea that he might be a spy was, on the face of it, preposterous. He knew damn well, at least he thought he knew damn well, the nature of this officer's secret mission. Rumors of hidden wealth outside the country were rampant. This man was obviously here to get one of the high-ranking party cronies out of the country. While the army stayed and fought and bled until there were no more bullets and no more blood.

Schaft took a deep drag on the delicious American cigarette. "I will take your case up with a higher authority," he said. "In the meantime, we are short of officers in this sector, Lieutenant. We will turn you over to a small SS detachment which is shoring up a Volkssturm regiment. You are hereby ordered to report to SS Major Boltar in Sector Seven. My men will see that you get there safely."

Jonathan sniffed. "I am SS, or have you forgotten? I take no orders from the Wehrmacht!"

Schaft said, "If you prefer, I will have you shot."

Jonathan spread his hands. "You have persuaded me, Colonel. Your logic is invincible."

The Russian gunners were punctilious. One half hour on, one half hour off, all day long. Jonathan stood in the entrance to the bunker with Schaft's men waiting for the shelling to stop. Meanwhile, a British bomber group was raining bombs down on the southern part of the city.

One of Schaft's men said to Jonathan, "Will the Fuehrer's super weapons be here soon?"

"Any moment," Jonathan said. "Have you not seen the jet planes?"

"We've seen them. They are fast, but few in number."

"Soon there will be thousands of them. They will knock the enemy from the skies."

The soldier smiled, but it was obvious he didn't believe it.

At last the shelling stopped. Jonathan and the two soldiers emerged from the bunker. It was in Jonathan's mind that he might have to kill these two men in order to get on with his mission. They were his own age, just plain soldiers. Not Nazis. They could have been playmates of his when he was a child. If they could survive another few days perhaps they would grow old and die great-grandfathers. The idea of killing them made Jonathan slightly nauseous.

But he told himself to remember his training. The mission comes first. If he had to kill, he had to kill.

The three of them made their way through the rubble. Russian Yak fighters were buzzing around overhead like wasps. One occasionally peeled off to dip down and strafe something in the rubble.

"They kill anything that moves," one of the soldiers said.

"Common murderers," said the other. "They kill civilians, too."

The three of them stayed under cover, making their way from building to building. Jonathan guessed it was noontime now. They continued up the street, scurrying through the bombed-out buildings, keeping an eye on the Yaks overhead, ducking for cover whenever one came in for a strafing run.

A few blocks later they arrived at their destination, a bombed-out church with the steeple hanging precariously off the side. They went down a stairway and into a network of sandbagged hallways where hundreds of young boys in Hitlerjugend uniforms filled sand bags.

The two soldiers asked for Major Boltar and were told where to find him. It turned out he was supervising the construction of the fortifications and the placement of two howitzers and a few machine guns. A detail of men were collecting bottles and filling them with gasoline to be used against tanks. There were crates full of Panzerfausts—hand-held, single-shot bazookas, which Jonathan knew had a short range and weren't accurate.

The Volkssturm recruits were civilians. There were a couple hundred of them that Jonathan could see, receiving instructions in small arms handling from a dozen or so SS troopers. The Volkssturm had no uniforms. The only thing distinguishing them was a red-and-white arm band with a swastika on it. The Hitlerjungend were boys from age eight to fourteen. Boy Scouts with guns.

Major Boltar was extremely tall and probably in his early sixties, Jonathan figured. He had a gaunt, death-like face, and his right arm was in a sling with blood oozing through. Boltar took one look at Jonathan and his eyes brightened. "Where have you come from, my friend?"

"I am on a mission to see the Fuehrer and the idiots in charge have to check this and check that before I am allowed to see him."

"Well, in the meantime we're glad to have you. As you can see we're making hasty preparations. Since Germany was thought to be impregnable, there was no need to build defenses around the capitol. The Fuehrer should have kept a closer watch on the general staff, no? But now, what can we do?"

"Pay for our mistakes," Jonathan said. With these school boys and old men in their path, Jonathan figured the Russians would overrun the city in half an hour with fifteen minutes out for a cigarette break.

Boltar gave him a cross look, but didn't say anything. Just then the shelling started again and they quickly ducked inside a doorway that led down into a basement. There were three large rooms: one for communications; one that served as a long, dark and narrow barracks and mess hall; and one that served as an infirmary, where there were perhaps a hundred patients lying on the floor and being tended by doctors and medics.

Boltar led Jonathan to the communications room, where he asked an aide for a status report.

The aide was a Hitlerjungend, perhaps thirteen or fourteen. "Reconnaissance reports the enemy massing for an attack, sir."

"Where, can they tell exactly?"

"Beyond the plaza, sir." His voice squeaked.

Boltar rubbed his forehead. He turned to another aide, even younger than the first. "Call up reserves, son, have them reinforce the line between the church and the west wall of the theater, that's the south end of our sector."

"I know, sir," the boy said, saluting. He turned and ran out into the artillery barrage.

Boltar turned and studied a map, shaking his head. "The Russians know they're up against us and not regulars," he said. "Well, we'll have to show them that we're not the weakest point."

"What kind of artillery support can we expect?" Jonathan asked.

"Very little."

Jonathan lit a cigarette. "How many tanks will they use?"

"Sixteen, twenty. Fifty. Who knows?"

"Will there be any air support?"

Boltar shook his head.

Jonathan said, "It does not look good, Herr Major."

"We have our orders and we obey them. Now then, have you had any field experience?"

"None whatever."

"Then you'll have to learn quickly."

"I would prefer to help with the wounded."

"Wouldn't we all."

Above them the crackle of small arms fire erupted. "That's it!" Boltar shouted to the communications men. "All units take their positions, second and third company hold in reserve."

A few hundred men, mostly elderly, lame, or wounded, came pouring out of a tunnel putting on ill-fitting helmets. Some had standard-issue Mausers; some carried pistols; others carried captured Belgian, Czech, Polish, and French rifles; still others had sporting rifles and shotguns. None had submachine guns. Jonathan could see one mortar.

Baltar called the sergeant commanding the troops to him. "Here is your new leader, Lieutenant Herr Mohne."

The sergeant saluted and stood at attention. The major saluted and wished Jonathan luck. Jonathan followed the sergeant down a sand-bagged trench to a staging area that ran along a brick wall. Artillery shells were crashing overhead. Jonathan searched the narrow strip of sky for planes. The air was full of them, but they seemed to be attacking the few German artillery batteries still firing. One spot in particular had a heavy concentration of anti-aircraft guns.

Could that be Hitler's headquarters?

The sergeant was a grizzled veteran with battle stripes up and down his arm. He was missing three fingers of his right hand and a few teeth. His uniform was torn and filthy and blood-stained. His eyes never seemed to settle on anything. Jonathan offered him a cigarette, which he took eagerly.

"Well, sergeant," Jonathan said. "What are our orders?"

"On the other side of the wall is Herman Goering Plaza. Beyond it, the Russians are massing for an attack. Their start line is by the water fountain. We're to hold the line here. When the tanks come, we attack with gasoline bombs and bazookas. Our main job—yours and mine—is to see that the men do not run away. Our orders are to shoot anyone who does, but you can't shoot them all. Where is your side arm, Herr Lieutenant?"

"I'm afraid I lost it."

"I'll get you one." He ducked into an enclosure and came out a moment later with a Walther P-38 and a few clips of 9mm ammunition. An artillery shell fell close by and the two men ducked. Then a mortar shell hit nearby, raining debris down on them. The sergeant gave a chuckle. Whatever he saw that was funny, Jonathan had no idea.

Suddenly two of the men bolted and ran past them down the long trench. The sergeant stood up, pivoted on his heels, and fired his sten gun in a short burst. The two men went down. He went over to the men, now lying on the ground, and sprayed them again.

A young man, straining to look over the walls, suddenly yelled, "Tanks! Here they come!"

Chapter Fifteen

In the brief interludes between the bursting of the artillery shells, Jonathan could hear the sounds of diesel engines and crawler treads of tanks. It sounded like dozens of them, coming closer, closer. A moment of panic seized him. He looked up and down the street at the rubble burning and crumbling in a cloud of dust. He thought to run, but when he turned, there was the sergeant, and beyond him would be more SS men, sharpshooters with orders to kill deserters on the spot.

The artillery barrage suddenly stopped and the boom of tank cannon filled the air, the shells blowing apart the wall in front of Jonathan, showering debris over the men, who squatted down, wrapping their arms around their legs in terror. Jonathan moved forward, not sure of what he was going to do. He knew if the tanks overran them, infantry units would come next, swarming over the rubble, digging out every last German. If the tanks didn't get him, the infantry would. He'd be killed or taken prisoner, and no Russian combat officer would believe his story that he was a Jew and a spy.

Jonathan had heard that when the Russians captured an SS officer he was routinely and summarily shot. Panic washed over him in waves for a few moments, then, like a summer squall, it abated. For a moment he felt merely numb and the sounds of the artillery and the machine guns blended into one roar, like a hurricane. His body felt leaden, his joints stiff, his skin itched with fear, but he managed to move forward. He scrambled up a pile of bricks and looked through what once might have been a window frame. In front of him was a sea of rubble strewn across what was once a wide plaza. On the other side of the plaza was a row of tanks firing randomly, their shells whistling over Jonathan's head. Behind the tanks, Russian storm [illegible]e lined up, carrying machine guns and [illegible]

[illegible] the tanks were unbeatable. In des- [illegible]e steppes of Russia, a tank was an [illegible]on. Even in a tiny plaza, they were [illegible], to an infantry assault; the tanks [illegible]r machine guns, supported by more [illegible] from the infantry behind them. For [illegible]n infantry charge of old men and [illegible]hem was suicide, Jonathan thought. [illegible] tanks crossed the open and hit the [illegible], where would they go? He looked [illegible]penings in the rubble, openings that had once been small streets and alleys.

Jonathan turned and motioned for the sergeant to join him. The sergeant scrambled forward, holding his sten gun in one hand and his helmet on his head with the other. He crouched next to Jonathan.

Jonathan said, "Take a look."

The sergeant looked around, his eyes growing large as he took in the size of the enemy force massing for the attack. "We should strike quickly," he said. "If we get one or two of their tanks, perhaps they will withdraw."

"*Nein,*" Jonathan said. "What can they do once they get across the plaza?"

The sergeant looked around and shrugged. "We can't let them come that close, we would have to withdraw to the next street. Our orders are to hold here. We must attack."

Jonathan couldn't believe a man so dumb had managed to survive on the Russian front. Perhaps he was better at obeying orders than thinking.

"Look," Jonathan said. "They've been shelling for four hours, how many casualties have we suffered?"

The sergeant shrugged. "One, two.

"In other words, it has been pretty m
of time. Tanks are effective on open grou
they are merely shields for the soldiers.
tanks cross the open space, they will b
either to hold their positions in front of us,
we can shower them with gasoline bombs, o

or taken prisoner, and no Russian combat officer would believe his story that he was a Jew and a spy.

Jonathan had heard that when the Russians captured an SS officer he was routinely and summarily shot. Panic washed over him in waves for a few moments, then, like a summer squall, it abated. For a moment he felt merely numb and the sounds of the artillery and the machine guns blended into one roar, like a hurricane. His body felt leaden, his joints stiff, his skin itched with fear, but he managed to move forward. He scrambled up a pile of bricks and looked through what once might have been a window frame. In front of him was a sea of rubble strewn across what was once a wide plaza. On the other side of the plaza was a row of tanks firing randomly, their shells whistling over Jonathan's head. Behind the tanks, Russian storm troopers were lined up, carrying machine guns and mortars.

In the open, the tanks were unbeatable. In deserts and on the steppes of Russia, a tank was an awesome weapon. Even in a tiny plaza, they were not vulnerable to an infantry assault; the tanks would fire their machine guns, supported by more machine guns from the infantry behind them. For him to lead an infantry charge of old men and boys against them was suicide, Jonathan thought. But once the tanks crossed the open and hit the piles of rubble, where would they go? He looked around at the openings in the rubble, openings that had once been small streets and alleys.

Jonathan turned and motioned for the sergeant to join him. The sergeant scrambled forward, holding his sten gun in one hand and his helmet on his head with the other. He crouched next to Jonathan.

Jonathan said, "Take a look."

The sergeant looked around, his eyes growing large as he took in the size of the enemy force massing for the attack. "We should strike quickly," he said. "If we get one or two of their tanks, perhaps they will withdraw."

"*Nein,*" Jonathan said. "What can they do once they get across the plaza?"

The sergeant looked around and shrugged. "We can't let them come that close, we would have to withdraw to the next street. Our orders are to hold here. We must attack."

Jonathan couldn't believe a man so dumb had managed to survive on the Russian front. Perhaps he was better at obeying orders than thinking.

"Look," Jonathan said. "They've been shelling for four hours, how many casualties have we suffered?"

The sergeant shrugged. "One, two."

"In other words, it has been pretty much a waste of time. Tanks are effective on open ground. Here, they are merely shields for the soldiers. Once the tanks cross the open space, they will be forced either to hold their positions in front of us, where we can shower them with gasoline bombs, or they them."

The sergeant gave him a befuddled look, then saluted and headed back toward the command post. Jonathan noticed some brass standing behind them in a sandbagged bunker, looking his way with binoculars. Suddenly a small group of men left the bunker and started heading his way. He pretended not to notice them, and swung around and went back to his forward position. He scrambled back up the pile of bricks and took a look.

There were perhaps fifty tanks forming a spearhead, grinding their way across the rubble strewn on the plaza in front of him. His men were firing sporadically and haphazardly along a line of rubble to his right and left for five hundred meters either way. It was clear his units were to receive the brunt of the attack. Behind the attacking tanks were what looked like two or three thousand men. A squad of German infantry suddenly ran out into no man's land somewhere from Jonathan's right. They closed on the massive lead tanks. Machine-gun fire hosed the area. The Germans were cut down before they got within fifty meters of the tanks. One German managed to fire his bazooka, which missed.

Someone grabbed Jonathan and spun him around. It was an SS captain, his face bloated with anger.

"What are you doing, man, you're supposed to attack!"

Jonathan raised a finger. "At the proper time

and in the proper way."

"The enemy will be here in two minutes!"

"How astute of you to figure that out."

"I order you to attack now!"

Jonathan stiffened, made a bow, and clicked his heels. He summoned his sergeant, who was returning from getting the reserves into position. "The captain says we should attack at once," Jonathan said.

"But sir," the sergeant said, "the men are in position, well hidden . . . Tanks have turned down the alley, as you said."

A shell exploded nearby and the three men huddled in the shower of bricks. Jonathan said, "This way, hurry."

The captain and Jonathan retreated to the relative safety of the concrete slab. From there they could see the tanks squeezing down the alley, encountering only occasional rifle fire, which didn't bother them at all. There were now five of them in a row making their way, spraying their machine guns right and left. Suddenly a Hitlerjungend sprang up out of a pile of bricks and fired his bazooka point blank at the first tank. It burst into flames. The second tank fired its machine gun and tore the boy in half, but it was too late, the damage was done.

The other four tanks started backing up, seeing the position they were in. A half dozen Hitlerjungend sprang from their hiding places and swarmed over the last tank, setting it on fire. As the men sprang from the tank they were shot down by more boys behind them.

The other tanks were trapped. The Russian infantry units behind them charged to their rescue, but the Volkssturm unit Jonathan had placed above them had a clear line of fire and cut them down. That left only two places to go. They could retreat across the plaza, or they could charge over the wall and into an open area between the crumbling walls that made up the alleyways. They kept charging, thousands of them, right into the trap which Jonathan had waiting for them. The reserves needed only to open fire at the moment they were in the open.

But they didn't.

Jonathan headed backward down a trench, with Russian bullets zinging around him. He turned the corner and there was the sergeant lying on the ground in front of him, his guts ripped open. The Volkssturm unit was huddled in a corner, covering their heads.

"Men of Germany!" he yelled. "You stand before God and the nation, the last line of defense before the Russian hordes descend upon our women! Rise up, your courage is in your will, your will is iron!"

He grabbed a gun one of them had dropped and kicked open a box of grenades. He threw a couple of grenades and fired. He turned to see that a few of the men had joined him, a few others were running. He turned and fired on them. Then he pulled the pin of a hand grenade and walked toward them. They'd turned their guns on him.

"Kill the enemy or die now!" he screamed.

They looked at each other, then three of them headed toward their position, screaming a battle cry. Then a dozen more. Only half a dozen were left now. Jonathan approached them, holding the grenade in front of him. "You have your orders, will you fight like Germans or do I slaughter you like cattle?" He dropped the grenade at their feet. They ran toward the line. He picked the grenade up and threw it over the wall toward the Russians.

The Russians were almost on them now. They had knocked out the small group with the machine gun he'd left at the forward position and were advancing quickly. Jonathan's men heaved grenades and fired their guns at them. Then someone threw a gasoline bomb, and then another. A few Russians in front were ignited; the flames seemed to panic the others. Then the unit on Jonathan's flank fired their two field guns with shrapnel shells. Seeing they were cut off on either side and the tanks had stalled, they turned and headed back across the plaza in a disorganized retreat, the Germans picking off many of them as they went.

Jonathan watched until the firing stopped and the last Russian had either been cut down or had gotten safely back to his lines. He counted the tanks. Twenty-two were burning; two more were crippled and had been abandoned in the plaza. There were several hundred Russians dead and wounded. The captain came up to Jonathan and said, "Report to Major Boltar in one hour."

Jonathan wondered whether, perhaps, he intended to have him shot for not obeying orders. It was possible, but from the look in the captain's eyes Jonathan didn't think it was likely.

The Russian artillery barrage had ceased, and there didn't seem to be any Russian planes strafing the city for the moment. He had his wounded taken to an aid station, where he could hear the screams of the men having limbs amputated without benefit of anesthesia. He'd lost thirty-three men, including his sergeant; twenty-eight were wounded to the point where they could not return to duty; eleven had deserted. If the Russians were to mount another attack, they'd punch their way through, he thought, like an elephant through cardboard.

He reported on time to Major Boltar's bunker. He was right, the captain had no intention of having him shot. Instead, Jonathan was awarded an Iron Cross, second class.

The award ceremony took place in Major Boltar's cramped, sandbagged quarters. Lt. Col. Schaft was there, along with Major Boltar, and the SS captain. A fat SS general made a speech about the astounding level of courage inherent in the German character, and how proud he was to have been a witness to it, even at the gravest moment of this most momentous historic struggle. He personally pinned the Iron Cross on Jonathan's tunic.

Jonathan did his best to stay within the Mohne

character, to puff out his chest with pride, to fight back a tear. But the irony was not lost on him. He might be the only Jew in the war to win an Iron Cross.

They drank some warm champagne and congratulated each other on the afternoon's work. Then the fat general, von Voorhees, announced that the Allies would no longer be bombing the city, that the jet planes were too much for them. Finally, at the last moment, Germany was gaining air superiority. Even now, with the enemy at the gates of the capital, the Fatherland would yet win the war!

Jonathan knew better, of course. The western Allies had stopped the bombing because they didn't want to drop bombs on the Russians, who were already well within the city limits. A few jet planes with great speed but inadequate armament would not do it. The Allies could put two thousand bombers and sixteen to twenty thousand fighters in the air at one time if they wished. What could a few jets do, except be targets for gunnery practice.

The men drained a second bottle of champagne, toasted the Fuehrer, whose genius would yet bring victory it was all agreed, Jonathan was again congratulated for his courage and leadership ability, then the group broke up. Schaft asked Jonathan to speak with him alone for a moment.

Schaft looked him up and down for a few moments and said, "Your cover is nearly perfect, but not quite perfect enough."

Jonathan felt a shot of panic rise in him, but

smothered it. He smiled and looked at Schaft with one eye closed, cocky and arrogant as Mohne would. "What do you mean by that, Colonel?"

"I cannot believe you were only a lieutenant. I now believe that you did come here on a secret mission. I can see now you are a man with a lot of combat experience."

Jonathan gave him a short bow. "Thank you, Herr Colonel."

"Here is your pass to see the Fuehrer."

He handed him a slip of paper. Jonathan felt his heart leap, both with satisfaction and with a sudden cold dread. "Thank you again," he said, and saluted.

"One more thing," Schaft said. "You will of course have to get that pass countersigned at Gestapo headquarters."

Chapter Sixteen

"Name?"

"Lieutenant Friedrich Mohne, and I must be given clearance to see the Fuehrer immediately."

"Immediately? Not possible. Can't you see how busy we are here?"

She had on a spotlessly clean white blouse with frilly cuffs; the blouse was starched, pressed, immaculate. Her tweed suitcoat and skirt were also pressed and spotless. Hardly what he'd expected to find in the middle of a battle, Jonathan thought, even at Gestapo headquarters.

But then the whole underground facility was clean and spotless, as well as massive. Great arched beams held up the roof. The floor was inlaid parquet; the walls were covered with murals of Germans, contemporary and historic, in heroic poses. Dozens of clerks scurried about. The phones must have been working, because men at a sea of desks were talking on them. They were so deep underground that explosions of artillery shells sounded like faint thuds. The only effect was an occasional loosening of plaster, which looked like puffs of snow gliding down on the desks.

Jonathan showed the woman with the starched white blouse the pass from Lt. Col. Schaft. The woman looked at it, frowned, and told him to have a seat in the waiting room. She gave him a ticket which would admit him. And she warned him sleeping was not permitted.

"Can you tell me how long I will have to wait? My mission is of vital importance."

"Everyone's mission is of vital importance," she said dully. "I will speak to Herr Diefenbacher, he is in charge of such matters. He will see you at his discretion, or not see you at his discretion."

She nodded to a guard, who stood behind an iron-grill gate. The guard relieved Jonathan of his pistol.

Jonathan found the waiting room down the hall. An SS private who looked about fifteen saluted him and checked his ticket. Jonathan took a seat on a long bench. No one else was waiting. Magazines had been left around for people to read, like the waiting room in a dentist's office. The air was foul. The ventilator duct was obviously too small for the large room.

"How is it going up there?" the private asked in a soft voice.

"We gave them hell today," Jonathan said.

"That is good," the private said. "Wenck's army

is coming to relieve the city. Fortress Berlin will never fall to the Russians."

"Never," Jonathan said. The guard returned to his post by the door. Jonathan started leafing through a magazine, looking at the pictures. Battlefield scenes. War plants going full blast. Nazi officials visiting workers and giving out medals. In the magazines it looked as if suffering was heroic and victory was at hand. There were no boy deserters hanging from light poles.

It felt good just to sit. Rest. Be safe from the bombs. He felt sore from some minor cuts and bumps, but he felt good. He'd survived. Maybe he was being saved for something special. It was a comforting thought. It took away the fear of the Gestapo.

He had, of course, faced the Gestapo many times. If one's papers were in order and one had on an SS uniform and acted arrogant, there was no problem with the Gestapo. Not that he had experienced. The door opened and a couple of men came in. The private didn't ask them for a ticket. One of the men was told to sit on the bench across from Jonathan. Then he was handcuffed to the heavy arm rest. The other man left.

The handcuffed man said, "Good evening or good morning, whichever it happens to be." He said it to no one in particular.

Jonathan nodded a greeting. The man looked vaguely familiar to Jonathan, but he couldn't place him. He was heavy-set, shabby and dirty, and his face looked puffy and black and blue, as if he'd been beaten with a club.

"You wouldn't happen to have a cigarette?" the man said. "I'm dying for a smoke. I know, we are all dying for something. Look at me, I look terrible. I know I shouldn't complain, at least they haven't shot me. Not yet. Have you seen the city? They flew me in two weeks ago and already it was a wreck. The airport is going to be closed, I hear. My back is feeling like a tank rolled over it. Soldier, have you a cigarette?"

"Not for you," the soldier said. "All I have for a traitor is a bullet."

"A simple 'no' would be enough," the man said. "I am not a traitor," he said to Jonathan. "This is all a huge misunderstanding. Lieutenant, if I told you all my troubles, you would not believe it. I am from Rothbaden, not far from Switzerland. Not originally, but I was with the Gestapo in Rothbaden. I was the Chief of District Four. Never had a single reprimand in my personnel record. I ran a model operation despite the fact I was not sent the best men. Knuckleheads, most of them. I hope I'm not boring you, we have nothing to do but wait anyway. When you hear my tale, you won't believe it, how a man can be a victim of circumstances. A Jew I arrested, who ended up shooting himself, is the cause of all my troubles."

Jonathan slowly realized who it was, and a cold terror came over him. It was Stuckurt. The Gestapo man who turned over Julius Shapiro to Jonathan when he was posing as Captain Hans Shroeder.

Stuckurt continued:

"It wasn't just the Jew, it was this fraudulent SS man, he is the one who caused my downfall, and perhaps some bad judgment on my part, although no one, not one single person can tell me where I failed to comply with the procedures outlined in our operations manual." He looked at the guard. "You must know someone, Private, who could get me a smoke—It is torture being without tobacco if you're addicted."

The private ignored him.

Stuckurt shook his head, leaning forward to rest his arms on his knees. "I was caught going over the border. I panicked and ran. That was a mistake. They have charged me with dereliction of duty. I, who have been doing nothing but my duty since I joined the party back in '24. You want to see my party card? My number is 28091. Practically a founding member. I knew Himmler personally, on a first-name basis. Heinrich. He called me 'Bern.' I used to bring him smoked sausage for his Czech girlfriend. Heinrich liked girls. 'Cunt madness,' he said it was, when he was in a jovial mood, which wasn't often. I hope I'm not shocking anyone. Himmler has been denounced, I'm sure everyone knows that. It is permitted to talk about him now. The truth always comes out in the end. Tell me, Lieutenant, what is your business here?"

He peered at Jonathan. Jonathan put his helmet on and pulled it down over his eyes. "I do not speak with persons under arrest."

Stuckurt leaned back and crossed his legs.

"There's no reason to act like that. We both have to sit here and pass the time, don't we? How long we'll be here neither of us knows. The Russians may come thundering down Hermann Goering-strasse at any moment. I was a first-rate administrator. I only ask that my record be taken into account. Am I not entitled to a trial? No charges have been brought against me, yet they flew me here. They think I am part of some vast conspiracy, in league with Himmler. Do you know they've arrested Eva Braun's brother-in-law? He was Himmler's adjutant, Fegelein. I've known the man for ten years. Totally loyal to the Fuehrer. Something about some papers in his brief case. I'm telling you, what's Germany coming to? A man can be shot for nothing."

The man who had handcuffed Stuckurt to the bench returned and removed the handcuffs.

"Well, what's happened now?" Stuckurt asked. "Has my request to see the Deputy Reichfuehrer been acted upon?"

"I think they've decided to tear your balls off and stick them up your ass."

"A funny fellow, are you? Is that something to joke about? We are brother agents, you know. After I'm cleared I may be your supervisor. I suggest you watch your mouth."

Stuckurt was ushered out of the room.

Jonathan wiped the sweat off his forehead.

The private said, "Traitors are everywhere."

A moment later a young woman appeared in the doorway and said, "Lieutenant Mohne? Herr

Diefenbacher will see you now."

Jonathan knew if he didn't get past Diefenbacher, his mission might well be doomed.

As he followed the young woman down one hall and then another, fear rose in him that he was too late. She was leading him past a row of offices where men and women were hastily packing records and dragging them on carts down the hall to where? The answer was obvious. To be incinerated. The Third Reich was in its death throes and the only thing for the criminals in charge to do was to destroy the evidence.

Jonathan would have to convince them that there was still hope, that if he could get in to see the Fuehrer immediately, the Red tide could be turned back.

The woman took him into Diefenbacher's office, then left them alone.

Diefenbacher was a squat little man in a gray suit, the vest unbuttoned. He was bald and had a beaked nose, so he would have resembled a penguin where it not for his eyes, which were deep-set and icy blue. He was busy packing his papers into trash barrels. The room was large, well lighted, and in complete disarray. The lights swayed back and forth to the rhythm of the artillery barrage that could barely be heard above them.

"Well," Diefenbacher said, "I understand you wish to see the Fuehrer. Tell me why, I could use a good laugh right about now."

"My mission is a state secret. I have come from Argentina where I have spent the last two years working on a project for Herr Himmler."

Diefenbacher grinned at him and took a cigar out of his desk. It had been half-smoked before. He lit it with a kitchen match and looked at Jonathan with his ice-blue eyes. "Do tell me more."

"I have not been authorized to tell anyone else. In fact, my oath prohibits me from discussing my mission with anyone."

"Pretend I'm a priest, you're in confession." He sucked on his cigar, making a cloud of blue smoke around his head.

"I can tell you this," Jonathan said, "that my mission has to do with super weapons that even at this hour might turn the fortunes of war."

Dr. Goebbels' Propaganda Ministry had been claiming for months that there were super weapons on the way. Jonathan expected Diefenbacher to brighten, but he didn't. He stared, grinned, then burst out laughing. He said, "What do you think, I'm an idiot? Maybe you've had a little battle fatigue. You start believing that crap the Propaganda Ministry puts out, you're ready for the lunatic asylum."

Jonathan gave him a hard look, hard and arrogant. "I am Friedrich Franz Mohne, my father was General Mohne, I expect to be addressed in a correct fashion." He clicked his heels.

Diefenbacher grinned at him and went back to stuffing papers in barrels. "Tell me why you really want to see the Fuehrer, and we might be able to arrange something."

"Is the Fuehrer here in Berlin?"

"That's a military secret. You want to see him or don't you?"

"I *must* see him."

"Then you'll have to convince me. And the only way to do that is to tell the truth."

Jonathan stepped closer. "I will break my oath, because there is no other way. But you must tell no one else."

"You have my word."

"We have a supply of a secret weapon, a nerve gas called Tabun, in the hold of a ship in Spain. Arrangements can be made to have it flown to Prague, where the Skoda works are still in operation. Tabun, a few ounces of it, can kill a thousand men. Ten thousand. No mask or filter will stop it. It is fatal if a tiny droplet touches your skin. Two weeks from now, the Russians will be suing for peace.

Diefenbacher dropped into his chair and stared blankly at Jonathan. "Is this true?"

"It is absolutely true."

"I will have to have this checked out."

"There is no time to have it checked out," Jonathan said, pounding on the desk. "You must get me to see the Fuehrer immediately!"

Diefenbacher stood up, his cheeks reddening. "I have to speak to my superiors." He left the room.

Jonathan took a seat by the door. His stomach was growling and he felt suddenly fatigued. It occurred to him that if they bought his story, he might be repeating it to Adolf Hitler five minutes from now. It was possible, even likely, that Hitler was in this very bunker. That thought gave Jonathan a cold shiver. He told himself, *stick to your cover.*

Suddenly an alarm went off, an oscillating, high-pitched buzzer. A moment later he heard a commotion in the hall. Jonathan opened the door. Hundreds of people were rushing past. One called to him, "The Russians are in the Wilhelmstrasse!" Others cried, "Evacuation! Evacuation!"

Jonathan shut the door. The lights flickered. The booming of the artillery grew louder. What should he do? Every damn minute lost was going to make it tougher. If he was going to see Hitler it had damn well be soon.

Diefenbacher came back into the room with three other men. One was gaunt and officious, wearing a dark suit and a tie. The other two were young men, blocky, tough. They closed the door. "This is the man," Diefenbacher said.

"Friedrich Franz Mohne, sir," Jonathan said, standing at attention.

The gaunt man in the dark suit stared at Jonathan for a long moment. "Do you know who I am?"

Jonathan shook his head.

"Maximilian Cronin."

The name meant nothing to Jonathan.

Cronin suddenly backhanded him across his face. "I sent you to Argentina! You and Linz, and Habermans. We have ordered your arrest! The three of you, who were supposed to invest and make plans, what did you do? Live it up, spend money on women and drink!"

He took a gun out and hit Jonathan on the side of the head, knocking him to the floor.

Jonathan stayed down as the room whirled around him. Blood ran down his cheek. What the hell was this? Was it possible Mohne wasn't such a staunch follower of the Fuehrer as he pretended to be? Damn Willis never checked him out. So that is why Mohne confessed so quickly—he had not done his duty. There were no hidden villas. He had been tempted, and he had abandoned the cause, and goddamn Willis and the rest had believed him because he seemed so fanatical.

One of the young toughs hoisted Jonathan to his feet.

Jonathan said, "Our seeming to disobey orders was only a cover for the Tabun operation. I have never once faltered in my duty."

That earned him a blow in the abdomen and another crack in the head. He fell onto the floor. Diefenbacher kicked him in the side.

"If we had time," Diefenbacher said, "we would get the whole story of your betrayal out of you. As it is, consider yourself fortunate that you get a bullet."

"You fool," Jonathan said, getting up on his knees. "Do you think I'd come back here if I were a traitor? We have Tabun that can win the war for Germany! Take me to the Fuehrer, are you all imbeciles?"

Cronin shook a fist at him. "The Fuehrer has sworn never to use gas! You use gas, it gets used on you. Have you never read *Mein Kampf?* Take him out and shoot him. Be quick about it."

The two thugs dragged him out of the room and down the hall. Jonathan could hear machine gun firing down the hall. Finishing off the prisoners, no doubt. People were pouring out of offices, leaving burning records behind. The records should have been burned earlier, of course, but since "Fortress Berlin" was impregnable, there hadn't been any reason to. At least that's the way Jonathan decided they had it figured. The hallways filled with smoke, which sent one of the thugs into a coughing fit. They turned a corner. Lights flickered. Jonathan's brain froze with fear. It was time to see whether Ott's attack methods worked.

This hallway was empty and dim. No smoke. From the far end, at a distance of about a city block, a machine gun chattered away. Any sensible thug would simply shoot him where they stood but, the Germans being neat, Jonathan thought, they would do all their shooting in one place.

Jonathan knew he had to make his move quickly. He felt his sleeve, and there was the piano wire. That might do for one, but it surely wouldn't do for both. Neither of them had a gun out. One had hold of Jonathan's arm; the other was just walking along next to him. Jonathan was limping and moaning, trying to make them believe he was hurt worse than he was.

Another alarm sounded, a pulsing wail. The

thugs paused to listen to it. Jonathan took this as his chance. He turned and plunged the fingers of his right hand at the thug on his right, stabbing into the warm gelatin of the man's eyes. The man shrank back, howling and grabbing at his face. Jonathan twisted and stabbed at the other man with his left hand, but missed, his hand sliding over the man's head; the man was pulling away, jerking his gun out.

But Jonathan already had hold of the wire and looped it around his neck, drawing the wire tight. The man dropped his gun as he reached for Jonathan's hands, but it was too late. His body melted onto the floor. The blinded thug was holding a hand over his face, crying, "Where is he, what's happening?" He had his gun in his other hand, but had no idea where to aim it.

Jonathan picked up his partner's gun, cocked it, and shot him in the forehead.

Chapter Seventeen

There were fewer people in the halls now, and most of them were running for the exits. The hallways were black with smoke. He could see flames now behind the glass doors of many of the offices. Two SS men swept by him pushing a cart with incendiary bombs. No doubt they intended to torch the whole place. The lights flickered. Time was short, and fear was wrapped around him like the piano wire.

He made his way back to Diefenbacher's office. Diefenbacher, alone, was busy packing papers into a brief case. He turned and looked at Jonathan with the gun in his hand and froze. The office was thick with smoke.

"A pass to see the Fuehrer, Herr Diefenbacher," Jonathan said.

Diefenbacher's lower lip trembled. He glanced at the door, then at Jonathan, as if having Jonathan come in didn't make any sense at all. "B-But how?" he managed.

"Don't trouble yourself, just write me the goddamn pass. If you wish to live, you'd better write it quick."

"And if I do give it to you?" He stiffened.

"All I want is that damn pass. I give you my word of honor as an officer in the SS, no harm will come to you. I serve the Reich, I'm not interested in petty vengeance. Hurry, they're setting incendiary bombs, this whole place is going to be an inferno." His eyes started watering.

Diefenbacher looked skeptical. He moved one way, then stopped. He said, "This is not about Tabun, is it?"

"Never mind what it's about. Just give me that pass!"

Diefenbacher straightened his necktie as indecision danced in his eyes. Then he shrugged and said, "If you're a traitor, they will kill you. Why should I worry?"

"That's correct. Why should you worry?"

Diefenbacher took a pen and wrote something on a piece of paper and handed it to him. It was permission to be admitted to the Fuehrer's headquarters, and Diefenbacher had signed it.

"Now where is Hitler?" Jonathan said.

"With his whore in Berchtesgaden."

Jonathan pointed the gun at Diefenbacher and fired, hitting him in the belly. Diefenbacher looked at the wound in disbelief. "A present from a Jew, Herr Diefenbacher. Have a nice time in hell." Jonathan shot him in the chest; Diefenbacher fell to the floor, twitching. Jonathan aimed at his stomach and fired a few more times. Then he turned and headed out of the bunker. There was a mass exit in progress, hundreds of people pushing and screaming, jamming their way to the exits. The smoke gagged him, blinded him. He could hear incendiary bombs going off on the lower levels. He kept pushing in the sea of people. Finally he was through the front security entrance and on the stairway, climbing over people, elbowing, shoving.

At last he burst through into the evening air. Shelling everywhere. The people exiting the Gestapo headquarters scattered, running off in panic. Jonathan sought refuge in a nearby shelter, where he found a wounded colonel, a Frenchman from the Charlemagne Division, sitting in the doorway; a young medic was bandaging him up. The colonel said his men had counterattacked and pushed the Russians back, at least temporarily. He added that it looked as if Ivan had had enough for today, that they would simply go boom boom with the big guns throughout the night.

After a while the shelling stopped. The Gestapo headquarters gushed flames and smoke from its entrance and air vents.

Jonathan headed back to the Volkssturm unit; his stomach was growling and he felt exhausted. He had not told the Gestapo what his unit was. If they sent anyone looking for him, which was extremely unlikely because they had plenty of problems of their own, they would not come to the Volkssturm unit first. They would no doubt go to the SS units, which were in the northern part of the city taking the brunt of Zhukov's frontal assault.

At the Volkssturm unit the evening rations were being passed out. The other officers and men congratulated Jonathan for winning the Iron Cross. Somebody had found some barrels of beer and most of the men were pleasantly drunk, singing and laughing. The rations included canned ham and potatoes, along with the field rations and strong imitation coffee. Major Boltar ordered the men to clean their weapons and then bed down, but as soon as he disappeared into his quarters the men were back drinking beer.

Jonathan found a place to curl up near the door that led to the main mess. As he drifted off to sleep, he could hear the thudding of artillery shells, but the bombardment was not intense. Occasionally he could hear return fire from German artillery, and the chatter of machine guns. But it was fairly quiet. The Russians had to sleep too.

Jonathan awoke at one. The shelling had stopped. The only thing he could hear was the snores of his men and the wailing of the men in the infirmary. Someone had put a blanket over him. He stepped over a sleeping corporal and went down the trench that served as a hallway and up a ladder, where a couple of sentries were standing by.

They saluted him. One was broad-shouldered and blond, the ideal Aryan specimen; the other was short, fat, and swarthy, like a Greek. Jonathan gave them cigarettes and lit one up himself. He told them he just wanted to get some air and stretch his legs.

It was a bright, moonlit night.

"We're not supposed to let anyone out without written orders."

"I promise not to run away. Surely a man who wins an Iron Cross can be trusted to take a short stroll."

They shrugged and let him go. Discipline in the German army, Jonathan thought, had gone to hell. That was good for him and the success of his mission. He was glad for another reason. He didn't particularly like the idea of killing those two young soldiers.

The city was strangely quiet. Fires burned around him. Smoke and the smell of death clung in the air. In the distance an occasional artillery round was fired. Above him, an ocean of stars sparkled on the vast mantle. Someday, he thought, this fight would all be over and the world would go on. This war would be just like all the other wars in the dust of history.

As he made his way through the rubble he came upon a small group of soldiers who had put up a makeshift roadblock. They checked the pass that Diefenbacher had signed, whispered among themselves, and let him pass. Nearby a Hitlerjungend hung from a twisted lamppost with a sign pinned to his shirt. No doubt it labeled him a deserter or a coward. He was probably all of about eleven or twelve.

"I'm afraid I got turned around," Jonathan said. "Where is the Fuehrer's headquarters? Am I heading in the right direction?"

"Report to General Weidling's headquarters first," one of them said. "Just beyond the statue of Bismarck. Can't miss it."

A shell whistled overhead and exploded a couple of blocks away.

Jonathan continued down the street. He was getting closer. A feeling of dread came over him. He paused. To his right, a column of flame rose into the sky. The feeling that somehow this was all fated and controlled by some higher agency once more took hold of him. Here he was, about to confront Adolf Hitler, the evil lunatic who had brought ruin on the Jews, on Germany, on the whole world, and he was just a few meters away. And somehow he, Jonathan Zalman Becker, was to become involved in the final act of this horrible world tragedy.

It was a miracle that he had made it to the center of Berlin. He had survived a battle, a plane crash, the Gestapo. But if it were true that he was fated, why was it that his limbs were now shaking? The night air was cold, yet sweat poured down his face and his back.

He passed by the statue of Bismarck and the entrance of a bunker with flags flying. That would be the bunker of General Weidling, he thought, who was in command of the pitiful forces defending Berlin. He looked around. It was surrounded by anti-aircraft and artillery batteries amid the burnt hulks of huge gothic buildings.

Jonathan knew this was the Citadel area of Berlin, where most of the government ministries, the embassies, the grand hotels and expensive shops had been before the war. He remembered being there once as a child. There had been a parade of stormtroopers goose-stepping with jackboots, huge flags and banners, bands playing music. He remembered his mother saying, "Men who believe in their own power controlling the destiny of the world are fools."

His mother believed in the power of God. He did not. Most of the evil in the history of the world had been done in the name of God.

He remembered how wonderful it all seemed, at that age, how it stirred his blood at the same time it terrified him. He remembered Hitler standing on the balcony of the Reichchancellory, screaming into a microphone, and the great crowds screaming back: SIEG HEIL! SIEG HEIL! SIEG HEIL!

Even the memory of it made his blood race. He did not tell his mother that day, but even now he could remember saying a silent prayer:

Lord God, let me be with them.

Jonathan stopped in his tracks. He was looking at the Brandenburg Gate, the arch that he knew was once at the center of the district, just a few blocks from the Reichschancellory. Could it be that Hitler was still there? Could it be that he was not in the field conducting the defense of Berlin as the Propaganda Ministry claimed, or at Berchtesgaden as the Gestapo claimed? Could it be that he was in the Chancellory?

He turned around and looked over the rubble, trying to get his bearings. He looked for the Little Bear in the sky, used it to find north, then turned southeast. That was the best he could recollect. He jogged down the street. Here he encountered drunken soldiers with women, crowds of them, singing and yelling.

He came to a corner and looked around. Part of a grand gothic building was still standing. It was huge, and there above the street was the same balcony he'd seen Hitler standing on years before. The top of the window had been blown away and the wall around the corner was gone, but it was the same balcony.

SIEG HEIL! SIEG HEIL! SIEG HEIL!

He approached. The place was packed with soldiers and officials, singing, arguing, yelling at each other. He could see them going in and out of the bunker across the street, bringing in women and loot. The sentries looked like idlers.

He felt a momentary gloom come over him. Hitler must be dead, he thought. Or he is too far gone to know what's going on around him. Or he's run away someplace.

Jonathan approached the sentries. These were ordinary Wehrmacht soldiers; he had expected them to be SS.

Jonathan stiffened, saluted, and said, "I wish to see the Fuehrer."

They looked at him strangely. "You have dispatches?"

"*Nein.* More important than dispatches." He handed them his pass. They handed it back. "These are no longer being honored. The Fuehrer does not wish to see anyone."

"Take me to an officer, corporal."

"As you wish."

The corporal led him into the Chancellory. The bottom floor was in amazingly good condition; the furnishings were intact, the paintings were still on the walls. A young woman ran by, half dressed, followed by a colonel with no pants on, giggling like a school boy. Jonathan watched in amazement. Another officer was having sexual relations with a woman under a blanket on a couch. Everywhere there were half-eaten sandwiches and bottles of liquor and beer.

"Please wait here, Lieutenant," the sentry told him. He disappeared down a stairway. He came back a moment later with an SS major. The major was stout, sandy-haired, with an expression as morose as an undertaker's. He looked at Jonathan's pass, then handed it back to him.

"The Fuehrer is seeing no one."

Jonathan gave him the same story he had given before, that he had vital information involving super weapons, information he was to give to the Fuehrer and the Fuehrer alone.

"You have come too late," the major said. "The Fuehrer has determined to die at his own hand very soon. His decision is unalterable. Whatever information you have, it has come too late."

"Does that mean we are surrendering?"

The major shook his head. "Not until the last bullet is fired. The fighting continues."

And, Jonathan thought, *so does the killing of the Jews.*

"I suggest you return to your unit," the major said. "Kill as many Russians as you can." He walked away and down some stairs.

Jonathan went back outside. He was momentarily dispirited. How near and yet so far. The moonlight seemed even brighter. A sheet of orange flame lit the southern horizon. The songs of the SS troopers in their barracks wafted across to him.

He went down the street and turned up another. There he saw a gang of SS troopers digging through the rubble in search of deserters. He pulled into a doorway and watched them. They found a couple Hitlerjungend crying for their mothers. The SS troopers laughed, then shot them in the back of their heads.

Jonathan felt a wave of nausea. The SS troopers moved on. One of them had spotted someone running, and they went after him. Jonathan turned another corner, and then another. He was directly behind the Chancellory now. Part of a high wall still stood, surrounding what? A garden perhaps. He started down a path through the rubble which seemed to be going in the right direction. He'd gone about twenty meters when he passed what looked like a cellarway leading down into the rubble. He paused for a moment. Someone was moving.

"Who's there?" Jonathan asked, reaching for his pistol.

A woman's voice: "At last you've come."

He recognized the voice. It was Heidi's.

Chapter Eighteen

Jonathan could barely make out her form, huddled in the tiny cave in the rubble. Heidi was wearing an army jacket with the collar high up around her neck. She motioned for him to follow her. He ducked down and lowered himself in. He crawled on his hands and knees through an opening and into a little room. She lit a candle.

"I had almost given up," she said. "I thought you might have been killed. But then I knew you hadn't been." Her mad eyes glistened in the candlelight.

"Where is Hitler, Heidi? Do you know?"

"I know. He lives like the mole people, deep under the ground. He only comes out to walk his dog at night sometimes."

"Have you seen him do this?"

"Oh, yes. Yes. Right over there, on the other side of the wall."

"How about his guards?"

"They stay in the doorway away from the shelling. I see them smoking and talking. The bombs have stopped falling, so it is only the cannon they fear. I think God has answered our prayers and has forbidden the planes to fly."

Jonathan squatted down and leaned back against a board. A series of small explosions went off in the distance like a string of firecrackers. The Germans were blowing bridges or tunnels, Jonathan figured. It meant that they still had an organized resistance.

"There are suicides everywhere," Heidi said suddenly, fanning her arms out. "I was in the U-Bahn station and saw two old ladies who had taken poison."

"Have you any idea when our friend Adolf will be coming out again?"

"No regular times. Every two or three hours when there are no bombs."

"The Russians must not know where he is or they'd be raining down shells on the place nonstop."

"I do not like the Russians. They are inferior Slavs."

"Well, nobody's perfect," Jonathan said. "Except the Germans."

She laughed. "I think you're funny," she said.

"Well, Heidi, I guess it's time to go meet Der Fuehrer, see if he's in the mood to get rescued." He said it glibly, but his stomach tightened.

They came up out of the opening onto the ground. A heavy black smoke clung in the air, and the smell of death was overpowering. And there was an eerie quiet.

Heidi grabbed hold of his hand.

"I think you shouldn't come with me," he said.

"Why not?" she said. "It's my dream and I have every right to it."

He had no idea what that meant, but he didn't want to ask. "Stay behind me, in case the guards shoot first and ask questions later."

"That's a funny thing to say."

"Haven't you ever been to a John Wayne movie?"

"No, but he must be very funny if he says things like that."

They made their way through the rubble. There was no longer any pathway. They had to be careful not to turn their ankles or cut themselves on shards of glass. At last they made it to the wall behind the Chancellory. No guards around. They crouched down behind the wall. The moon was low on the horizon; it looked bluish and strange through the smoke.

"It is an evil time," she said.

"The war is almost over."

"I won't see any more wars. I hate them."

"Somebody must like them, people keep having them."

Jonathan patted her on the cheek. He could hear

the revelers' voices coming from the Chancellory. Singing the Horst Wessel song. Some pistol shots went off a few blocks away. Deserters getting it, Jonathan supposed.

"Cowards," she said.

"Yeah," he said. "And some of them ten years old."

"A German must know how to die," she said. "The Fuehrer taught us that."

They heard a dog bark. Jonathan got up and took a look. Someone was moving around the rubble. A guard, maybe. It looked as if he had a machine gun slung over his shoulder. Jonathan slid back down and said, "Looks like something's happening. I'm going on alone from here."

"I want to talk to Der Fuehrer, too."

"No, they might shoot on sight."

"I want to ask him why he has done this to the world. What did we do to deserve this?"

"He'll have you shot."

"Not when he sees that I love him. I just want to understand."

"No. Stay here."

Jonathan stood up and moved down the wall to a broken place. He knew Heidi was behind him, but there wasn't much he could do about it. He took a look through the broken place in the wall. There was a small courtyard, once no doubt a garden. The earth had been completely churned up by shells and bombs and littered with pieces of masonry and torn pieces of metal. Across the way was the back of the Chancellory, which was in fact two buildings joined together. The older one to Jonathan's left was missing the upper stories, but the lower stories were pretty much intact. The newer part appeared to be a shell surrounding a pile of rubble.

Next to the new section was a concrete blockhouse with a doorway, and next to the blockhouse was a tower with an unusual conical hat. Jonathan guessed it must be the airshaft for an underground bunker. A guard stood by the conical tower, a machine gun across his chest. A couple more guards were just above him in the rubble, with a good open field of fire to protect anyone walking in the courtyard. Whoever it was who had been walking around had apparently gone back inside.

He slid back down. His heart pounded in his chest. He wiped his hand on his shirt. A large block of ice had formed in his belly. He took a couple of deep breaths.

"He's just a man," she said.

"Yeah, just a man."

"He is strong only because he is evil," she said.

"And he's got a lot of people who will do what he tells them to."

"He's the Fuehrer," she said. "Everyone must obey him, even if he is evil."

"You're bound and determined to go along, aren't you?"

"Yes," she said.

"Okay, come on then."

He stood up and took her hand and together, crouching low, they moved along the wall to a pile of wood and stones that once might have been a shack for a building maintenance crew. Part of it was still standing. They squeezed into it. From inside they could see part of the courtyard and most of the blockhouse. She put her arms around him and rested her head on his shoulder.

"Dying sometimes seems so pleasant," she whispered.

"This war is going to be over. Survive it, that's all you've got to do."

"I'm not going to survive it," she said. "I've known that for a long time."

"Shhhhhh. Someone just came to the door."

The door to the bunker had opened. A red light in the bunker doorway outlined a figure. He was hunched over, almost like a hunchback, and was wearing a stiff-brimmed officer's hat; he was gesturing with his hands, talking to someone inside. Then a dog on a leash appeared, and the man in the doorway took the leash and came outside.

Now Jonathan could see his round face and the mustache under the nose.

Hitler.

The soldiers came to attention and saluted. Heidi pressed her face close to Jonathan's to get a look through the small opening in the rubble. "Ahhh," she said, "there he is. Satan has come out of hell to walk in the garden."

"He's just a man," Jonathan said. "An evil, evil man, but just a man nevertheless."

"He's Satan."

"Shhhhhh."

Jonathan licked his finger and tested the wind. It was blowing toward him, so it was just possible the dog might not get their scent. Hitler walked slowly, letting the dog sniff and pee. Except that the ground had been blown to hell, Jonathan thought, he might have been any dog owner out walking the dog in the moonlight.

Sweat rolled down Jonathan's back. He could feel it soaking through his shirt. Heidi dug her fingers into his arm. Jonathan kept trying to swallow, but his throat had closed up. Suddenly he thought, *I can't go through with it.*

But then an image of Julius Shapiro flashed into his mind. And the men and women he'd seen, the walking skeletons, behind the barbed wire at the camps.

Then he saw his mother and remembered her saying, *They have been killing us for centuries and we are still here.*

Hitler disappeared around the corner of the wall out of Jonathan's sight. Jonathan shoved his head up further into the opening, but part of the wall blocked his view. He held his breath and waited. And waited. A few distant artillery pieces fired.

Then the night was still again. Jonathan breathed in and out through his teeth.

Suddenly Hitler was in front of him, having looped around the courtyard; Hitler was walking back up toward the blockhouse, no more than ten or fifteen meters away, walking with a shuffling gait.

Jonathan, paralyzed with fear, couldn't breathe. Suddenly Heidi grabbed the gun from his holster and stood up. *"Nein!"* Jonathan cried. She pointed the gun at Hitler and pulled the trigger. Click. Jonathan grabbed Heidi and flung her behind him, sending her tumbling backward. The dog turned and started barking, straining at the leash. Hitler was no more than five or ten meters away, ignoring the dog's barking.

A hail of machine gun bullets sprayed around Jonathan. He fell backward, next to Heidi. Heidi said, "The gun didn't fire!" It took Jonathan a moment to realize he'd emptied the damn thing in Diefenbacher and hadn't reloaded. He grabbed the gun out of her hand and threw it away.

Heidi turned and crawled into a hole beneath the wall.

Suddenly half a dozen men appeared, surrounding Jonathan and pointing guns at him.

Jonathan put his hands up. He looked around. Heidi was gone. They marched him over the bricks and into the courtyard where Hitler was waiting.

Hitler appeared frozen, standing in the moonlight with his hands on his hips, his dog heeled to his side. Hitler looked Jonathan over carefully. Then he said, "I've been expecting you."

"But you don't know who I am."

"Do not contradict me!" He gestured to his men and they took Jonathan into the bunker.

Book IV

Chapter Nineteen

The room in the underground bunker was small and square, with a few chairs and a table. It was stuffy. Red rust marks streaked the walls and the air smelled vaguely of sewage. A diesel generator droned on.

Jonathan sat on the floor in the corner to stay out of the way of his roommate, Hans Georg Otto Hermann Fegelein, an SS general. Fegelein, about forty, was tall, blond, very military. He was Eva Braun's brother-in-law, and an adjutant to Heinrich Himmler, the now disgraced SS Reichfuehrer.

"But I hadn't even read the damn papers," Fegelein said aloud, more to himself than to Jonathan. Jonathan gathered the papers were incriminating, but that's all he knew. Fegelein stopped pacing and said, "How the hell was I supposed to know what they said if I hadn't read them?"

"I'm sure I can't tell you," Jonathan said.

Fegelein resumed pacing. "Haven't I done everything I was expected to do? I married Eva Braun's sister even though she's got a face like a goose's ass, and damn it, I was a good husband to her. How can they make this stupid trumped-up charge against me? 'Collusion to conspire with the enemy.' How is it possible when I was only obeying the orders of my superior? Now Bormann says they might try me for treason. How can they try me? I'm a general. Who is here with enough rank? The Fuehrer himself signed the SS charter. Have you read it? In it it says that no officer can be tried except by a tribunal of his fellow officers of equal rank. There are not enough officers of equal rank in all of Germany left to hear the case." He waited for Jonathan to respond, but Jonathan just looked at him.

Fegelein continued: "If they do try me, I will be found innocent. My name will be cleared completely. I can't believe this is happening. My wife is Hitler's mistress' sister. My closest companion, who I get drunk with every night, is Martin Bormann. How can this happen? What has happened to loyalty? I have spent my life fighting for National Socialism. I won the Knight's Cross with oak leaves—here, see? It was I who put down the rebellion at Theresienstadt—we killed two hundred thousand in four days. Four days! I have given National Socialism my very soul. Tell me, do I deserve this? To be charged with treason. To be disgraced?"

Jonathan knew of the rebellion at Theresienstadt,

a death camp in Bohemia. The reprisals took the form of burning inmates alive. Stabbing children in front of their mothers. Cutting off testicles and forcing them down the victim's throat. And here before him was the man responsible. A violent rage rose in Jonathan, but he managed to remain still.

Fegelein continued to pace, his hands behind his back, his head bowed. Finally Jonathan said, "Perhaps you should have acted differently in your career, Herr General? Is that what you've concluded?"

Fegelein looked at him strangely. "Of course not, whatever gave you that idea?" He tucked his tunic into his belt, even though it did not need tucking. Then he dropped onto a chair. He looked at Jonathan and said, "What have they got you in here for?"

"I have come to Berlin from Latin America on a mission of utmost importance to the Reich. Unfortunately I, too, have been associated with Reichfuehrer Himmler. And my papers were out of date."

Fegelein's eyes narrowed. "What kind of mission?"

"We have a secret weapon of great strength on its way to the Skoda works in Prague. Once this weapon is put into the field, it will mean victory for Germany. I can tell you no more than that. My orders are to speak with the Fuehrer directly. I have done everything I possibly can to get to see him. I was waiting outside the bunker when the Fuehrer came out to walk his dog. When I confronted him, he said he had been waiting for me. But then he had me taken here."

"You don't understand," Fegelein said. "The Fuehrer no longer has the power to reason. The traitorous acts of his generals, I mean of course the generals of the Wehrmacht, have let him down at every turn. He is surrounded by fools. He no longer trusts anyone. He is suspicious of even those of us who love him most. If I could just get to see him for five minutes, I could convince him that what I was doing was simply my duty. That the papers Himmler had given me were shocking, and I only had them to give them to the Fuehrer himself in order to prove Himmler's treachery. I was not participating in it myself. Hasn't my record been exemplary? Do you think you will get to see the Fuehrer soon? If you do, will you plead my case? We should make a pact to help each other. I will help you and you can help me, what do you say?"

"All right," Jonathan said. "We will plead each other's case if we get the chance."

Fegelein's face brightened with momentary hope. "I am still young and in vigorous health. I do not want to die. There are too many women in the world left unbedded."

Jonathan smiled.

At that moment the door opened. The guard looked in for a moment, then stepped back and a woman came in.

"Eva!" Fegelein exclaimed.

It was, Jonathan assumed, Eva Braun. Jonathan came to his feet. If the desperate situation Germany was in distressed her at all, she didn't show it. She was dressed in a frilly blouse and a full skirt and her hair was combed down over her forehead in a schoolgirl kind of way.

Fegelein went to her and tried to hug her, but she backed away. She wouldn't even let him hold onto her hand.

"You asked to see me, Hans, and so I've come," she said, signaling the guard to close the door.

"I thank you for that," Fegelein said, bowing.

Eva Braun said, "You are, after all, married to my sister and so there is an obligation to at least listen to what you have to say, but I'm not very inclined to help you. After all, you have not been a good husband to Gretl, and you certainly have not been loyal to Dolf."

Fegelein did not get angry over this as Jonathan thought he might. Instead he stiffened and backed away from her, a hurt, offended look coming to his face. "Darling, Eva," he said silkily, "I think my enemies have been talking against me and you've been listening." He glanced at Jonathan with a look that seemed to say, watch me wheedle this simpleton. "Believe me," he continued to Eva, "I have not even considered for one moment being disloyal to the Fuehrer. I can and will explain those papers in my brief case to the proper authorities and at the proper time. I only ask that you do one thing for me, Eva darling, and that is that you see to it that the Fuehrer will see me for a few minutes. I know he's busy, but I also know how fond he is of you. He would allow me to see him if you asked. You do have a way with him. When he's with you, his goodness and kindness shine through."

He took her hand as if to kiss it, but she drew it back. "It's too late for soft soap, Hans. I know what you did with Lise up at the Burghof."

"Lise?"

"The second maid."

Fegelein's mouth dropped open.

"One of the soldiers on sentry duty saw you. The sentries tell me everything, so don't try to deny it, Herr Don Juan."

It took Fegelein a few moments to regain his composure. "But surely a weak moment with that little tart of a maid that meant absolutely nothing could not debase our friendship, Eva."

"I'm sure it would mean something to my sister. Besides, Dolf tells me that what was found in your brief case is unforgivable, that you are a traitor to the Reich and he can't possibly do anything for you, that justice must take its course."

Fegelein shook his head dumbly. "But Eva. They mean to *kill* me."

"When I was in the convent school and I spoke

out of turn they used to hit my hand very hard with a ruler. All the girls got the same treatment. Whenever I spoke out of turn, they took me to the head of the class and I had to put my hand out and take my punishment. When you don't do what you're supposed to do, you have to take the punishment."

"But Eva, they are not going to slap my hand with a ruler, which I would happily let them do if they wanted. They are not interested in disciplining me, they are going to *execute* me, don't you understand?"

"I understand perfectly."

Fegelein turned to Jonathan. "I'm going to the wall because I kissed a chambermaid!"

"That isn't exactly true," Eva Braun said. "I'm sorry, but we haven't been introduced, Lieutenant, I am Eva Braun."

Jonathan bowed. "I am extremely pleased to meet you, Fraulein Braun. I am Lt. Mohne. Has the Fuehrer spoken to you about me? I met him tonight in the garden."

Her eyes got large. "I didn't know you were an actual person."

"I'm sorry, Fraulein, but I don't know quite what you mean."

"The Fuehrer that said when he was out walking the dog he met Death in the garden. I thought it was some kind of apparition."

"The lieutenant is on a secret mission, Eva,"

Fegelein said. "He knows of a secret weapon that could alter the outcome of the war, even now. The Fuehrer must talk with him."

"But Dolf has already made up his mind to kill himself, here, in the bunker. He is determined to die in Fortress Berlin, and I am going to die with him." She raised her chin high. Heroically.

"Is there any reason to die when we could still win the war?" Fegelein asked.

"Dolf has made an unalterable decision, and so have I."

She turned and walked out the door.

Fegelein turned to Jonathan and said, "She wants to be a martyr. Dying is a grand and glorious thing to her, like in the fifth act of a bad opera. You see what I'm up against? The kind of mentality I've been dealing with?"

The door opened again. A rat-faced SS colonel came in. He looked battle-worn and brittle. Jonathan saluted him. He didn't bother to return the salute. He sneered and turned to Fegelein, "General Fegelein, it is my unpleasant duty to inform you that you are to be shot immediately."

Fegelein's face turned gray. "But how—I have had no trial! A general of the SS cannot be shot without a trial!"

The colonel looked puzzled for a moment, stroking his chin. "Haven't you had one?"

"I've just been interrogated."

"Most unusual," the colonel said.

"I demand a tribunal be convened!" Fegelein cried. "I demand the Fuehrer be told that the SS charter has been violated."

The colonel nodded vaguely and left the room.

"We'll get this straightened out yet," Fegelein said to Jonathan. Beads of sweat had formed on the top of his forehead. He resumed pacing.

Jonathan said, "Is Hitler insane?"

Fegelein started to answer negatively, but then he sat down and said, "I guess it is too late in the game to lie. He's always been a little mad, I thought, but he was at least predictable. He is no longer predictable. He broods, then bursts out laughing. He rails like a man possessed. I think he is possessed."

"Is there any way to get through to him?"

"Sometimes he has great moments of clarity. His eyes are almost always clouded over these days, and when he rails they turn red and bulge out of his sockets. But every once in a while, his eyes are clear and his old genius returns. Watch his eyes for his moment of clarity."

The door opened again and the rat-faced colonel came back in; two SS storm troopers carrying machine guns were with him. The colonel said, "I have discussed the problem with the Fuehrer. He said it is true that no general of the SS can be executed without a trial."

Fegelein breathed a sigh of relief and wiped the beads of sweat from his brow.

"Therefore," the colonel said, "the Fuehrer has ordered that you be reduced in rank to private, effective immediately. Come along, Private Fegelein, we have to get our executions done while the Russian artillery men are not doing their business."

Fegelein screamed: "I refuse to die as a private!"

"But you have no choice," the colonel said.

Fegelein looked pleadingly at Jonathan.

"I guess the Fuehrer had a moment of clarity," Jonathan said.

In the doorway Fegelein wailed and his legs went out from under him. The two storm troopers had to drag him down the hall, wailing and screaming.

And that, thought Jonathan, is the end of the hero of Theresienstadt.

Fifteen minutes later the rat-faced colonel and the storm troopers returned. The colonel said, "Herr Lieutenant, you are to come with me."

Chapter Twenty

Jonathan still had the piano wire in his other sleeve, and he was ready to use it as he had the evening before at Gestapo headquarters. Only this time there were three of them and they were ready to shoot. The prospect of making a successful attack did not look good.

Jonathan and his captors went through a narrow passage and down a flight of stairs, then turned down another hallway. Men in uniform were everywhere, many of them drunk. Jonathan could hear a lot of arguing and shouting as they passed by the men's rooms. This was the command post of a defeated army whose mad leader refused to surrender. There was nothing to do but get drunk and rail against one's fate.

"Might I ask, sir," Jonathan said to the rat-faced colonel, "where it is you are taking me?"

"You'll find out."

"Am I to be shot?"

The colonel turned and grinned. "We'll just have

to see about that now, won't we?"

"I guess we will," Jonathan said.

They descended another flight of stairs to the lower level of the bunker. Here it was quieter. They passed two SS sentries, who nodded at the colonel and allowed him through, but not the storm troopers. The colonel motioned to Jonathan to follow him. Jonathan was amazed to hear the laughter of children coming from a room down the hall. A young girl in a white dress sprang out of a doorway and quickly disappeared into another. Whose children? he wondered.

Jonathan and the colonel went into a small waiting room. A young SS private stood up, saluted, and ushered them into a stuffy, crowded sitting room, where a meeting was going on.

Jonathan had seen photographs of some of the people squeezed into the room: Martin Bormann, the Nazi Party Chief and Hitler's scheming personal secretary, was there, as was Dr. Joseph Goebbels, the Propaganda Minister, who had made lying a virtue and an art form. Next to him was Army General Keitel; next to him, Air Force General Brauer; over by the wall, Hitler's two lady secretaries. Another woman sat next to Goebbels; Jonathan figured she was Goebbels' wife. Next to her was Eva Braun, who sat stiffly like a young girl who'd been told to behave herself. An SS general Jonathan didn't recognize sat near the door. Jonathan supposed he was General Kraft, head of the remaining SS troops in Berlin, a veteran of the

Russian campaign and, according to Allied Intelligence, one ruthless, vicious, bloodthirsty bastard.

There was another doorway at the other end of the room, covered with a curtain. The curtain suddenly parted and Hitler entered the room. Everyone stood; the military men saluted. Hitler returned the salute perfunctorily. He was hunched over and took shuffling little steps. His face was puffed up like bread dough, Jonathan thought, and he looked half dead. An aide helped him into his seat.

"What is the latest?" Hitler asked.

"The Russians are still advancing on all fronts," Keitel said. "They are in Friedrichstrasse. Five or six blocks away. They will be here within two days."

"And Wenck, is he not going to relieve the city?"

"Wenck has ordered his men west, to surrender to the Americans," Keitel said. "It was in Monday's report, don't you recall?"

"Damnable treachery," the SS general said. "The Zoo station is still holding out. Led by an SS detachment." He swelled with pride. "And the 56th Panzers are supporting Weidling in the Citadel. Without them, all would have collapsed by now."

"The Frenchmen of the Charlemagne Division fight the fiercest," Goebbels said. "Without them, your panzers would be crushed." The SS general shot him an angry glance but said nothing.

Hitler sighed. Jonathan could see the irony of Hitler's fiercest supporters being Frenchmen, which was true.

"The Hitlerjungend fight too," Eva Braun said cheerfully.

"Yes," one of the secretaries said, then covered her mouth, realizing she had no right to speak.

"And many more desert," Goebbels said bitterly. He looked as if he could not understand how someone would not want to die for such a glorious cause.

"Yes, treachery is everywhere," Hitler said wearily. "The whole General Staff let me down, let the nation down. They were not the same as the men in the Great War. The generals in the Great War were outstanding men who could be relied upon to do their duty."

"Absolutely," Bormann said.

"I never wanted this war," Hitler said. "None of us did, isn't that right?"

"Absolutely," Bormann said.

"That is true," Goebbels agreed.

"It was international Jewry," Hitler said. "And their lackeys, the British and the Bolsheviks. If only the damned British had understood all we wanted was living space. Are not we and the British of the same race? It was that damnable Churchill. If not for Churchill, I could have made peace with the British in '41."

"Yes, yes," most agreed.

"Damned Jews," muttered Goebbels.

Jonathan nearly laughed. Here were the most villainous monsters in the history of the world trying to post blame everywhere and anywhere, as long as it didn't stick to them.

Hitler shook his head, his eyes half closed as if he was either praying or in pain. Then he opened them again and nodded to Bormann, as if to say the first part of the ritual was over, now they could get down to business. Bormann looked at Eva Braun and said, "Is this the man?" He indicated Jonathan.

Eva Braun nodded.

"We've been told that you have some news," Goebbels said to Jonathan.

"I do." He drew himself to attention and took a deep breath. "A large shipment of Tabun gas, the most powerful gas ever invented—no mask or filter can stop it—is on its way to the Skoda works. Three large tank cars of it. It is now in Spain. If it can be flown to Prague within twenty-four hours, it can be operational by the end of next week."

General Keitel said, "The use of gas is a violation of the Geneva Convention."

"And so is the bombing of civilians," Jonathan said. "Two months ago, the Allies totally destroyed Dresden. Is not that a gross violation of the Geneva Convention? Dresden had no military significance whatever."

"I don't see how this gas will do anything," Bormann said, "except blow back in our faces. If we use gas, they will use gas." Bormann glanced at Hitler, who nodded in sad agreement.

"The Allies do not have Tabun," Jonathan said. "Tabun needs only to contact the skin. No mask or filter can keep it out. Yet it will not linger more than a few hours in the air. It is the perfect weapon. A month after it goes into the field, our victorious armies will be at the gates of Moscow."

Jonathan glanced at Hitler for a reaction. None registered on his face.

"I want nothing to do with it," Keitel said. "I knew gas in the Great War, I don't want to see it again. I want no part of it. Might I be excused, Mein Fuehrer?"

Hitler waved him off with a sweep of his hand. Keitel saluted and left hurriedly.

The SS general said, "We have a duty to win the war for Germany at all cost. If this is the cost, it must be paid."

Goebbels said, "The world has already judged us a criminal nation. What penalty it will impose on us if we lose the war only a madman could imagine. If we have an opportunity to win and we don't take it, what will our children and our children's children think of us?"

"That we are cowards," the SS general said.

Jonathan noticed Hitler's expression had not changed, but his eyes seemed sharper. He was peering off into space, lost in thought. Everyone was looking at him, waiting for him to speak. Finally he said, "I have made my last testament to my people. I have resolved to die here in Berlin fighting the enemies of Germany. How do I know what you say is true? How do I know you are who you say you are? My inner voice spoke to me and called you Death. That is who you are. You are Herr Death."

"We have done some checking on Herr Lieutenant Mohne, Mein Fuehrer," the SS general said. He reached into his tunic and took out a paper. "He is reported to have shown up at a Luftwaffe base near Prague four days ago, demanding to be flown to Berlin. The Luftwaffe obliged him, and flew him to Berlin in an old Messerschmitt 109, but they were shot down by enemy aircraft. The lieutenant crashed the plane in a pond and was found two days later wandering around by elements of the Berlin Guard Battalion, who didn't know quite what to do with him. They didn't believe his story, but while they checked with headquarters he was put in charge of a small detachment of Volkssturm, where he personally rallied his troops and they threw back a massive Russian assault force. He was awarded the Iron Cross, second class, in the field. The next thing we know of him, he is taken in the garden."

"And before Prague?" Hitler asked.

"Of that we know nothing, except that he was sent to Argentina by the traitor Himmler in the beginning of 1943."

Hitler said, "I want to know more about this man, and about this gas." He stood up and shuffled out of the room. "Get hold of Speer." Speer was the Armaments Chief.

"Speer is presumed to be in enemy hands," the SS general said.

Hitler's eyes bulged. "Then get whoever is running things in his ministry and bring him here! Do I have to do all the thinking for everyone!" He yanked back the curtain and disappeared into the next room.

The SS general saluted even though he was gone. Everyone else simply filed out of the room.

Martin Bormann was a worrier.

He worried about the fate of Germany and the world. He worried what would become of him. He worried most about the hundred and twenty million gold Reichmarks he had managed to get out of Germany and safely put away in Swiss banks and South African gold stocks.

Martin Bormann was a squat, dark little man with a sloping forehead and thinning hair he combed straight back. As a member of the far rightist *Freikorps* in 1924 he had helped a comrade hack to death Walther Kadow, who was alleged to have betrayed one Leo Schlageter, a right-wing saboteur, to the French occupation authorities in the Ruhr. That Walther Kadow had been Martin Bormann's third-grade teacher did not help his cause one iota.

For his part in the killing, Bormann received a one-year jail sentence. It was in jail that he met members of the Nazi Party and immediately saw the possibilities. He was already an extreme anti-Semitic and nationalist, and the party and its leadership gave direction and purpose to his feelings.

Martin Bormann was a high school dropout at the time he joined the party, but he did have good penmanship, was a hard worker and assiduously neat, punctual, efficient, and ingratiating. He was made for secretarial work. He attached himself to Rudolf Hess, the Deputy Fuehrer; Bormann did his best to make himself indispensable. Bormann's title, from 1933 to 1941, was Chief of Cabinet in the Office of the Deputy Fuehrer. It was in that position that he first got his hands on a great deal of money and experienced the sweet taste of power.

He was the developer and chief administrator of the Adolf Hitler Endowment Fund of German Industry. His duties were simple enough. He collected "voluntary" gifts from German businessmen and doled them out to party functionaries. This fund, in 1942, amounted to half a billion marks annually. By then he had also gained control of the commission that set the pay scale and determined the living standards of the party. These two functions guaranteed him practical control over the party machinery, and the party controlled the Reich. Martin Bormann had made himself the most powerful man in Germany, with the exception of Adolf Hitler.

In order to become Number Two, the first thing he had had to do was get rid of Rudolf Hess. Hess, like Bormann, had started in the party as a secretary: Hitler's. Hess was blindly loyal to Hitler, shy, quiet, sincere, and, Bormann thought, a little stupid. With all the political acumen of a four year old.

At all mass meetings and party functions Hess announced his personal declaration of loyalty to Hitler and asked that all his followers join him: *The National Socialism of all of us is anchored in uncritical loyalty, in the surrender to the Fuehrer that does not ask for the why in individual cases, in the silent execution of his orders.*

Hess was also fond of saying that Hitler was *pure reason in human form.* When Hitler designated Hess as his successor, Martin Bormann thought it proved that Hitler was the furthest thing from pure reason on the planet.

Early in 1941 when the Battle of Britain was underway, Martin Bormann hatched a plan to get rid of Hess once and for all without killing him, which would have been risky in the extreme. Hess was, after all, the Deputy Fuehrer. No, killing him would not do. Instead, Bormann convinced Hess that if he were to go to England as a peace emissary, he could talk the British into making a separate peace with Germany. To make his story convincing, Bormann brought along two astrologers who convinced Hess that the stars were right and his mission could not fail. Bormann even arranged flying lessons for Hess so he could do it all on his own. Hess flew out of Germany on the night of May 10, 1941, and parachuted into England near the home of the Duke of Hamilton, whom Hess had met briefly at the '36 Olympics and thought he could trust. He shouldn't have. The British simply locked Hess up as a prisoner of war and never gave five minutes' thought to his absurd peace plan.

It was not quite as easy for Bormann to get rid of his other chief rivals: Hermann Goring, the head of the Luftwaffe; Heinrich Himmler, the head of the SS; and Albert Speer, the Armaments Chief. He had to wait three and a half more years, until the crumbling days of the Reich. When these rivals had dared to talk of peace, Bormann was able to brand them traitors and get Hitler to go along with it.

Now that Bormann had brought down all his enemies and even eliminated some of his friends (like Fegelein) who he thought of as *potential* rivals, he was ready to help Hitler in his mania for martyrdom. So Hitler would be gone, as was everyone else who had stood in his way.

In the case of Joseph Goebbels, who had come to the bunker to die with his Fuehrer, the problem would soon take care of itself. Hitler would shoot himself, then Goebbels would do the same, which would leave Bormann the undisputed leader of the Party and the nation. Since this fit perfectly with Bormann's plan, he had no quibbles with Goebbels at the moment, and regarded him as an ally. Just as long as he or the Fuehrer didn't change their minds.

Martin Bormann was not a man given to vague dreams, fantasies, and illusions. But he had seen the crushing defeat of the Great War turned around, and the new Germany rise up out of its ashes. And he knew a new Germany would rise again. And so would the party, the sacred tenets of which were holy writ and would endure forever. And it would rise more quickly if well funded, and well guided by a hard core of true believers like himself. The mistakes of the past could be rectified. The rebirth of the party would not allow one man's megalomania to bring the country to ruin. The movement would now be guided by a more patient hand. His. From the ashes of the Third Reich, he would build the Fourth.

If only this Lieutenant Mohne, whoever he was, did not spoil everything.

Chapter Twenty-one

The city to the east and south of the Fuehrer-bunker was ablaze. Jonathan watched the spectacle at a blown-out window in the new Reichschancellory above the bunker. The officers encamped in the Reichschancellory seemed more subdued. Many were drunk, but they were merely sitting in small groups murmuring to each other.

He was no longer under guard. He knew, though, he was being watched. After eating and catching a little sleep, he had strutted around acting as he thought Mohne might, telling soldiers not to forget to salute officers, making them tuck in their shirt tails, getting them to keep inventory of what little ordnance was left.

The Russians were shelling heavily now with incendiary shells and they had managed to set the entire industrial district on fire. Bright red and orange flames climbed into the sky. Jonathan was profoundly saddened by it. The death of the Nazis and the end of their reign of terror gladdened him, but to witness the total destruction of one of the great cities of the world was a terrible thing.

And he hoped Heidi was safe.

Suddenly a plane flew in low. Jonathan instinctively ducked, taking cover from possible machine gun bullets. But the plane wasn't on a strafing run. It circled around the Chancellory, coming in low over the street in front. The plane was a Fieseler Storch, a Luftwaffe trainer. It made a third loop around the building, clearly visible in the light of the fires. Jonathan could see flak holes in its wings and smoke pouring out of its fuselage. It made a right turn, then dipped down and looked as if it would crash near the Brandenburg Gate a few blocks away.

He listened for an explosion, but didn't hear anything.

He had to know how the battle was going, to know how much time he had, but he sure as hell didn't want to ask a lot of questions around the bunker. While the sentries were off chasing after the plane, he decided to take a tour of the medical station in the bunker across the street. The recently wounded would certainly know how things were going. At the medical station he found three nurses and two Lutheran nuns trying to take care of thousands of wounded, laid out on the floor shoulder to shoulder, most of them crying in agony because there was no morphine. One lone doctor was doing surgery and no one had carried away the sawed-off arms and legs, which were simply put in tubs and left near the entrance to the bunker. Bandages were being boiled and reused. Jonathan felt faint. He kept telling himself these were the people who were putting other people in ovens and whatever horrors were being handed out to them, they had it coming. But looking at the anguish on the face of a blinded twelve year old, he had trouble conjuring up those feelings. He didn't ask any questions about the battle, he would find another way to gather intelligence.

When he returned to the Reichschancellory he found a major general and reported that assistance in the infirmary was desperately needed. The major general told him that all available manpower was needed to fight the Russians.

"I beg the general's pardon," Jonathan said with a click of the heels and a bow, "of course the general is correct." He saluted.

Jonathan went back to the new Reichschancellory and drank some schnapps. The Nazis were out of bandages and bullets were low, but there was plenty of liquor everywhere. He still wanted to know the state of things. He had to know the escape route. He went outside and wandered up and down the street. Near the entrance to a bunker, he found a battle-weary young sergeant eating meat out of a tin can. He had bandages around his head and left hand, and his uniform was charred and torn. Jonathan offered him some schnapps. The sergeant drank it out of the bottle.

Jonathan sat down to have a chat with him. At that moment the Russians opened up a rocket barrage with *Katushkas,* "Stalin Organs," which fired sixteen rockets at a time. The target, as far as Jonathan could tell, looked like the Zoo station to the west of the Fuehrerbunker on the other side of the Tiergarten, the huge park at the center of Berlin. Tongues of flame shot up at intervals and huge columns of black smoke billowed into the night sky.

"What is happening out there is beyond a human being's mind to take in," the sergeant said.

"But it does," Jonathan said. "Sadly, it does."

"We have passed the definition of war as fought by men," the sergeant said. "This is a war of demons in hell. Did you hear what happened in the Zehlendorf District? Six hundred Volkssturm guardsmen were trying to make a stand in the square when the Russians hit them with tanks and a massive artillery barrage. They were totally annihilated in six minutes. Everywhere our barricades are being smashed down like piles of matchsticks." He stuffed some more food in his mouth. "There are pockets of resistance, but our men are deserting in wholesale numbers. Volkssturm arm bands litter the streets. In Weissensee the workers' houses have red flags flying from them." He spat.

"We who have the spirit to fight on," Jonathan said, "must thank God that He gave us a backbone."

The sergeant laughed. "Fighting on is not going to be possible much longer. This morning I saw a phalanx of artillery knock down a row of houses in half an hour so that nothing was left more than a meter high. Suicides are everywhere. The civilians are wandering the streets in madness."

"Have the Russians taken the airports?" Jonathan asked.

"Yes."

Jonathan felt a pang. So it seemed he wasn't going to fly out.

"Are all avenues out of the city closed?"

"I don't think so. They can't blow all the bridges because they are out of explosives, I've heard. They blew the tunnel under the Spree and drowned perhaps a hundred thousand civilians who were hiding in it. There is a way out through the Spandau District, which the Fuehrer has ordered to be kept open at all cost in case the Fuehrer wants to try a breakout."

So hope was not lost, Jonathan thought. There still was a chance.

Jonathan let the sergeant keep the bottle of schnapps and went back to the Reichschancellory and into the Fuehrerbunker. No one stopped him. There was a celebration going on with a lot of drinking, even the popping of champagne corks, and singing. The plane he'd seen earlier had not crashed and the two pilots were being congratulated. One of the pilots was wounded and was having shrapnel removed from his foot. Jonathan was astounded to find that the second pilot, the one who had actually landed the plane, was a woman. Her name, he learned, was Hanna Reitsch. Hanna Reitsch was about thirty, a small-boned dishwater blonde, who hardly looked the part of a heroine.

Jonathan didn't know much about Hanna Reitsch, though he had heard of her. An avid Nazi, she was a test pilot and had set some flying records as a glider pilot before the war. She had survived a few crashes and had been awarded the Iron Cross, first and second class.

"So, Hanna, why have you come to Berlin?" a tipsy SS colonel asked.

"To fly the Fuehrer out if he wants to go."

"And if he doesn't?"

"To die with him," she said resolutely.

The colonel smiled benignly. "Then we shall drink a toast to your courage."

So, Jonathan thought, that little plane was still operational. A two-seater. One seat for him, one for Hitler. Just right. If he could get fifteen minutes alone with Hitler, he figured, he could talk him onto that plane.

Now that he had a plan, Jonathan's spirit soared. He made his way through the crush of people downstairs to Hilter's private quarters, where he was informed the Fuehrer was giving battle orders to his generals and could not be disturbed without written authorization from Herr Bormann. In fact, no one at any time could see the Fuehrer without Bormann's permission.

Jonathan clicked his heels. "Where can I find Herr Bormann?"

"If there is a celebration upstairs, he will probably be celebrating," the guard said.

Jonathan knew he wasn't at the celebration. He went back upstairs and found Bormann's office, which was, Jonathan noted, strategically located next to the Fuehrerbunker escape tunnel. He knocked on the door and Bormann said to come in.

Bormann was sitting behind a desk piled high with papers. He was wearing an SS Reichfuehrer uniform. Jonathan saluted him. Bormann scowled and said, "What do you want?"

"I am afraid time is growing short, Herr Bormann. The city is nearly encircled, the airports are closed."

"How very perceptive of you, Lieutenant. Why are you telling me?"

"I want to get the Fuehrer out of Berlin. I want to get the Tabun into operation. I think we can still win this war."

Bormann ran his finger around the collar of his new uniform. The insignias indicated his rank was ceremonial.

Bormann said, "The Fuehrer does not quite believe your story and neither do I."

"Hanna Reitsch has just landed a small plane, which is still operational. It can fly the Fuehrer out of here to safety in Prague or Bavaria, where we can regroup our strength and prepare for the Great Counteroffensive. If you would support the plan, I'm sure the Fuehrer would go along with it. Let's go talk to him."

"I'm sorry, but the Fuehrer is busy now, perhaps later." He smiled enigmatically. He had smooth, snake-like skin and beady little mean eyes. He said, "You don't understand what's going on around here, do you? It's completely lost on you."

"I wish someone would tell me."

"The war is lost and everyone knows it, but it is a treasonable act to say so. This is a Wagnerian opera building up to the Gotterdammerung, the destruction of the Germanic world by fire. You would not deprive us all of that now, would you? Deprive the Fuehrer of his grand exit?"

Jonathan stared at him. "In the meantime the killing goes on."

"Yes, the blood sacrifices. A necessary component to the ritual."

"I thank you for clearing this up for me."

"If I were you, I would get out of here before we find out who you really are and what you are really up to. Just because things are in disarray does not mean that I cannot get things done. It just takes a little longer."

Jonathan saluted him. "Thank you for the advice, Herr Bormann."

"Would you mind shutting the door on your way out?" He gestured for Jonathan to leave.

In the hallway, Jonathan noticed there was a line in front of the bathroom. With so much drinking going on, no wonder. He asked an aide where there was another bathroom and was told he would have to go into the lower bunker where Hitler's quarters were. The only other bathroom around.

Jonathan waited in line, went into the stinking little toiled that had only one commode, relieved himself, and joined the party. After a while, he could hear artillery shells breaking on the roof overhead. The party continued. The kitchen served up some hors d'oeuvres, the singing grew louder. Jonathan found a towel and shoved it under his shirt and got back in line for the bathroom. When he got inside he crammed the towel down the toilet, jamming it.

Then he went and had some more champagne.

Word spread quickly that the toilet was out of commission. No one could go outside or go up into the Reichschancellory, so the only thing to do was to go down into the lower level. Jonathan waited until the routine was established and dozens of people had made the trip past the guards. In the meantime he had a talk with Hanna Reitsch.

She was more than a little drunk. He congratulated her on her daring and her skill.

"Thank you, Lieutenant," she said with a grin. "I heard that it is your desire to fly the Fuehrer out of here. Surely your plane has been hit by flak getting in, would the wings have enough lift to get you out?"

Her eyes rolled around. "With me at the controls, she will rise into the sky. With anyone else . . ." She made a dipping gesture with her hand.

"Probably so," Jonathan said, "Can the wings can be patched?"

"It is supposed to be being done at this very moment," she said boozily.

Jonathan had one more glass of champagne before steeling his courage and making his move. Wouldn't it be a great irony, he thought, if the war ended two weeks earlier because of a stopped-up toilet?

The shelling had brought more soldiers in the bunker; some of them had women with them. Jonathan threaded his way through the hallways and down the stairs. The line for the bathroom snaked down the corridor past the Fuehrer's rooms. Jonathan waited at the bottom of the stairs for a few minutes trying to decide what to do, when the doors to Hitler's quarters opened and Keitel, Kraft, and a few colonels came out, causing a crush of bodies in the hallway. The guards had given up trying to keep order.

Jonathan started down the hall, murmuring, "Coming through—dispatches, coming through, coming through. Dispatches. . . ."

When he got to the crush of bodies, he squeezed through and into Hitler's quarters and closed the door. Jonathan found himself in the sitting room he'd been in the night before. No one around. He went through the curtained-off doorway and down a short hall. Here a door was open. Inside, Hitler sat at a desk poring over some maps. On the wall above him was a somber, dignified portrait of Frederick the Great.

Hitler looked up at Jonathan and said, "I'm glad you've come, I have a plan."

Chapter Twenty-two

In the soft light, Hitler appeared like a ghost. He looked at Jonathan for a long moment through his wire-rimmed glasses with a puzzled expression, then motioned for Jonathan to come closer.

"Here, look at this," Hitler said in a raspy voice, running his hand over the map. It was a map of Germany with arrows and lines and circles all over it. "See here," Hitler whispered, "I have worked out an operational plan for the relief of the city. Follow this closely. Wenck's Twelfth Army will attack from the southwest while Busse attacks from the southeast. Together these two forces will defeat the Russians south of Berlin, then they will drive north and meet up with Steiner, where the joint force will make a massive frontal assault on Zhukov and push him back across the Oder. Once we have the damned Russians off our backs it will not be difficult to deal with the Western Allies. There now, what do you think?" Hitler sat back with a self-satisfied smile on his face.

Jonathan said, "I believe the map you're studying is a week old. I think Steiner's army is no more. In fact, he has surrendered to the British. The Russians and the Americans have already lined up on the Elb in the south, so that Germany has been cut in two. Your Army Group North is cut off. The only viable force left to you is Kesselring's Army Group South, which can hold off several more weeks while we supply him with Tabun."

"But we have to think of Berlin," Hitler said with exasperation. "The capital. Am I to turn over the capital to the Russians?"

"They already have most of it," Jonathan said, marveling at himself for being so little afraid in the monster's presence.

"I won't hear of it!" Hitler said, his face bloating. "Defeatist talk, I won't listen to it!" He banged on the table, then covered his ears with his hands.

"Is it defeatist talk to say the truth?" Jonathan said. "You are not going to win a war commanding phantom armies."

"I do not let people talk to me this way. I could have you shot!"

Jonathan bowed. "What does your inner voice say?"

Hitler's eyes closed and his face contorted with pain. "I've been listening for it, waiting, wanting to hear it, but nothing. Not a murmur!"

Jonathan said, "Listen, then. Listen to me. If it

were to speak, it would tell you that I am your savior, that I have a way for you and Germany to yet win the war, just as Frederick the Great was saved at the last moment, when he too was surrounded and defeated in this very city."

Hitler's eyes opened wide. He looked at the portrait of Frederick the Great on the wall. "If only it were true. I've been sitting here concentrating and it is as if my mind were linked to his."

"History is speaking to you. I've come to bring you victory."

Hitler took off his glasses. Tears came to his eyes. "I am a fool," he said. "The traitorous acts of my closest followers, of my generals, of the German people, have set my mind in turmoil. Oh, how I have suffered for my people! I want to believe you, only Bormann says the super weapons are just something that Goebbels dreamed up and you are a fraud. Part of Himmler's treachery. Oh why is it that my inner voice has departed me just when I need it most!"

"Mein Fuehrer, if you will only hear me out. I have a plan. You can leave the city immediately."

"But how? The corridor that is still open is too risky. The Russians are shelling it constantly. It is an avenue of death." He was whining now, like a child. His weak side was surfacing; Jonathan could see it in the way his eyes suddenly softened.

Jonathan said, "There is a plane waiting not two blocks away, *Mein Fuehrer.* I could have you out of here in an hour. You need not die. Listen to me. What if you could fake a suicide, then we could get on the plane and fly out of Berlin? When the Allies think you're dead they'll start fighting among themselves over the spoils."

"Yes, yes! I've always said that!" His eyes came alive now.

"A cease fire will be in effect while the terms of surrender are drawn up. Then, with the Tabun gas made operational, you could strike a quick blow, drive them out of Germany, and regroup. Victorious German armies would once more sweep across Europe, the Jews and their lackeys will be destroyed by a German tide, and the Reich will yet last a thousand years!"

Hitler came to his feet, trembling. "Yes, you are right. It's a plan worthy of the wolf. All the traitors who have not stood with us will be eliminated. Those who have stayed true to their oaths, to our cause, will be given honors and lands in the new, greater Germany. Yes! I can see it! I'll be like Napoleon, only for me there will be no Waterloo." He grabbed Jonathan's shoulders. "Yes! You are my salvation! I will do as you say. Eva wants to die for the glory of the fatherland. Well, we'll let her. I need only find someone's body the same size and shape of mine. There are bodies everywhere in the city. Yes, I can see it. First I shall marry Eva, make a big show of it. I'll say goodbye to everyone. I've already discussed it with Eva, she's all for it. What is dying, she said, you just bite into a little capsule. I admit I never liked the idea. What a load off my mind! I'm feeling better already. Yes, well, we shall have much to do, won't we? I'm about to be a married man and a widower in one day. Then we shall fly out of here. I must get some orders sent to Admiral Doenitz, who's my designated successor, to make sure he does not surrender. He is at Obersalzberg. Yes, this is going to work. As for you, you should be a guest at my wedding. Yes, we'll have a feast! Go now, I've things to do. Rest up. Eat. Have a drink. From the ashes Germany will strike with a terrible vengeance!"

If anyone on earth ever loved Adolf Hitler as a god, it was Magda Goebbels, wife of the Propaganda Minister. At the moment Hitler was talking with Jonathan, Magda Goebbels was sitting in her small room down the hall thinking of ways to kill her children.

Two days before, Hitler had given her a gift—his own Nazi Party badge. She wore it pinned over her heart and didn't take it off even when she slept. She was a consummate actress, with natural good looks and a charming personality. Her role was the *perfect* Nazi wife. On the stage of life, she had played the part of a forgiving wife to perfection when faced with her husband's many blatant affairs. Always appearing at major functions hanging on her husband's arm, gracious, charming, dutiful. She had wanted a divorce in 1939, but when Hitler appealed to her to stay with her husband for the good of the party and the nation, she did as he asked. In public she made a great display of being the loving and adoring wife; in private, in her heart of hearts, she hated the man she had married. She loathed him. She wanted him to suffer the way she had suffered.

Now that the end was near, rather than giving up the pretense of the perfect wife, she did just the opposite. She lavished affection on her husband, who had publicly expressed his desire to die with the Fuehrer. Joseph Goebbels was a myth-maker, and he knew better than anyone that if the Hitler myth was to continue Hitler would have to go down in flames. The messiah must die. If Hitler were taken by the Allies and made to confess to crimes against humanity, the myth would be gone.

So she steeled herself to play the martyr's role with him.

The problem was what to do with their children who were with them in the bunker. There were five girls: Helga, 12; Hilde, 11; Holde, 8; Hedde, 6; and Heidi, 4. The boy, Helmut, who never did well in school, was 10. The children were blond, lively, fun-loving, and had no inkling whatever that their perfect Nazi mother was planning to kill them.

Afterward, Magda Goebbels planned to announce publicly that she had killed the children because she didn't want them to grow up in a world dominated by the victorious Allies, where they would be brought up to believe either in democracy or Bolshevism, both of which she considered decadent. She claimed that the Allies would make them ashamed to be Germans, and she could not go to her death thinking her children would grow up to be like that. She had borne them for the Third Reich, and they were not intended to outlive it. But there was more to it than that.

Magda Goebbels wanted to kill her children because she wanted to punish her husband. He loved his children above all else. She would see to it that he would go to his death knowing they were already dead. It would be revenge of the sweetest kind. That they were her children too didn't matter. He would suffer; that was all that counted.

Her husband had wavered on the question of what to do with the children. He had had plenty of opportunity to send them off to stay with relatives, but Magda found an excuse each time why the plan wouldn't work. Now it was too late. All the avenues of escape were shut. Letting them be captured and raped by the Russians was unthinkable.

Her meditation on how and when to kill her children was interrupted by one of Hitler's aides, who announced that Hitler had decided to marry Eva Braun at eleven-thirty that evening and the

Fuehrer would appreciate it if she would help with the preparations.

She felt a stinging sensation in her heart. She knew what it meant. If the Fuehrer was getting married, he was preparing to die. That meant the Goebbels family did not have long to live. If the Fuehrer died, what right did she have to live? As for the children, she would make some hot chocolate. They all loved hot chocolate. She would mix in some fast-acting poison, and that would be it. As soon as the Fuehrer was dead there would be no reason to delay.

Having reached a decision and having a concrete plan, she went into the kitchen to help with the wedding preparations feeling light-headed, almost giddy.

An hour later, Hitler received Alfred Huff, one of his orderlies, into his study. Huff was large, broad-shouldered, and had been used occasionally as a chauffeur and bodyguard. Hitler had called him because he was strong, dullwitted, and absolutely obedient.

"I have decided to kill myself tomorrow," Hitler said to Huff.

Huff nodded. The junior staff had been talking about little else for days, so Huff wasn't in the least surprised. Some of the SS guards had even started a lottery. Unlike most of those in the Fuehrer's entourage, Huff was not particularly in awe of the Fuehrer. Feared him, yes, because of the ease and swiftness with which he could inflict death, but he was not in awe. To Huff, Hitler was like a stern father, distant and cold, but Huff knew he was somewhat unbalanced and not in the least godlike. Huff waited for Hitler to speak. Hitler was looking better than he had been in weeks. His eyes were clear, he was holding himself upright.

"Now then," Hitler said, "I will be wearing my regular uniform, the dark one. With my Iron Cross."

Huff nodded again. He had had no idea a suicide required one to be properly dressed.

"It will be done out there in the sitting room," Hitler continued. "Fraulein Braun, who will then be Frau Hitler, will be with me. Now then, I want you to carry my body into the garden and burn it. Nothing is to remain. Not a trace."

"Jawohl, Mein Fuehrer. I will get some petrol and will make sure nothing is left."

"Good. And no one—I repeat, no one—is to see me after I am dead. You may notice that I will not look like myself. In fact, when I am dead, I may look entirely different. Show my body to no one, just take it up the back stairs and burn it."

"Jawohl, Mein Fuehrer." He clicked his heels and saluted.

"After seeing to the burning, go to my study and remove everything that belonged to me—clothing, personal effects, personal papers, official things, maps, everything—and take them out and burn them."

"Jawohl, Mein Fuehrer."

"Everything except the portrait of Frederick the Great. For that I have made other arrangements."

Huff bowed and left the room. He heard they were cooking up a feast in the kitchen and he wanted to go and see what delicacies he might sample before the big shots ate it all up.

The wedding did not begin on time. There was no one to conduct the ceremony. SS men were scouring the city looking for a justice of the peace. Meanwhile, Hitler and his bride remained in seclusion while those who had been invited to attend—Dr. and Frau Goebbels, Bormann, Generals Krebs, Burgdorf, and Kraft, Hitler's three secretaries, a few lower-ranking military men, a few petty Nazi Party officials, and Jonathan Becker, milled about, sipping champagne and talking of the good old days, and how the Jews were responsible for everything that had gone wrong in the history of the world.

Finally at midnight the SS men returned with a minor official, Walter Wagner, who had the authority to conduct the ceremony, but he had been dragged from his post in a Volkssturm unit and had come without his official certificates. Eva

Braun came out of her quarters and spoke to him, refusing to go through with the ceremony without having a certificate. She'd waited for this for twelve years and wouldn't have it any other way.

Jonathan wondered what she'd think if she knew Hitler intended for her to die and had no intention of dying himself.

More drinks were served, but the food was left for after the ceremony. People drifted off into small groups. Jonathan sipped champagne and stood near the door to Hitler's quarters. Finally at 12:30 the official, Walter Wagner, returned with the proper certificates. His suit was dirty and torn and he seemed exhausted, but he was ready, he said, to perform the ceremony.

The bride came out wearing white, a few spring flowers in her hair. Hitler was in his best uniform, but even that was spotted and wrinkled. He was smiling like a nervous bridegroom, looking around as if slightly embarrassed.

Hitler and Eva Braun stood in front of Wagner, who was all smiles. "And who shall stand up for the couple?" Wagner said.

He wrote something on a marriage application card and said to Hitler, "Since you are personally known, I will not have to ask you for an identity card."

Everyone laughed at that.

"But you don't know me," Eva Braun said. She produced a police card and said, "And I live at

Wasserburgerstrasse, Number 12. I was born on February 6, 1910, in Munich." Wagner wrote it all down. Jonathan noticed how everyone had polite smiles on their faces, as if this farce were a real wedding, and afterward the couple was going to honeymoon in Rome. As far as everyone else knew, these two were going to kill themselves very shortly. Yet everyone was pretending.

Wagner asked whether both would swear they were of pure Aryan descent and suffered from no hereditary disease which would preclude them from marriage. The crowd laughed again.

They both swore.

The two witnesses were Goebbels and Bormann. They did not have to produce identity cards either, as they were known to Walter Wagner. Wagner then cleared his throat and began the ceremony. He simply asked Hitler and Eva Braun whether they were willing to take each other for husband and wife. They both answered they were, then Walter Wagner said, "I declare that this marriage is legal in the eyes of the law."

Hitler and his bride, the two witnesses, and Walter Wagner signed the document. The bride, Jonathan noted, looked exceptionally radiant. The reception began. The men kissed the bride's hand, the women kissed her cheek. Champagne was drunk all around and even Hitler seemed to get tipsy. Then Bormann whispered something in Hitler's ear and he left the room with him. Hitler came back a moment later looking pale and shaking.

Hitler said, "It is all finished. Death will be a relief for me. I have been betrayed and deceived by everyone." He signaled to Jonathan to come with him. Jonathan followed Hitler and Bormann down the hall and into Bormann's office.

There, waiting, a big smile on his bruised face, was former streetcar conductor Bernhard Stuckurt of the Gestapo.

Chapter Twenty-three

Stuckurt came to his feet and gave a sloppy and awestruck Nazi salute to his Fuehrer, then another one in Bormann's direction.

Bormann said, "Is this the man, Herr Stuckurt?"

Stuckurt looked at Jonathan closely, one eye pinched closed. Then he nodded. "Yes, yes, that's the man. He passed himself off as Captain Shroeder, he had false papers and he took my prisoner. We went after him, but he managed to get away, possibly with the help of Satan. Twenty-two crack SS storm troopers fallen. He had an airplane. Two armed Hitlerjungend he killed, too. Boys, they were. I swear that's the man. On my oath."

"Well?" Bormann asked with an eyebrow raised, his arms folded across his chest. "It will do you very little good to lie. I have several good men at my disposal who can get the truth out of you quickly enough."

Jonathan told himself not to lose his head. He

still might pull it off, if only he didn't lose his head. He said, "I might as well admit it, then."

Hitler glared at Stuckurt and then at Jonathan, and started trembling so badly he had to sit down, his skin ashen. "A spy," he mumbled.

Bormann said, "Thank you, Herr Stuckurt, you are free to go."

"Thank you, sir." He saluted Hitler, then saluted Bormann, then bowed, then moved to the door and made a stiff-arm salute. "Heil Hitler," he said, backing into the hall.

Hitler bent over and buried his face in his hands.

"Now then," Bormann said to Jonathan. "Just who are you?"

"My name is Jonathan Zalman Becker. I'm a Jew."

Hitler sat up and glared at him.

"That's right," Jonathan said. "I am a Jew. I work for Allied Intelligence. Our branch is called SOC—Special Operations Corps, our main job has been getting important people out of Europe who would aid the Allied cause."

"A Jew," Hitler said, muttering.

"Yes, rather remarkable that a subhuman could manage to get to Berlin, find you here in the bunker, and sell you a load of horse manure."

"And then you were to kill the Fuehrer, no doubt," Bormann said.

"It was never my intention to kill him."

"How could you ever have believed you could put this over on us?"

"If I got caught I was to offer a deal to Herr

Hitler. A deal we feel is irresistible. Do you want to hear it?" Jonathan felt the sweat running down his back, but he showed no fear outwardly.

Hitler blinked, but he didn't say anything.

Bormann said, *"Mein Fuehrer,* let me just have this man shot."

Hitler said, "I want to hear what he has to say."

"Here's the deal," Jonathan said. "You know and I know that as soon as this war is over, the Allies are going to start fighting with each other over the spoils. Already the Soviet-sponsored radio broadcasts in Lisbon are calling America an imperialist warmonger."

Hitler nodded. "Yes. True. I've been saying that all along."

Jonathan leaned back against the desk and folded his arms. "Our intelligence agencies are already making plans for a covert war against the Soviet Union. It's simple enough. You already have a vast network of Abwehr agents, you have the underground saboteur network called Werewolf which we could use. The deal is this. If you'll go over to us, we agree not to put you on trial. As far as the world's concerned, you'll be dead. We guarantee that we'll keep you comfortable, you'll have a suite of rooms, a garden to walk in, and your own household staff. You'll of course have to be listed as officially dead."

"What do you think, Martin?" Hitler said.

"I would never trust a Jew."

Jonathan said, "I have a code name for you and a short wave band you can call on. Speak to my superiors."

"I will have to think about it," Hitler said. "Give me the code."

"Not until you first order the killings stopped at the death camps which are still operating."

Hitler shook his head. "You want to put me in touch with your superiors, I might talk to them, but I will not save a single Jew."

"Then no deal."

Hitler's face bloated with anger. "How dare you! I am the Fuehrer of Germany!"

"Let me get rid of this Jew now," Bormann said.

Hitler nodded and got up to leave.

"Hold it," Jonathan said. "All right, here's the frequency and here's the code name." Jonathan wrote it on a piece of paper and handed it to Hitler, who shoved it in his pocket mechanically and started for the door.

"This deal is not for you, *Mein Fuehrer,*" Martin Bormann said. "Do you wish to be a bird kept in a cage? Like Napoleon? What would history say? While the capital burned and the people fought, their Fuehrer was making a deal with the enemies of the Reich to save his own neck."

Hitler stopped with his hand on the door latch and turned back toward Bormann. "You are right of course, Martin. I thank Providence sent me you." He went over to Bormann and patted him on the shoulder. "See to it that Hanna and General Greim fly out of here as soon as possible, I don't want them staying in the bunker. Have them go to Obersalzberg, I want Greim to take over as head of the Luftwaffe."

"It will be done, Mein Fuehrer."

Hitler opened the door and said to a guard in the hall, "Have Radek come in here."

Bormann opened the door and after a moment the rat-faced SS colonel who had taken Fegelein to be shot came in. The colonel saluted Hitler and Bormann, then turned to Jonathan. "So now it's your turn, eh?" he said.

THE LAST WILL AND TESTAMENT OF ADOLF HITLER

Although during my years of struggle I believed I could not undertake the responsibility of marriage, I have now, at the end of my life's journey, married the young woman who, after many years of true friendship, came of her own free will to this city, when it was already almost completely under siege, in order to share my fate. It is her own desire she will go to her death with me as my wife. This will compensate us for what we both lost through my work in the service of my people.

What I possess belongs, in so far as it has any value at all, to the Party. Should the Party no longer exist, it belongs to the State, and should the State also be destroyed, any further decision from me is no longer necessary.

The paintings in the collections I bought over the years were never acquired for private purposes, but always exclusively for the establishment of an art gallery in my native town of Linz.

It is my heartfelt desire that this legacy shall be fulfilled.

As executor of this testament I appoint my most faithful party comrade: Martin Bormann. He is authorized to make all decisions which shall be final and legally binding. He is permitted to give everything of value either as mementos or such as is necessary for the maintenance of a petty bourgeois household to my brother and sisters, and also above all to my wife's mother and to my faithful co-workers male and female who are all well known to him, principally my old secretaries, Frau Winter, and so on, who have assisted me with their work over many years.

My wife and I choose death to avoid the disgrace of defeat or capitulation. It is our wish to be cremated immediately in the place where I have done the greatest part of my work during the course of my twelve years' service for my people.

Hitler awoke at eleven in the morning. He bathed and shaved, dressed in his best uniform, and had a light breakfast in his study with Frau Jung, his secretary, where he dictated his farewell to his people. He was interrupted by General Krebs at one-fifteen in the afternoon. Krebs wanted to give him a status report on how the battle of Berlin was going.

Krebs, like most senior military officers, handled stress well. He showed no nervousness. As always, he spoke in a calm, level manner. It was only his tone that seemed to carry a hint of apprehension.

Hitler listened while sipping coffee and munching a biscuit. The Russians had crushed nearly all pockets of German resistance, the general said. The Zoo station had fallen and the Russians had advanced deep into Grunewald in the southwest sector of Berlin. Ammunition was nearly depleted. Ordnance was nonexistent. Desertions were at a fifty-percent level. Field commanders up to and including generals refused to obey orders and were surrendering or simply refusing to advance on the enemy.

General Krebs, of course, had expected Hitler to go into a tirade, cursing traitors and cowards and demanding arrests and executions of all offenders; instead he simply looked up and said, "And what is your recommendation, Herr Fieldmarshal?"

"You must send a personal emissary immediately to General Wenck and urge him to exert himself to the utmost to break through the ring around Berlin."

"An excellent suggestion," Hitler said. "Anything else?"

"I think Admiral Doenitz should act against all traitors with lightning speed."

"Order it done," Hitler said. "And tell them all they prove their loyalty to the Fuehrer by coming to my aid at the earliest possible moment."

Krebs thought he detected a smile on Hitler's lips.

"You know, General," Hitler said, "the people and the armed forces have given their all in this long and hard struggle. A truly enormous sacrifice. But my trust and confidence have been misused by many people. Treachery and ill will have undermined everything I've tried to do. It was not granted to me to lead the Volk to victory." He said this in a tired, mechanical way, as if it seemed to settle everything.

Then he dismissed his general and returned to his study.

By late afternoon the Russians were reported to be a few hundred meters away and driving toward the Reichschancellory, which was now reduced to a single story by the constant artillery bombardment. The chancellory itself was now unoccupied. Except for the German Southern Army Group, still intact and digging in in the hills of Bohemia and Bavaria, Hitler's once mighty army now numbered less than five thousand and were squeezed into a few blocks of downtown Berlin.

There were only a few stalwarts left in the upper bunker. The army and SS officers and party officials had either joined the men at the battlements or had made a run for it. In the lower bunker there were less than thirty people, including Martin Bormann, Eva Hitler, and Joseph and Magda Goebbels and their six children. Ever since the wedding everyone was exceedingly grim. At four in the afternoon Hitler called everyone except the guard staff into the map room and personally passed out vials of cyanide. He said that it was up to each one personally to decide his or her own fate. The diesel engine that drove the generator and the ventilator was sputtering and the lights kept flickering. Chunks of plaster kept falling off the ceiling. The toilets kept backing up and the smell could not be gotten rid of.

Hitler thanked everyone for staying with him until the end. He personally shook their hands. He looked weary, but he was smiling and exchanged pleasantries as if he and his wife were taking a vacation trip. Only Magda Goebbels was terrified. She threw herself on her god Adolf Hitler, wrapping her arms around him. "*Nein! Nein!* You must save yourself! Germany will be finished without you to lead it!"

Her husband and one of the generals pulled her away gently.

"Now, Magda," Hitler said in a consoling tone. "The Russians know perfectly well that I am here in this bunker. A few years ago we developed a gas that will put a man to sleep for twenty-four hours. Intelligence tells us that the Russians now have that gas, too. They could pump that gas in here and make everyone go to sleep. Can you imagine what would happen if the Russians caught me alive? They would put me in a zoo cage and bring busloads of school children to laugh at me and throw tomatoes. No, Magda, we cannot have that." His mouth drew tight. "Besides, I have no taste for living anymore among traitors and cowards."

It was then that he read his last public statement, standing amidst the stink of the backed-up sewer, the flickering lights, the falling plaster. His eyes teared up and his voice cracked, but he managed to deliver it:

> Since 1914 when, as a volunteer, I made my modest contribution in the Great War which was forced upon the Reich, over thirty years have passed.
>
> In these three decades only love for my people and loyalty to my people have guided me in all my thoughts, actions, and life. They gave me the strength to make the most difficult decisions, such as no mortal has yet had to face. I have exhausted my time, my working energy, and my health in these three decades.
>
> It is untrue that I or anybody else in Germany wanted war in 1939. It was desired and instigated exclusively by those international statesmen who were either of Jewish origin or working for Jewish interests. I have made so many offers for the reduction and limitation of armaments, which posterity cannot explain away for all eternity, that the responsibility for the outbreak of this war cannot rest on me. Furthermore, I never desired that after the Great War that a second war should arise against England or even against America. Centuries may pass, but out of the ruins of our cities and monuments of art there will arise anew the hatred of the people who alone are ultimately responsible: international Jewry

and its helpers!

He let the paper he had read from fall from his hand. He removed his glasses. Tears flooded down his face. He was shaking all over, but his left arm was shaking so much he could barely control it. Eva put her arm around him and led him through the doorway.

Magda Goebbels called after him: "If only Germany had been worthy of you!"

Chapter Twenty-four

"Are these phials of poison perfectly dependable?" Hitler asked Dr. Haas, summoned from the infirmary.

The doctor, who had been sawing off the shattered limbs of old men and young boys for three straight days and nights, at first had no idea what the Fuehrer was talking about. Then he nodded and said, "If it is cyanide, yes, absolutely. Only the tiniest drop of pure cyanide will bring death instantly."

Eva said, "That's good enough for me." She was sitting on the couch, prepared for death. She was facing death calmly, having long ago come to terms with it.

Hitler was not so sure about cyanide. He studied the phial, holding it up to the light, shaking it.

"I wish to see it work," Hitler said finally.

The doctor was momentarily horrified.

"On an animal," Hitler said.

The doctor nodded and was shown to the kennel by Hitler's valet; Hitler and Eva tagged along behind. Hitler's Alsatian dog, Blondi, was nursing her litter when they arrived. Hitler had his valet open the dog's mouth while the doctor opened the capsule and shoved it in. Blondi's eyes rolled back; she stiffened, then relaxed and was dead, without making a sound.

"There, you see, Dolf," Eva said. "Nothing to it." When she turned to him she could see that he had not watched. He said, "I see, I see." The puppies started barking wildly. Hitler told his valet to get rid of the puppies quickly. Hitler, Eva, and Dr. Haas went back to the sitting room.

Hitler sat in a chair biting on his thumbnail, obviously deep in thought. The doctor didn't know what to say or do. He simply stood there, putting his hands in his pockets and taking them out again.

Hitler got up suddenly and started pacing up and down, his left arm trembling at his side. The valet returned and the doctor was given some real coffee and a piece of Eva's wedding cake. The doctor nibbled at the cake and sipped the coffee, all the while keeping his eyes on Hitler.

"Even if it *appeared* painless," Hitler said, "How do we know the animal was not in fact feeling intense and excruciating pain? After all, how can we tell if a dog feels pain or not?"

"But it didn't last more than a few seconds," Eva said. "I'm sold."

"What do you think about a gunshot?" Hitler asked the doctor suddenly. "Would it be more sure, more quick and painless?"

"A gunshot," the doctor said, "is potentially very gruesome. If your hand falters at the critical moment it can take off your face or even part of the brain and leave you still alive. I'm sorry, Frau Hitler."

"Not at all, I'm used to gruesome things."

Hitler said, "What if the cyanide didn't kill you right away, I mean it is possible, is it not?"

"Possible, but highly unlikely."

"Say it was very impotent."

"Then you might have convulsions, like a stroke."

"That is the last thing I want for myself and my wife," Hitler said. "If I am to die, I want it to be as quick and as painless as possible."

The doctor thought for a moment, then said, "You might take both the poison and shoot yourself at the same time, that way you would be doubly sure. You might have a trusted comrade stand by and finish the job when you are through. Thank you so much for the cake. If it's all right, *Mein Fuehrer,* I'd like to get back to work. I have really said all I know about the subject."

Hitler grumbled, but gestured it was all right for the doctor to leave. As the doctor went out, Martin Bormann came in.

"I have terrible news," Bormann said. "Mussolini and his mistress, Clara Petacci, have been killed by Communist partisans. What's worse, their dead bodies were taken to a gas station in Milano and hung up by their heels."

Eva's mouth came open in horror. "There, you see, Eva," Hitler said with disgust. "We must be absolutely certain that does not happen to us."

The evening briefing of Hitler by General Krebs was short. Wenck's army was pinned down south of Schwielow Lake, a hundred kilometers south of Berlin. The Twelfth Army was disintegrating and could not break through the circle of death around Berlin. General Weidling, commander of the garrison defending Berlin, had told Krebs that the Russians would be at the bunker the following morning.

Hitler said nothing in the face of this news. He took it calmly, nodding, then dismissed Krebs and spent a few minutes with Eva. He told her how much he wished things could have been different for them, and they talked about how much they had enjoyed the brief vacations they'd spent at Berchtesgaden. Then he went into the corridor and told the guards to have everyone line up for one more round of leave-taking.

There were eighteen loyal followers left in the bunker, not counting the SS guards. Hitler, accompanied by Bormann on one side and Eva on the other, shook everyone's hand, this time without saying anything. His eyes were moist and vacant, and his left arm trembled out of control. Whatever was said to him, he made no response, as if buried in thought. Then he retreated into his quarters once again with Eva.

Ten minutes later Hitler opened the door and gave a message that he wanted sent to the forces still fighting in the south. The message read: *Der Fuehrer lebt und leitet Abwehr Berlin.*

The Fuehrer is alive and directing the defense of Berlin.

But most everyone in the bunker knew that the defense of Berlin was a myth and that Hitler would soon kill himself. The result was a general release of all inhibitions.

Cigarettes, which Hitler had forbidden inside the Fuehrerbunker, were lit, phonograph records blared, booze bottles appeared. Martin Bormann was in his office packing up his papers when the bacchanalian goings-on started. He kept yelling at everyone to tone it down, but nothing got toned down. Finally he went scurrying around trying to restore order. SS men were chasing naked girls up and down the corridors. Bormann found one SS colonel and two women under the table in the map room and told him that if order was not restored he would have the colonel shot.

The colonel paid no attention to him whatever.

There was no one around at the moment to do any shooting.

Defeated, Bormann returned to his room and had a few drinks himself. He was feeling, at the moment, quite satisfied. He was soon to be the one and only master of the National Socialist movement. Finally, he was going to have it all.

Now all he had to do, he figured, was be sure he stayed alive to enjoy it. And, of course, to make sure that Der Fuehrer went through with his suicide. Siegfried, after all, must ascend his funeral pyre if he's going to be immortalized.

Huff, Hitler's orderly, was summoned to Hitler's quarters at 2:30 a.m. There was only one guard in the hall outside Hitler's suite of rooms. The other was too drunk to report for duty. As Huff was about to enter, Magda Goebbels showed up screaming she had to see the Fuehrer. The guard would not let her in. *"Nein! Nein! Nein!"* she screamed to Hitler through the door, twisting violently in the guard's grasp. "There is still hope!" she cried.

Hitler told the guard he didn't want to see her. Then he asked Huff to wait exactly ten minutes and then come in.

Hitler closed the door, shutting off Magda Goebbels' sobs. He smiled wanly at Eva. She looked curiously radiant, as she had at her wedding. She wore a navy blue polka-dot dress, nylon stockings, her favorite brown shoes. Her hair had been carefully combed over her forehead the way she liked it. She produced the vial of cyanide and sat down on the couch. Hitler sat next to her and brushed a few specks of lint off his uniform. He had his Iron Cross pinned over his heart. He reached down and picked up his 7.65 Walther pistol and cocked it.

She leaned over and kissed him on the cheek. "It's all right," she said. She put the small vial in her mouth and bit it. Her eyes suddenly closed, her body twitched once, and she fell over forward.

Bormann was still in his office when one of his aides, half drunk, burst in with the news:

"Adolf Hitler is dead! He has finally done it! Shot himself!"

Bormann leapt to his feet with an odd feeling of power, as if his veins had suddenly been infused with blue blood. He followed his aide down into the lower bunker, walking with quick, sure strides. The drunken commotion that had been going on earlier had now come to a complete stop. Everyone in the hallways was looking bewildered. The shelling had stopped, as if even the Russians knew the great man was dead.

As he approached the Fuehrer's quarters, Bormann felt dread rise in him, followed by a momentary confusion. Now he, *Martin Bormann,* who had never even finished school, was the head of the Party, and the direction of the movement was now totally in his hands. His knees nearly buckled under the weight of this realization. The fact that the Party was now nothing but smoldering cinders on the junk pile of history didn't trouble him. He would resurrect it, of that he was absolutely certain.

Bormann's aide stood aside at Hitler's door. The guard saluted and opened the door for him. Bormann glanced back down the hallway. Fifteen to twenty people, standing very still, were watching him. He stepped inside. Huff was there. He'd covered one of the bodies with the Fuehrer's overcoat. Bormann started to say he'd get blood on the Fuehrer's coat. Part of him didn't accept that the greatest man in the history of the world could be dead, even though another part of him was reveling in it.

Then he looked at Eva. She was slumped down on the couch, her head at an awkward angle, as if she had gotten drunk at a party and had passed out. But she wasn't breathing. Her lips were blue and her skin was translucent yellow.

"I wish to see the Fuehrer," Martin Bormann said.

"It was the Fuehrer's wish that no one see him when he's dead," Huff said.

"I'm in charge now," Bormann said angrily.

Huff sighed and reached down and pulled back the overcoat. It was a gruesome sight. Hitler had botched it, apparently. Bormann guessed he had meant to shoot upwards through the roof of his mouth, but he must have jerked the gun to one side at the last moment and the bullet tore through his upper lip and went into the cheekbone directly under his right eye, tearing off the left side of his face. His left eye was compressed up into the socket and Bormann could see the bone. His face was waxy and the lower part was flattened in death because, Bormann guessed, the muscles had relaxed. It hardly looked like him, Bormann thought, draping the coat back over him.

"I'll carry Eva myself," Bormann said to Huff.

Together they carried the bodies up the back stairs into the garden, where four hundred liters of gasoline were waiting.

The bodies were put into a shell hole near the ventilator. As the smoke rose it was sucked inside the Fuehrerbunker, stinking like burning bacon grease.

Jonathan Becker, handcuffed to a water pipe in a small room on the second floor, could smell it, but didn't know what it was. He had heard the revelers in the hall and had wondered what that was all about, also.

Jonathan was feeling cold with fear. Every man must die. What had Willis said? *I believe in destiny.* Well Jonathan, Jonathan said to himself, *it looks like your destiny to die on a fool's errand in this madhouse.*

He tried to look into the void and imagine what it was like to be dead. To be or not to be. To *not* be. And he could not imagine it. The void terrified him. He would fight to the last breath. He made up his mind to do that. Whatever chance there was, no matter how desperate, he would take it.

The burning bacon smell continued for about half an hour, growing worse by the minute. Then the shelling started again, and just about that time the generator faltered and the emergency battery-operated lights came on.

He listened. There was a lot of furious activity in the hallways. Someone was shouting, "The Fuehrer is dead!" Jonathan felt a burst of elation. The era of horror was over! He found himself giggling with joy.

A few minutes after that the door opened and Bormann and the rat-faced SS colonel named Radek came in. The colonel was in uniform, but Bormann was wearing a trenchcoat over an old, battered suit and was carrying a thick briefcase under his arm.

"Herr Bormann," Jonathan said, "If you are wise you will listen to me. I can get you through the American lines. I can save you."

Bormann hit him in the mouth. "I want nothing from a Jew!" He turned to the colonel. "See to it that he takes the uniform off before you do it," Bormann said. "I don't want a Jew to die in our glorious uniform."

"Jawohl, Herr Reichfuehrer," the colonel said, drawing his pistol.

"Strip him naked and shoot him like a dog."

"Jawohl, Herr Reichfuehrer."

Bormann turned to the colonel. "Now that the Fuehrer is dead, there is no reason to stay in this wretched place. You have your escape route, you know where to contact me. Heil Hitler!"

They saluted each other. Bormann hurried out of the room and down the hall.

The colonel turned Jonathan toward the wall and put his pistol to Jonathan's head. Then he clamped handcuffs onto Jonathan's wrists behind his back.

"My last duty," the colonel said.

"Listen," Jonathan said, "You're a fool if you keep obeying orders of a dead man. The Reich is finished. I'm an Allied agent. You help me and I can see to it you will not only never spend one day in prison, but you'll be living fat in South America."

"If I want you to speak to me, you filthy Jew, I will tell you. Is that clear?"

"I'm offering you life!"

The colonel jerked Jonathan's arm, propelling him out the door. Then he shoved him hard in the back to get him moving down the hall.

Jonathan felt his throat close up.

The party had started again in the map room with a lot of loud laughter and singing. A heavy artillery barrage started and plaster chips rained down. The Russians had closed the circle so tight they could now concentrate just on the inner city.

As they made their way through the bunker, Jonathan and the colonel passed a lot of SS guards coming the other way, dressed as civilians, lugging bundles of their belongings. Jonathan and the colonel went into the lower bunker. No guards. It was quiet. Then Jonathan heard a woman whining. As they passed by, he glanced in and recognized Magda Goebbels standing alone at the head of a table where her six children were sprawled out dead, mugs of hot chocolate spilled all over.

Magda was trembling all over, but there was a triumphant look on her face.

"Just keep moving, Jew," the colonel said.

They turned down a hallway and the colonel directed Jonathan through a door and into another corridor in an adjoining bunker. Jonathan then realized that the entire center city was honeycombed with bunkers. They went through another door and down a few steps into another corridor, this one damp and dark. The shelling above was muted and distant and the vibrations were hardly noticeable.

At the end of the tunnel was a blank wall, as if the tunnel was unfinished. The colonel reached up and twisted a pipe; the wall fell open, revealing yet another tunnel on the other side, pitch dark and smelling as musty as a sarcophagus.

The colonel took out a flashlight and they started down the tunnel. Fifty or sixty meters into the tunnel there was a heavy metal door. The colonel pushed it open. Jonathan stepped inside. It was a small, cavelike room, hollowed out of the limestone. And sitting on a rock was a white-haired man with a puffy round face and dark, piercing eyes. He was wearing a shabby private's uniform, but he didn't get up to salute when the colonel came in.

The man said: "I spoke to your Mr. Willis, and we've made a deal."

It was Adolf Hitler.

Book V

Chapter Twenty-five

"You look most amazed, Jew," the colonel said with a sneer.

Jonathan felt a cold chill spread through his body. So the Great Evil was still alive! The world is not free of him yet.

For a moment Jonathan felt dazed, overcome by a powerful feeling of hopelessness. And then it struck him that there was still a chance to get Hitler in front of a judge, to make him answer for his crimes before all the world. Yes, there was still a chance! Jonathan felt his heart race and his face flush.

"We're taking you to German-held territory," Hitler said. "If on our way there we encounter advance units of the American army you will give them your recognition code and make sure we are allowed to go on our way. If necessary you are to have them speak with Mr. Willis in London."

Jonathan said, "Has the killing in the death camps been halted?"

"No SS operations will be halted," the colonel said, "until the Fuehrer and Willis have come to terms."

"Until the killings in the death camps are halted, I will not help you."

"I won't have you or anyone telling me what I must do!" Hitler screamed, his face bloating red. He shook for a moment, his left arm swinging out from his body and back again like a gate in a windstorm. Then he inhaled deeply and seemed to regain his composure and said, "I will negotiate the fate of the Jews with Mr. Willis at the proper time. I am still the Fuehrer of Germany, Mr. Becker."

The colonel gestured with his weapon for Jonathan to get moving.

Jonathan shook his head. "I said I will not help you until the killings in the death camps have been halted."

Hitler scowled. Without his mustache, his face looked strange and distorted. He had a jagged scar on the right side of his mouth that made him look like he was snarling. "I need only to say the word," he said, "and you'll be killed here and now. I give you ten seconds to make up your mind."

The colonel pulled back the receiver on his submachine gun and pointed the gun at Jonathan's face. Jonathan looked down the barrel and felt his knees go weak under him.

"Well, Jew?" the colonel said. "Do I shoot you or do I not shoot you?"

"I have the American recognition signs. You will need me if we encounter the Americans."

Hitler said, "I will not sit here and dicker with a Jew."

The colonel grinned.

A lump formed in Jonathan's throat. He looked at Hitler, who glared at him with the snarl on his lips. "He doesn't move in five seconds, kill him," Hitler said. He meant it.

"Wait," Jonathan said. "I'll do what you want."

"Then get moving," the colonel said, jabbing Jonathan with the barrel of his gun.

Hitler mumbled something to the colonel. Something about how you can always back the cowardly Jew down.

They snaked their way through several tunnels, Jonathan leading the way holding a bright phosphorus flare the colonel had given him. As they went, they sloshed through pungent sewer water and foul mud. Hitler was behind Jonathan, breathing hard, occasionally slipping and pushing Jonathan in the back. The colonel, lugging a large backpack and his submachine gun, trailed behind Hitler. Gradually the sound of the shelling grew dimmer and dimmer, and finally disappeared altogether. The only sounds they heard were the hissing of the burning flare and the sloshing and sucking sounds made by their feet in the mud.

As they went, Jonathan tried to figure out why Hitler was so insistent the camps keep going. They were going to be stopped soon enough anyway. Was the hatred of the Jew so great that five or six million wasn't enough? That he had to have every drop of blood he could get?

That didn't seem plausible. He started asking himself questions about what would happen if it did stop and it suddenly hit him. Yes, of course—once the killing stopped, it might not be easy to get the death machinery started again. Hitler, no doubt, was using the lives of the camp inmates as a bargaining chip with Willis!

That meant that it was just possible that Hitler might escape justice. Hitler might make a deal with Willis and somehow escape the hangman. That thought made Jonathan feel sick to his stomach. He swore a silent oath to himself that somehow, someway, Hitler was going to get what was coming to him.

"Move faster!" the colonel yelled at Jonathan.

Whenever a flare would start to die down, the colonel would light another from his pack and hand it to Jonathan. The flares made grotesque shadows on the rough-cut walls. Often the tunnels were so narrow as to be almost impassable. Hitler would say keep going, and they kept going, squeezing through narrow spaces, at times on their hands and knees. Finally the tunnel ended in a boxlike little room with a low ceiling. A square piece of steel was built into the far wall. It took Jonathan a few moments to realize it was a door.

The colonel worked a key into a slot, unlocked it and pushed it open. A blast of putrid air hit them. Jonathan turned and retched. Hitler stood firm, but the colonel stepped back, rocking on his feet, holding his hand over his mouth. They stepped through the opening onto a small platform. Jonathan's flare was dying out, but he could see they were in a huge cement tube, which Jonathan thought at first might be a sewer pipe. The colonel lit another flare and instantly the place glowed bright as day.

They were in the U-Bahn, the subway, and it was half full of water. There had been more than a hundred thousand people in the U-Bahn when the SS flooded it to prevent the Russians from using it to attack the inner city. More than half had been drowned. Bloated, blackened, stinking corpses floated everywhere on the water.

The colonel went back into the tunnel, leaving Hitler and Jonathan alone for a few moments. Hitler remained absolutely silent. Jonathan fought back the impulse to throw up. The colonel returned a few minutes later with a rubber raft and a couple of paddles, which must have been kept hidden back in the tunnel someplace. The three climbed in. Hitler sat in the front, his head high, like an Egyptian Pharoah floating down the Nile. He held the flare now. Jonathan and the colonel paddled away as fast as they could.

Blackened ghostlike faces glowed from the light

of the flare in the black water. Jonathan kept turning away, holding his jaw tight to keep from choking. Hitler sat perfectly rigid in the front of the rubber raft, his arms folded across his chest, his face as cold and hard as a death mask.

They had gone about a mile when Jonathan thought he noticed the tunnel ceiling was closer to them. Could it be the water was rising? Not possible, he told himself.

Jonathan and the colonel continued paddling at a steady pace. The stench was acrid. After a few more miles Jonathan noticed that the ceiling was much closer, he could almost touch it with his paddle.

"What's this?" Hitler asked, suddenly coming alive, looking around.

The colonel stopped paddling. He said, "They're flooding the tube again so that the Russians cannot use it to get into the Citadel!"

"I ordered no more flooding be done!" Hitler screamed, his voice echoing down off the concrete walls.

"You're supposedly dead," Jonathan said. "No one is obeying your orders anymore."

Hitler turned to the colonel. "You've got to get us out of here! We'll drown!"

"Look for a manhole ladder," the colonel yelled at Jonathan. "They're every seven hundred meters. Get paddling, hurry!"

Jonathan started paddling madly, pushing the

bodies out of the way as he stroked the blade deep into the water. A few moments later they had to duck down under the curving support beams that ran like ribs every few meters under the overhead. The water kept rising. They kept paddling.

"There's a manhole!" Jonathan called. Their flare was fading and they had almost missed it. The colonel steered them over to a ladder, barely squeezing under the last support beam.

"Get me out of here!" Hitler cried. The colonel climbed up the ladder. It took him a few moments to turn the latch and open it. Finally the three scrambled out into the cool night air. They lay on the ground filling their lungs with fresh air. Gradually they stood up and looked around.

They were in the middle of an open field. To the northeast, the center of Berlin was a massive inferno, the flames boiling into the sky. Between them and the city center they could make out Russian artillery firing, the guns volleying in rippling crescendos.

Hitler stood silently gazing at the city, scowling. The colonel turned his back to it. After a few moments the colonel said, "We should get moving, it will be light soon."

Jonathan said, "I think the American lines could be no more than a few kilometers to the west."

"But we are going south, where Kesselring's army is still fighting," the colonel said.

Jonathan said, "Since you plan to deal with

Willis, why risk encountering the Russians?"

"Because there are details yet to be worked out by the Fuehrer."

Jonathan knew what that meant. Hitler was going to bargain as hard as he could. In fact, it might even be possible Hitler had not decided to surrender. That he might have another scam up his sleeve. If they were heading south, once they got behind German lines once more, Hitler might just slip away. He could fly to Switzerland or Italy. It was possible Hitler might just be pretending to go along with Willis to get help making his way south.

Hitler was still facing the firestorm. He cried out suddenly: "I never wanted this! It was the Jews who conspired against me. And my own officers, they opposed me at every turn. I had many visions for Germany, but never this."

Jonathan said, "What if you were to blame, what would it matter? No man can shoulder as much blame as you have brought upon yourself."

Hitler turned an angry eye toward him as the colonel hit Jonathan with the butt of his machine gun, forcing him to the ground. "Let me kill him, please, *Mein Fuehrer.*"

"I'm afraid we need him, but if he speaks disrespectfully once more, I will let you disembowel him alive." He paused and looked around. "The sun is coming up, we must find someplace to hide."

"But where?" the colonel asked.

Jonathan got to his feet, dazed from the blow.

He considered for a moment what a great pleasure it would be to kill the colonel, but then thought better of it. He might need him.

Jonathan said, "How far are we from the botanical gardens?"

Jonathan was ecstatic to find Heidi alive. He hugged her and held her and they danced around her little room in the candlelight. Then Heidi's eyes fell on Hitler, who was standing in the doorway.

"The monster has changed his clothes," she said. "And cut off his mustache."

"He is surrendering to the Allies," Jonathan said.

Hitler said, "Do you not love your Fuehrer, child?"

She spit at him. The colonel raised his gun to fire, but Hitler shook his head. In the candlelight Hitler, his whitened hair shimmering, looked like a specter. "What is your name, child?" he asked Heidi.

"Heidi Luden."

"And you have helped this Jew?"

"He is my friend."

"But you are German. No Jew is a friend of a German."

"The Jews corrupt the race," she said mechanically.

Hitler smiled, and gestured for her to come to him. She moved across the room with halting steps.

Hitler held her face in his hands and stared into her eyes. "You have a duty to your people, my child. I am your Fuehrer, I am the will and the conscience of your people. You must obey your Fuehrer."

"Jawohl, Mein Fuehrer," she said, as if in a trance.

"That's a good child," Hitler said. "Now then, we'll rest and have something to eat."

The colonel carried field rations in his pack. He handed each of them a box. They contained tins of meat and packages of crackers. Hitler didn't eat the ones with meat. Jonathan could still smell the rotting bodies and he still felt nauseous, but he forced himself to eat. He didn't know when he'd get another chance.

When they were finished Hitler said, "Let's get some sleep."

Jonathan slept on a pile of rags in the corner, the colonel took the cot, and Hitler a mattress near the door. Heidi slept near him on the dirt floor, curled up like a dog.

When Jonathan awoke it was dark and quiet. He could hear rain falling outside. The colonel was sleeping sitting up on the cot, leaning against the wall with the machine gun in his lap, snoring. Jonathan went past him through the doorway into the passageway leading outside. He went up the ladder at the end of the passageway and pushed open the tin covering over the entrance.

It was late afternoon. The rain poured down steadily. It smelled wonderfully fresh and clean. The artillery shelling had stopped and he couldn't see any flames, but black smoke hung over the city like a blanket. He wondered if the German defenders of Berlin had quit. He looked to the south and west. A column of civilians were slowly making their way out of the city under the watchful eyes of Russian soldiers. They were no more than half a mile away, passing by the twisted iron of what once had been the entry gate to the botanical gardens. Occasionally the soldiers would yank someone out of line. Jonathan figured they were looking for high-ranking Nazis, military and civilian, and were no doubt looking for telltale clues like nice shoes or manicured fingernails.

Wouldn't they be surprised to find who was nearby hiding in a hole in the ground? he thought. He chuckled. He let the rain fall on his face, then he crawled back inside. He could hear the rats moving about in the debris along the passageway. Back in Heidi's room he found the colonel just waking up.

"We can't move until dark," Jonathan said.

"A soldier knows how to wait," the colonel said, checking his watch.

Hitler spent the next few hours sitting with Heidi, mesmerizing her with tales of the greatness of Germany and Aryan superiority, while the colonel spent his time cleaning his machine gun. Jonathan studied Hitler. Mr. X's prediction that Hitler would go into a total withdrawal seemed totally false. If anything, Hitler's mental state seemed to be good. He was lucid. Sitting on the mattress talking to Heidi, he seemed genuinely contented. He was showing his soft side. The contrast was indeed striking.

Hitler had always portrayed himself in Nazi propaganda as loving children and Jonathan had thought it was make believe stuff, but seeing him here with Heidi, who was childlike in her madness, Jonathan was ready to believe that perhaps he was capable of affection.

Then Jonathan thought of the Jewish children who had been shoved in the ovens and he was filled with a sudden and terrible rage. He turned away and stared at the wall. He had a mission, he had to think of the mission and nothing else.

When it was time to leave, Heidi kissed Hitler's hand. Jonathan put out his arms to hug her, but she refused.

"You're a dirty Jew," she said. "Corrupting the race."

The colonel laughed.

Jonathan ignored him and said to Heidi: "Soon the Americans will be here. Go to them and they will take care of you."

She nodded, keeping her eyes on Hitler.

"Come now, Jew," the colonel said.

Hitler and the colonel went outside. Jonathan

stayed with Heidi for a moment. "You're going to be fine," he said.

"Why did you corrupt the race?" she asked, a tear coming to her eye.

"You know better than that, Heidi. You'll wait for the Americans?"

She nodded. Tears flooded down her face. She hugged him.

Jonathan went outside into the darkness. The rain beat down violently. No artillery fire in the distance. Hitler was whispering something to the colonel, but stopped when he saw Jonathan.

Hitler and the colonel started walking off to the south. The colonel suddenly stepped back and said, "My apologies, *Mein Fuehrer,* but I've forgotten my maps."

"Well get them," Hitler said, "and be quick about it."

The colonel went back inside the tunnel while Hitler and Jonathan stood in the rain silently with their hands in their pockets. Then it suddenly occurred to Jonathan that the colonel was too well organized to have forgotten anything . . .

Jonathan dove back into the passageway, Hitler calling, "Halt, I order you to halt!" Jonathan crawled down the passageway and into Heidi's little room.

The colonel was standing over Heidi's body, wiping his knife on her shirt. He had cut her throat clear through to the neck bone. Jonathan started toward him, but the colonel fanned the air in front of him with the knife. Jonathan froze. "Come on, my Jewish friend, I'd love to cut you, too."

"But why?" Jonathan stammered. "She was completely harmless. Her mind was gone!"

"She had seen the Fuehrer and might have talked. You brought us here. You condemned her."

"No one would have believed her!"

"Just get moving, I don't argue with Jews."

Chapter Twenty-six

They made their way south through the rubble, moving in the rain from building to building. They passed makeshift camps where Russian soldiers were drinking, singing, dancing, making love to women who cooperated, raping those who didn't. To these soldiers, the war was over. They were the victors, and to the victors go the spoils.

The few Russian sentry posts Jonathan and his two companions encountered were easily skirted. And Jonathan knew why. For the Russians to try to stop the floods of civilians and straggling soldiers moving south wasn't worth the trouble. So what if they crossed German lines? Hitler was dead in his bunker, as far as the Russians knew; the fighting in the south would soon stop. If they took all the stragglers prisoner they would have to feed and shelter them, and the Russians didn't have the resources. Besides, a flood of refugees would make things even more chaotic for the Germans still fighting in the south. So they let them go.

By midnight Jonathan, Hitler, and the colonel were fifteen kilometers further south of Berlin. Jonathan was soaked to the skin and he had an annoying blister on his right heel. But he was feeling good about the mission. The feeling that he was somehow fated to deliver Hitler to justice had hold of him.

Hitler was breathing heavily now, apparently on the point of exhaustion. But he was taking it stoically, marching with a steady gait, his head tilted into the wind. A little before one in the morning they found shelter in a bombed-out house. The colonel shone a flashlight around to make sure there was no one hidden in the shadows. Jonathan caught a glimpse of Hitler. Whatever he had used to color his hair white was running down his face, giving him a sickly pallor.

They ate some of the colonel's field rations: crackers, meat spread, and gouda cheese. Again, Hitler didn't have any meat.

For some reason, sitting there in the darkness, the rain running down the walls, Jonathan thought of Miss Melrose at the theater telling him about epiphanies. Why was it he had gotten so angry at her and her silliness? It all seemed like a faraway dream.

They rested half an hour, then resumed their trek. Hitler kept silent, trudging forward, his shoulders hunched, his left arm twitching sporadically.

An hour later they came to a Russian field hospital set up in what had once been a Strength

Through Joy recreation center. Hitler took the colonel aside and spoke to him for a few moments, then the colonel came over to Jonathan. "The Fuehrer orders us to secure transportation. You will come with me."

"Without a weapon?"

He gave Jonathan a knife.

"Have you forgotten," Jonathan said, "the Russians and I are on the same side?"

"Your mission is to help us get to where we are going. If you have to kill a few Russians to do it, that is the fortunes of war."

Jonathan took the knife. It was the one the colonel had used to murder Heidi. It felt heavy in Jonathan's hand.

The colonel and Jonathan left Hitler sheltered in a broken culvert pipe. There was no water running out of it. It was four feet across, sticking out of a hillside. Hitler sat in it with his knees up under his chin and with his collar raised high around his neck, looking, Jonathan thought, like an old bum.

Jonathan and the colonel crawled along a drainage ditch through ice-cold water to the field hospital road. No sentries were posted that they could see. Jonathan and the colonel crawled up out of the ditch and into some thick brush and took a look at the place. Kerosene lamps made flickering lights in the windows. Ambulances, some Russian-built, some confiscated from the Germans, were parked along a loading dock of some sort. At the far end was a makeshift ramp going up to the back door. Beyond the ramp, the building protruded beyond the back of the ambulances. Behind that section of the building there appeared to be a pile of rubble.

"We'll take one of those ambulances," the colonel said.

They crawled through the mud of the parking area. Jonathan kept the knife in his hand. The colonel had his machine gun on his back. When they got to the ambulance the colonel got into the driver's seat. "No key," he said. He started to work on the wires under the dash. "Make sure no one bothers me."

Jonathan went around the back of the ambulance, keeping the knife in his hand. A couple of Russian soldiers stood under a porch overhang in the light of a lantern smoking cigarettes and chatting. They had broad Russian peasant faces and wore baggy uniforms. One was short and barrel-chested; the other, tall and gangly. They didn't seem to be paying much attention to what was going on in the parking area.

Jonathan went back around the ambulance and looked inside. The colonel was sitting there watching the two Russian soldiers. He turned and glanced at Jonathan, then silently rolled down the window.

"I'm ready to start it up," he whispered.

"What about the two on the porch?" Jonathan asked.

"Kill them," the colonel said.

Jonathan glanced over at them. A lump formed in his throat.

"Well?" the colonel said. "You don't, I will."

"I'll take care of it," Jonathan said.

Jonathan made his way down behind the row of ambulances past the doorway. The rain had lightened up some, but it was steady and misting. He could hear the groans of the injured men inside. The smell of astringents and chloroform came at him. In the distance, he heard the drone of airplane engines. Britishers on their way to bomb German-held territory to the south, Jonathan thought.

As he rounded the last ambulance he discovered that what he thought was a pile of rubble had been cut for firewood. Jonathan found a stout piece of rough wood to use as a club. Then he moved along the wall back toward the ramp. The moaning inside was louder now. A young man's voice whined. A deep voice shouted. The whining stopped.

Jonathan made it to the edge of the building where the makeshift ramp led up to the doorway. The two soldiers were still there. Jonathan had seen enough Saturday matinees in America to know what to do next. He knelt down and felt around for a rock. He picked one up and and tossed it over the first ambulance. It pinged off the hood of the second.

The two soldiers started down the ramp, their rifles at the ready.

One said something in Russian.

Jonathan held his breath and waited. The barrel-chested one went around the ambulance away from Jonathan. The gangly one repeated what the first one said, only louder. He was coming toward Jonathan, but he was facing the ambulances, circling around them, so that he would pass in front of Jonathan.

Jonathan swung his club at the top of his neck, just below his knit cap, connecting with a thud. The soldier's knees spread and he fell face first into the mud. Jonathan turned the man's head so he wouldn't drown, then took the rifle out of his hand. He looked up over the hood of the ambulance nearest to him. The other soldier had ducked out of sight.

Jonathan started to circle around the ambulance when he sensed movement behind him. He turned and there was the second Russian soldier, who must have come around the back of the ambulance. He had his rifle pointed at Jonathan.

"Halt," he said in German.

Suddenly a shadow moved behind the soldier: the colonel, his hand covering the man's mouth, was pushing the rifle up in the air. Jonathan leapt at the soldier, burying his knife into his chest. Jonathan felt him stiffen as warm blood squirted into Jonathan's face. The rifle fell, and the soldier dropped into the mud.

"The other one dead?" the colonel asked in a whisper.

"No."

"Finish him."

"No need. Let's get out of here."

The colonel went over to the unconscious soldier, lifted his head, and cut his throat with a swift stroke.

Jonathan worked the knife free from the soldier's chest where he had plunged it in, pulling with all his strength. Jonathan and the colonel dragged the bodies to the wood pile and covered them up. Then they went back to the ambulance and got in.

"I should have known better than to trust a Jew," the colonel said. "Inherent weakness."

"That's right," Jonathan said. "You're a superman, I'm not." He found his hands were shaking. He felt simultaneously lucky to be alive and sick at the idea of killing the two young soldiers. If he had handled it right, he thought, they wouldn't have died.

The colonel laughed. He cranked over the engine and pulled out of the driveway.

They picked up Hitler and headed south with their blackout headlights barely lighting the road. The colonel had a Russian sergeant's jacket in his pack that he put on. When they stopped an hour later at the last Russian checkpoint before crossing into no man's land, a Russian officer asked the colonel something in Russian, and the colonel answered in Russian and gave him a piece of paper. The Russian officer went into a tent and made a call on a field telephone. A minute later they were passed on through.

Jonathan wondered whether Willis had arranged it all to go smoothly and concluded that of course he had. He wondered, too, what lies he'd told the Russians.

Which made him wonder, tôo, about the lies Willis had told him.

They had crossed the Elb with the ambulance on a raft, which had been waiting for them, hidden in some rushes, with two hundred liters of gasoline. They kept moving south. They moved slowly because of the bomb craters and had to ford streams because the bridges were blown, but they made steady progress. When exactly they had moved into German-held territory Jonathan had no idea, but he knew they must have because the colonel had thrown away his Russian army jacket and gotten rid of the Russian markings on the ambulance. They hid in a forest the next day, fearing the Americans wouldn't respect the red cross on the ambulance. There was a small cottage nearby which Hitler and the colonel used, but Jonathan preferred to stay by himself in the ambulance. The following night it continued to rain, making the roads muddy and progress slow. The colonel found a disabled tank and siphoned out some gasoline to keep them going.

By dawn they were in a hilly area full of scrub pine. The colonel pulled off the road and parked in a stand of trees. Jonathan and the colonel got out and cut pine boughs and covered the ambulance with them. The colonel got back in the ambulance and lay down on a stretcher. Jonathan sat on the edge of the hill and looked out over a peaceful valley. Beyond, in the far distance, were snowcapped mountains. The Alps. The rain had turned into a cold drizzle. He could see a couple of towns nestled into rolling hills. Nothing moving on the roads but long columns of civilians heading south toward the mountains in the distance.

After a while he saw some American fighter planes, dozens of them, strafing the town at the base of the hill.

Hitler joined him. "You see up there?" he said to Jonathan, pointing to the mountains in the far distance. "Up there is my redoubt, that is where we're going." He grinned. "You see, Jew, Providence has brought me through impossible difficulties once again."

"I got you here. And the colonel. Not Providence."

Hitler chuckled, then paced back and forth with his hands behind his back and a grin on his face. He was wearing a helmet with the strap tight under his chin. After a few moments he turned to Jonathan and said, "One thing troubles me. Why you, a Jew, would help me to escape. This truly baffles me. It cannot be for the reasons you've stated. What do you think Mr. Willis has in store for me?"

"I do my duty," Jonathan said. "It's none of

your business what Mr. Willis wants to do with you."

"You think they are going to put me on trial, don't you?"

"No."

Hitler laughed deep in his throat, which came out like a growl. "You are so transparent, you Jews. I know what you are going to think before you think it. That's what they told you, all right." Hitler laughed again. "You must think me a fool. How little you understand anything. The war, all this killing, don't you know what it's about?" Hitler had a strange, faraway look in his eyes.

"Why don't you tell me?" Jonathan said.

"It is about power. Do you know what power is? It's land. It's space. The human animal has to have land. To get it, the Americans slaughtered the Indians. The British slaughtered everyone in the world for the last three centuries. Who now has the land? The Russians have the land, and they want more. No matter how much land a nation has, it always wants more. Land is power. Politics feeds on power. What has this war been about? It has been about land. The Japanese took it from China and the Europeans, and whoever they could get it from. Now that the Russians have so much of it, the Americans will want to make sure they don't get any more. The Russians will want Poland and Germany and Czechoslovakia, they will push south and west. They will want Afghanistan and Mongolia and Japan. They want it all. Land is what the human animal craves like the wolf craves blood."

"Then why did you make the Jews your enemy? They have no land."

"Why I hated the Jews? It's so obvious. I have hated the Jews because it was necessary. Necessary and logical, if you understand human nature."

"Nothing to me is less logical."

Hitler's eyes shone in the light of morning. "My inner voice spoke to me one night when I was still in Austria. It spoke to me and said I was to be the savior of the German people. Have you no idea what it was like in Germany after the Great War? Germany was like a man who had been taken out and beaten within an inch of his life every day for four long years. Spit on. Told he was worthless and cowardly and not a man. And then this man, terribly humiliated, thinking himself worthless, is told he must pay a million marks to the man who has beaten him. Then he is told he cannot make weapons to fight back in case the men who have beaten him want to come and do it again. What man of honor would not feel rage over such an injustice?"

"What has this to do with the Jews? The Jews did not beat Germany. The Jews did not make Germany pay reparations. The Jews didn't force Germany to disarm."

Hitler shrugged. "I had to put the spirit back into this defeated man."

"But what has this to do with the Jews?"

Hitler looked at Jonathan as if he was a thick-headed child who couldn't see that one and one equaled two. "The Jews were merchants and poor people always think the merchants are cheating them and gouging them. The children of the clothing merchant always are well dressed and the people envied them. You see, I only watered the seeds which were already planted in men's hearts. Had not the Christians paved the way for me by blaming the Jews for crucifying Christ and not accepting the truth of the Christian religion? What was the Inquisition, if not five hundred years of hatred against the Jews? It is in the blood of the Germans to hate Jews. What was the Enlightenment but a temporary thing? Reason does not guide men, hatred is what guides men. I was lying on a cot in my boarding house when my inner voice spoke to me. To bring the beaten people back to life I needed an object of hatred, something or someone to hate and to hate intensely. The Jews, how perfect! If I blamed the Jews for everything, blamed them not only for the war and the economic disasters, but blamed them for polluting the race, for ruining crops, for *everything,* then I could mold the German people together." He paused, turning to look out over the valley. "The final solution was the inevitable result, which I did not foresee in the beginning, but once ancient hatreds are ignited, a conflagration inevitably results."

"And if you had foreseen it?"

He paused for a moment, then said: "I wouldn't have done anything differently. It was necessary; if you are to lead a great people, you must do what is necessary."

Jonathan stared at him for a long time, then said, "But why did you personally hate them? What did the Jews do to you?"

"Nothing."

"Nothing?"

He shrugged. "My mother had a doctor who was a Jew. She thought he was the kindest, most generous man who had ever lived. I saw to it he was not bothered during the past few years. I had a friend in Vienna who was a Jew. We went to the museums together and spent many hours discussing art. He was a fine comrade and a good friend. I had nothing against the Jews myself. I saw that it was necessary for the Jews to be blamed for everything. And now it is necessary for the Americans to hate the Russians and the Russians to hate the Americans. The pressure will be off the Jews for a while, but for just a while. For now, the Russians will blame America for all the troubles of the world and the Americans will blame the Russians. The Americans will need some guidance and that is what they want me for. I have set up the Werewolf underground, which I alone control. When the Russians take over, our network will be reporting back their every move. The Americans want to control this network, and they can, through me. So there, you see? This war is over, but everything is in place for the next one to begin."

Jonathan felt cold suddenly. Was evil logic and

calculation? And could it possibly be true that he had saved Hitler so that he could be used in some future war?

Jonathan remembered, back at the training camp, the others who were being trained there. Already they were calling the Soviet Union "the enemy."

Hitler stood up. "You see," he said, "you think I'm evil because I murdered. Don't you realize that the weapons of the future will make mass killing a matter of pushing a few buttons? I will be seen as a great prophet. Do you want to hear my prophecy? I'll tell you anyway. The world cannot survive the coming technology of total destruction."

Chapter Twenty-seven

Hitler returned to the ambulance. Jonathan went wandering around the hillock, feeling perplexed. Why had Hitler bothered to tell him all that? Was he somehow making excuses for what he'd done?

One of the American planes made a low pass through the valley, scattering refugees, but not opening fire. Then it turned to the right and disappeared over the next hill.

Jonathan ambled down a trail chewing a twig. It was just possible a fighter might spot him in the open and fire on him, so he kept in the trees. It had stopped raining, but the grass and trees dripped from the rain the night before. His thoughts tumbled in his head. It was all so cold-blooded. Could it be Hitler's vision of the future was true? The U.S. and the Soviets at each other's throats, each with superweapons ready to annihilate the other?

He'd heard that Soviet propaganda broadcasts in Portugal were already calling the Americans imperial warmongers, blaming the Americans for all the political repression on the face of the earth.

He came over the crest of the next hill and looked to the south. In a tree-lined gorge was a camp of some kind made up of identical white wooden buildings and surrounded by barbed wire. In the middle of it were two white wooden buildings with a brown smoke stack sticking up between them.

He knew where he was. He was standing above the Bouhler-Gessler concentration camp. He felt queasy in his stomach.

Along the back side of the camp there was a long column of men in striped uniforms. Possibly they were evacuating the camp. Maybe they couldn't kill everyone fast enough in the gas chambers and they were going to get the prisoners out before the Americans got there.

Here it was in front of him. He wanted Hitler to explain this. He wanted to show it to him and let him talk about land and power. There were real flesh and blood human beings in that camp being killed and incinerated. Let him look at this and talk about his goddamn necessity!

Jonathan raced back to the ambulance and grabbed the rear door handle with one idea in mind—to show Hitler his goddamn inevitable final solution in action. Jonathan pulled at the door, but it wouldn't open. He went around to the front and grabbed the handle; the door swung open. But somebody was waiting inside, and swung something at his head. He ducked, but not quickly enough.

Jonathan opened his eyes and found a rifle barrel pointing at him. Americans?

"Get up!" someone said in German.

Two men pulled him to his feet. Jonathan shook the cobwebs out of his head and took a look around. A rat pack had him. German deserters in scruffy, tattered uniforms. They looked dirty and nasty. He counted six. One had a gun in the colonel's back, two were going through his pack. One stood beside Jonathan, pointing an automatic pistol at his head. He stank like death, Jonathan thought.

"Now what have we here?" one of them said, swaggering around with his hands on his hips. He had a woman's scarf tied around his neck. Jonathan took him to be the leader, although he didn't look much more than twenty. "A pretty sight," he said. "An SS colonel, an SS lieutenant, and a lowly army private."

Jonathan glanced at Hitler; he looked stunned. His eyes were fixed on the leader and he seemed to be holding his breath, his left arm trembling at his side.

"Let's kill them quick and take their boots," the

one next to Jonathan said. "They all got good boots—almost new."

"I demand you release us," the colonel said in his command voice. "If you do not release us immediately I will have you all shot!"

They laughed. The leader said, "Here's a man who don't seem to know what a bad spot he's in."

The others laughed again.

"Maybe I'd better inform him, eh?" The leader turned to the colonel. "You know who we are?" He strode over to him and said loudly in his face, "We're the shit you goddamn mighty SS been stepping on. We're the guys you been hanging and shooting because we didn't want to fight your goddamn war. You wanted us to go throw ourselves in front of Russian tanks and we said no. So you been tracking us down and hanging us and shooting us and grinding us up in your tank tracks." He pulled back, swaggering, his hands of his hips. "Well now, things have changed. Now we're hanging you. Got the rope, boys?"

One of them stepped forward. "Got it right here." He pulled a rope from a sack.

The leader said, "Only got one rope, so you're going to have to take turns."

Jonathan figured the odds. All armed. He could maybe get one or two, but he couldn't take them all. Even if the colonel could react quickly and get one or two, it wouldn't be enough.

None of them were bothering with Hitler, who

had drifted back to the edge of the hill. He stood there, his left arm flapping at his side, his features cold with fear, his eyes darting around.

The colonel screamed: "We're on a supremely important mission, the future of the Reich is at stake!"

"That limb over there looks like it might do," the leader said.

The one with the rope swung it up over the limb and let the noose dangle.

"You know how the SS does it?" the leader asked the colonel. "They don't let you drop so your neck breaks. They just stretch you out, let you kick and choke. We learned all your tricks when you were killing us."

"I demand to be taken to your officer!" the colonel stammered. "You will all be put on meathooks!"

The threat meant nothing. Three of them dragged the colonel yelling and screaming to the rope and put it around his neck. They tied his hands behind his back. "Do something!" the colonel screamed at Hitler. Hitler looked at him dumbly. "The lieutenant's a Jew!" he shrieked. "Arrest him!"

No one was listening.

Two of the men pulled on the rope and it tightened around the colonel's neck. He screamed, "I'm an SS officer, you can't . . ." The rope cut off his air as the men pulled. The colonel's face turned red. The rope cut into his neck. His body swung into the trees; he kicked out with his legs, trying to catch the tree, but he couldn't quite get his legs around it. His face turned purple, the veins on his neck standing out like snakes. Then his bladder let loose and a dark spot appeared on the front of his trousers.

He swung back and forth for a few minutes. Everyone was silent. The breeze rustled the trees. Jonathan remembered Heidi lying on the floor with her throat slit, but he was rigid with fear and couldn't take any joy in the colonel's demise.

Then the two men holding the rope let the body drop. One of them said, "Which one next?"

The leader looked at Hitler. "He's not SS. Let him go. We don't hang men for being cannon fodder. Hang that one." He nodded toward Jonathan.

Two of the men grabbed Jonathan and started marching him toward the noose. Jonathan said, "Wait, you're making a terrible mistake. I'm not who you think I am. I'm an Allied agent. Really. You heard what the colonel said. It's true. I'm a Jew. I'm working for the Americans."

"Hold it," the leader said. "Let's hear him out."

Jonathan composed himself. He looked at Hitler, who was slipping away, heading for the edge of the hill. Hitler turned suddenly and started running.

"I am an Allied agent," Jonathan repeated, "and that man you've just let go is Adolf Hitler."

They all laughed. The leader said, "Bring him back, let's have a look." One of them went after Hitler and brought him back, dragging him by his good arm.

"Herr Hitler?" the leader asked.

"What an absurd thing," he said. "These SS me were taking me to Obersalzberg to have me executed. I am one of you. Horst Wrynick is my name. I have identity papers if you wish to see them."

"Identity papers can be forged," the leader said, walking around Hitler, touching his white hair, rubbing what came off on his finger tips. Jonathan picked up a piece of dark stick and held it under Hitler's nose. "Look," Jonathan said. The others jumped back suddenly as if hit with an electric spark.

"See!" Jonathan exclaimed, "he's Hitler. He faked his death in Berlin and he's turning himself over to the Allies. If you can get me to a radio where I can make contact with London, I can have him picked up here. I guarantee you will be well compensated."

No one said anything, they were still staring at Hitler. They all backed away from him as if he might start firing lightning bolts at them.

The leader said to Hitler, "Is what he says true?" His voice sounded surprisingly meek.

"Yes."

He kept staring at Hitler in the eyes.

"Let's get out of here," one of them said.

"Wait a minute," the leader said. The meekness was gone. "This is the head devil himself, the architect of all our misfortune. I say we hang him and hang him now."

They looked at him.

Jonathan said, "You help me deliver him to the Allies and I'll see to it you are all given one hundred gold sovereigns each."

They looked at each other in disbelief.

"Yeah," the leader said, "And a nice comfy jail cell to spend them in? No thanks." He turned to his men. "You think the Allies are going to give you anything once they have their hands on him? Don't be stupid. You, Hitler, stand accused of blundering into Russia, of conscripting me into an army where I had no desire to be, of making me eat dirt and getting one of my balls shot off and of killing my friends, and making Germany into a pile of shit. I say you got to die for that, and die now!"

"Let's do it!" another one of them cried. "Do it now!" yelled another. They moved to grab Hitler, but he stopped them with an angry stare. His chest expended and he stuck his jaw out. "You are Germans," he said in a deep-throated voice. "You have a mission and a destiny just as I, as your Fuehrer, have a mission and a destiny. Providence has chosen me for my role just as it has chosen you for yours."

He stepped closer to them. They backed away. He caught them in his gaze. "Look at you, you have let yourselves decay and degenerate just as the lesser races have let themselves decay and degenerate." He stared at each one of them, one at a time, holding the look for a long moment. "You are Germans. Stand up! Where is your pride? You have been called for an historic mission. You must do your duty to the fatherland! If you must die for Germany, then you must die! You cannot judge me. I am your Fuehrer!"

One of them snapped to attention, glassy-eyed. "Sieg Heil!"

"Sieg Heil!" two of the others cried.

Hitler saluted them, each one, one at a time, and they saluted back. Then he came to the leader.

"I order you to go to Obersalzberg and join the defenders of the Reich! Go now, run! Run!"

The leader didn't move.

"Now!" Hitler cried. "History demands it!"

Two of them took off down the hill. Another dropped his rifle and ran after them. The others looked to their leader and then to Hitler, and then back to their leader again, who was standing firm in the middle of the clearing.

Hitler marched over to him and shook his finger in his face. "Providence has chosen me to be the leader of all Germany in these times, to turn back the tide of Bolshevism, to halt the decadent west, to preserve German unity and greatness for the next thousand years. That great and noble task still lies within our grasp at Obersalzberg! Are you a German?"

"Yes . . ."

"Then be a German, renounce your past foolishness, be ready to die with German steel in your hand, be ready to nourish the sacred soil of Germany with your blood!"

Hitler drew a knife and held it before the leader's eyes. "Be ready as your Fuehrer is ready!" He drew the blade across the palm of his hand; blood squirted out.

"Now go, your destiny calls to you!" Hitler yelled, his voice echoing across the valley.

The leader stumbled backward, an expression of awe and fear on his face, then he turned and started down the hill, and the other two ran after him. Hitler went to the edge of the hill and watched them go. He wrapped a handkerchief around his hand.

Jonathan caught his breath and marveled at the man. Hitler turned to him and smiled. How much he had changed, Jonathan thought, since he'd first seen Hitler. He seemed younger, more vigorous, he was standing taller, and the puffiness had gone from his cheeks. He was being reborn, Jonathan thought, remade, just as Mr. X had predicted.

"What do you say?" Hitler said. "Let's have something to eat, then we ought to be moving on." He went back into the ambulance.

Jonathan looked down the hill. The rat pack was still running. Hitler had frightened them, then took hold of their minds. Jonathan realized suddenly that Willis or whoever was going to keep Hitler to run his organization would soon be working for Hitler, whether they wanted to or not. No one was going to control this man.

Jonathan looked in the bags of stuff the deserters had left behind near the ambulance. He took out a Luger and put it in his belt. A silver tea service. Some drapery material. Striped inmates' uniforms with stars of David on the fronts. They'd been bloodied. No doubt the rat pack had killed whoever was wearing them for their uniforms. No doubt they had them so they could pose as escaped prisoners should they meet the Allies. He found a half-full bottle of very good brandy and took a long drink.

Jonathan knew if he brought the monster to Willis there would be no trial. Willis planned to use Hitler, and that wasn't possible. Before long, Hitler would be using Willis. Hitler had to be stopped now, whatever the cost.

If he killed Hitler, Jonathan thought, Willis might kill him for it. Might kill his mother. He'd do what he could to protect her, and himself. Whatever the price, it had to be paid.

Jonathan picked up an old sock from the ground and climbed inside the ambulance. He took the Luger from his belt and pointed it at Hitler. "Open your mouth wide," he said. "Do it!"

Hitler glared at him.

"You open your mouth or I'll kill you now."

Hitler opened his mouth. Jonathan stuck the sock in.

Chapter Twenty-eight

Gunther Jager, SS brigadier general and commandant of the Bouhler-Gessler concentration camp, was in a state of frenzy.

The American advance units were twenty miles away and the only thing slowing them down, he thought gloomily, were the frauleins they liked to wave at and throw kisses to from their tanks. Why hadn't he been given orders to get rid of the last of his prisoners earlier? Here, just this morning, he was still marching prisoners out to secret execution sites where mass graves were supposedly dug—supposedly—and now here he was left with only a few men and still hundreds of filing cabinets of records to destroy. How was he supposed to get rid of all the records without staff to do the job properly? You can't make milk out of water.

He had his men taking the records and shoveling them into the crematorium and incinerating them.

Records meticulously kept. It was a waste of a good facility, but what else could he do? Making a bonfire was no good, the wind would blow the papers around and it would make a horrible mess. They wanted the buildings knocked down, too, but the bulldozer they sent to do the job had a bad crawler tread and was proceeding very slowly. It seemed as if everything was broken down.

Brigadier General Jager was 45, having been born in 1900 in Heidelberg, where his father was an instructor in German literature at the university. He detested his father, who he regarded as having a rather weak personality and had allowed himself to be dominated by Gunther's mother, a shrill, empty-headed woman determined to get her own way in every circumstance.

He had hated them both from a very early age.

Gunther joined the army secretly in 1915 during the Great War to get away from his parents, though he told himself at the time he was doing his patriotic duty to the fatherland and all that. And he was a good soldier. He killed a lot of Russians. At seventeen he was made the second youngest sergeant in the German army. He received the Iron Cross, first class, for charging a machine gun nest and knocking it out single-handedly. Later, after the war, he served with the East Prussian Volunteer Corps for the Protection of the Frontier, which fought pitched battles in the Balkans, the Ruhr, and Upper Silesia. Gunther Jager, from a very early age, was an avid nationalist, militarist, and rabid anti-Semite.

While on leave in Berlin in 1924 Gunther heard a communist speaker in a beer hall, followed him down the street, and bludgeoned him to death. He received a ten-year prison sentence, but served only four years, being released in the General Amnesty of 14 July 1928.

During the next four years he worked as a clerk in a tax office and spent his evenings working for the Nazis, attending rallies, writing speeches for local politicians, smashing windows in Jewish businesses. In 1934 he joined the SS and was given the job of block overseer at Dachau, then a "protective custody" camp. He made captain in 1936 and was transferred to Sachsenhausen in 1938, where he rose steadily, achieving the rank of full colonel in 1942. Himmler promoted him to brigadier in June, 1943, when Bouhler-Gessler was opened and he was assigned there as commandant. It was the proudest moment of his life.

Gunther Jager felt passionately about two things: the Nazi Party, to which he had given his full measure of service, and "correctness," which was his personal philosophy of living that guided his every action.

He did his work in an orderly, organized way. He was punctual, efficient, and had beautiful penmanship; in speech he was slow, methodical, machine-like. In his job performance, as far as the SS hierarchy was concerned, he was a model, the standard for the other camp commandants to measure up to. He was a dedicated bureaucrat who did his job quietly, smoothly, and kept accurate records. Fewer SS guards—per inmate—were lost to disease at Bouhler-Gessler than at any other camp. Though epidemics among the inmates were inevitable, given the sorry state of their physical condition when they arrived, he was proud of the fact that the typhoid fever and cholera which were rampant at other camps were kept well under control in his. He had been repeatedly praised by Rudolf Hess, the Inspector General of the camps. Officials from the Interior Ministry were always parading through, admiring the efficiency of his operation.

His chief accomplishment was the refinement of Zyklon B gas, used first in his camp as a replacement for carbon monoxide, which was much slower acting and required much more volume. He personally supervised the test trials of Zyklon B, keeping scrupulous records of duration, volumes, pressures, temperatures, and so on. Himmler awarded him a certificate of merit for his work with Zyklon B. Himmler called him the epitome of efficiency.

He knew, of course, that the Americans would never understand what had gone on at the camp, how it was necessary for the purification of the race to get rid of the Jews and other undesirable elements in the population. America was, after all, basically a naive and ignorant, Jewified nation, completely incapable of understanding what the German nation had suffered at the hands of the Jews. In their ignorance, they would no doubt seek revenge through some sham courts. He had no fear for himself, of course. From the very beginning Himmler had told him that the total responsibility for the final solution of the Jewish question was his and the Fuehrer's, and that he, Jager, was simply obeying orders. Even the Jewified Americans could understand that.

But Jager knew in his heart of hearts that the Americans would not understand and he would have to face some kind of unpleasantness, at least for a while. He had done his duty and had nothing to be ashamed of.

If only the Fuehrer had not given his life in the defense of Berlin! The Fuehrer would make them listen.

A knock came at the door. He was in his office at the moment, sitting at his desk composing his last weekly activity report. "Enter," he said.

His aide entered and said, "A Lieutenant Mohne to see you, sir, he has a Jew with him."

"A Jew?"

"Yes, sir, he says he caught him in the woods. He must have escaped from the column this morning."

"What does he want with me?"

"I don't know, sir."

General Jager sighed. "Send him in."

The aide showed the young lieutenant in. The lieutenant was covered with mud and what looked like dried blood on his shirt. He had hold of a white-haired man in a striped uniform with a gag stuffed in his mouth and his hands tied behind his back. The prisoner was shaking with either fear or rage, the general couldn't tell which.

"I caught this man in the woods not far from here, I believe he belongs to you."

"This camp is officially closed," Jager said. "All of my prisoners were turned over to a Major Hoffmann this morning. If this man got away from Major Hoffmann, it is not my responsibility."

"He isn't my responsibility either."

"Why don't I just shoot him?" the aide said.

General Jager gave him a sharp look. He personally detested bloodshed. It was messy and sometimes the shooter missed. People could often take a large number of bullets and still be alive for a short time, crying and moaning. He liked gas; it was quick and clean. The correct way of doing the thing. "Can we activate the showers?" Jager asked the aide.

The aide nodded. "I suppose, as long as the tanks have not been vented."

"Well, go and see," Jager said with exasperation.

The prisoner continued to struggle in the lieutenant's grasp. His eyes looked, Jager thought, as big as oranges, and his face was bloated. Though his hands were tied behind him, his left elbow flapped at his side like the wing of a rooster trying to take off.

"You know, there's something familiar about this man," Jager said.

"Jews all look alike to me," the lieutenant said. "Would you like a taste of brandy?" He took the bottle out of his jacket.

"I wouldn't ordinarily," Jager said. "But you cannot believe how frantic things have been these past two or three weeks."

"I would believe it," the lieutenant said.

The prisoner sagged, obviously exhausted from fighting his bonds. He chewed on the gag in his mouth.

Jager produced two glasses and poured some brandy for both of them. "To the memory of our Fuehrer," he said.

They drank.

The prisoner shook violently.

The lieutenant said, "The prisoner has a hatred for the Fuehrer that knows no bounds."

"Well, what do you expect, he's a Jew isn't he? Funny thing, though. Look at those eyes of his, have you ever seen any bluer eyes than those?"

"Yes, I noticed. No doubt a strain of Aryan blood somewhere," the lieutenant said.

The prisoner glared at Jager. Jager glared back. "Almost hypnotic eyes," he said. "Demon eyes."

"Have another drink," the lieutenant said.

"I really shouldn't, but since we're closing up

shop, why not?"

The aide returned. "The gas is still operational, Herr General," he said.

"Good, good," the general said. "I believe procedures called for maintaining functional status for as long as possible. You should have seen our operation here, Lieutenant, when things were in full swing. We were handling twenty-eight hundred, forty-six a day. Twenty-two percent over maximum."

"Impressive. Congratulations, Herr General."

"Thank you so much."

The prisoner made a grunting sound, still glaring at Jager.

"He is a talkative one, isn't he? Well, we're operating the last camp in Germany. If the Americans overtook the column that left here this morning, he may very well be the last Jew to receive a treatment. What's his name and number, I'll write it in my book. I've kept that book perfectly accurate from the beginning."

"I don't know," the lieutenant said. "He sliced his arm where his number was. He keeps insisting he's Adolf Hitler. His mind may be gone, I don't know. Either that, or he insists on profaning our Fuehrer."

Jager shook his head. Blasphemy, that's what it was. A Jew using the Fuehrer's name. He opened the huge leatherbound book on his desk and said, "If he insists, that's what I'll put in the book.

Adolf Hitler, number unknown." Then he said, "I think I'd like to supervise the procedure personally."

"Come along, Herr Hitler," the aide said, grabbing the prisoner by the arm.

The prisoner started whining. His knees sagged. The aide, a squat, muscular young man, had to clasp his arms round the prisoner's chest and drag him, kicking and twisting in his grasp.

As they walked down the gleaming halls of the administration building, Jager showed the lieutenant various plaques and citations he'd received for efficiency. They were framed and hanging in a straight row. At the end of the hall was a special display with a certificate of merit signed by Himmler himself. A picture of Himmler standing in the quadrangle outside the main entrance presenting the citation to the staff was the centerpiece of the display. Jager saluted it as they passed by.

Going down the stairs Jager said, "How I have loved my work here. I think I will go to my grave saying to myself, Gunther, you have served your people well."

"I think I will be able to say the same," the lieutenant said.

Jager patted the lieutenant on the shoulder. Then he signaled for one of the gate guards to come and help his aide handle the prisoner.

"They usually didn't give us this much trouble," Jager said to the lieutenant by way of apology.

"Lately, of course, with the war coming to an end, we have been encountering a more spirited resistance. Hope does it, don't you think? Most of the time, of course, we overcame this regrettable tendency by the shower technique. As long as the prisoners suspected nothing, things went as smoothly as a picnic. Sometimes word got out, but we managed to keep order."

They walked down a path in the sunshine and through a wire gate. At the end of the path a small bulldozer, engine revved, was pushing down a white clapboard building. The boards cracked and split as one wall gave way, then the roof came down in a cloud of dust.

They came to another gate, which Jager opened with a key, then he told the two guards to take the prisoner away for "treatment."

"Might I go along?" the lieutenant asked.

"Regulations forbid it, I'm afraid," Jager said. "Forbid it absolutely."

The two guards took hold of the prisoner, who was kicking and squirming and making ghastly sounds out his nose like the grunting of a pig, and dragged him backward down the path.

Jager took the lieutenant by the arm. "Let me show you, Lieutenant, how through sound management practices and the latest scientific advances we became the highest rated Final Solution camp in Germany."

They continued down the pathway that ended at

a wood and barbed-wire gate. On the other side a wooden walkway led up to a train platform. Across the walkway were two white, windowless buildings. One marked for women, the other for men. A sign over the door to each read, "Clean Station."

"We'd unload them up there. You wouldn't believe it, but some of them would be in such poor condition after the train trip we would have to take them off in stretchers. Inexcusable. I left standing orders to hose down the cars with disinfectant after the prisoners were taken away. They were full of vomit and excrement. Terrible. I opposed such treatment right from the beginning. I always believed we should treat the subhuman people humanely. Such cruelties I found intolerable. I let Himmler know, too."

"Yes, death should always be dealt humanely," the lieutenant said, taking a swig of brandy.

"We'd bring them here from the trains in groups of fifty," Jager said, indicating a longish white building to the left. "We'd tell them they had to be de-loused before they could be fed. The men here, the women over there across the way." He pointed to a similar building on the other side of a high barbed-wire fence. "We had them take their clothes off here and leave them."

The bulldozer roared; another building fell.

Jager noticed the lieutenant looked pale.

"Are you all right?" Jager asked.

"I-ah-I'm just tired."

"I guess we all are," Jager said with a sigh, giving the lieutenant a pat on the back. "It has been a long war."

At that moment machine-gun fire erupted no more than a mile or two away to the west. Jager jumped back with a start. "T-The Americans!" he stammered. "I must see to my records. You will not want to be found here, Lieutenant. Run to the west, to the redoubt! Continue the fight until the superweapons are ready, and we will yet win this war!"

"But what of the Jew?"

"Never mind about him, his smoke will be going up the chimney in one minute."

Jonathan jogged down the path and out the unguarded front gate. The machine-gun fire was sporadic now, mixed with an occasional explosion of mortar fire and artillery. Jonathan dashed across the road and into the woods on the other side, hiding in a cluster of pine trees behind a rock. He watched for the smoke to come out of the tall brick chimney next to a brick building with a low roof and huge ventilators. That must be the crematorium, he thought. He waited. And waited. The gunfire stopped, except for an occasional burst. He couldn't tell whether it was getting closer or not.

A horrible fear was welling up in him, a terror that wrapped around him like steel bands, which were being cinched tighter and tighter. He had visions of Hitler getting the gag off his mouth, of his mesmerizing the guards the way he had mesmerized the rat pack. He would once again be saved.

Jonathan felt the taste of bile rise in his throat. His cosmic joke—having Hitler be the last Jew to die in the gas chamber—could have backfired, and the monster could live, and rise again!

Somehow, he told himself, he had to make sure Hitler was dead.

He got up and started to run down a little hill, heading back into the camp, when he saw a detachment of Waffen SS double-timing it down the road from the west. No doubt they were retreating from the advancing Americans. Jonathan pulled back into the pines. The SS detachment took up defensive positions in a ditch along the side of the road, while their captain went into the camp. Jonathan half expected the Americans to come storming around the bend any moment, but they didn't. He kept looking toward the smoke stack. No smoke. He looked through the binoculars and slowly scanned the camp. It appeared totally deserted. The SS men in the ditch were chatting with each other and smoking, scanning the camp with curiosity. These were fighting men, Jonathan thought, and they probably knew little about the camps and what went on there.

But still, if they found Jonathan, they would

either shoot him for having no orders, or press him into service in their detachment. There was nothing he could do at the moment but wait and watch for the smoke.

So far not a wisp. And he hadn't seen any activity in the low brick building he took to be the crematorium.

The Waffen SS captain came out of the administration building, jogged back down the path, and rejoined his men. At least he didn't have Hitler with him. The detachment started off down the road single file, keeping close to the ditch along the side of the road to be close to cover should a fighter plane come by on a strafing mission. Jonathan waited until he saw them disappear over the hill to the east before he started back toward the camp. Then he heard the clank of crawler treads. A tank. And it wasn't far away.

It sounded as if it was moving up on the other side of the camp. More SS? Americans?

As yet no smoke came out of the smokestack.

He turned and headed east, staying in the woods, running through thickets of brush and trees, stumbling, panting, pumping his legs, urging his fatigued body onward, until he was half a mile south of the camp. He crossed the road and headed into the woods on the other side. This woods had been thinned, and he made his way from tree to tree keeping hidden as best he could, pausing occasionally to catch his breath.

Still no smoke from the chimney. He felt cold and his skin prickled.

Suddenly he heard shots again; they sounded like pistol shots and they were coming from the camp.

He couldn't see anyone. The bulldozer had stopped working and the soldier who had been driving it was gone.

Jonathan continued circling the camp, staying outside the perimeter fence. Then he saw that the gate across the train track was open and the body of a soldier was draped over it.

More shots.

The woods behind the camp came close to the fence. Jonathan stayed in the woods. He could see the train platform now and next to it was a Sherman tank and two armored personnel carriers. A group of American GIs stood around looking bored, their rifles slung over their shoulders.

Jonathan studied them through his binoculars. They seemed to be waiting for something. Then he saw Willis, in a colonel's dress uniform, coming down the ramp; with him, wearing an American second lieutenant's uniform, was Friedrich Mohne. So he wasn't dead! Emma Rolf hadn't shot him, it was all staged!

Between Willis and Mohne was a man wrapped in a blanket, his head and face covered.

Hitler?

They were getting into the armored personnel carrier. Jonathan ran toward them, crashing into the chain-link fence.

"Willis!" he called.

Mohne and the man wrapped in the blanket disappeared into the personnel carrier.

Willis came to the edge of the platform, shading his eyes from the sun. Then he turned and said something to the soldier next to him. Willis and his men at the moment were fifty to sixty yards away. The soldier Willis had spoken to called an order out to the men standing around the tank. They raised their rifles in Jonathan's direction and fired. Jonathan spun around and dove behind a tree, bullets whistling over his head. He crawled quickly down a small depression, then got up and ran toward some trees, bullets zinging around him. As he headed up the hill, his legs burning with fatigue, he could hear men's voices in pursuit.

Jonathan thought of the ambulance up on the hill; he could use it to get to the Swiss border. Once in Switzerland he'd seek out Jewish relief organizations; they would help him.

If only he could get them to believe.

The men were still behind him. Gaining on him. He somersaulted down the hill and headed up the next to where the ambulance awaited. They were firing on him again now. Bullets slammed into nearby trees, hit near his feet as he ran.

He had to make it, had to. Halfway up the hill where the ambulance waited his legs cramped up. He stopped behind a tree to rub the pain out.

Then he took a look. He was perhaps a hundred yards ahead of his pursuers now, and they were coming fast.

He started running again, ignoring the cramp and the pain. And as he ran he turned and shouted over his shoulder:

"Hitler lives!"

And from the valley he heard a ghostly echo: Hitler lives! Hitler lives! Hitler lives!